WHO
WILL LOVE
POLLY
ODLUM?

WHO WILL LOVE POLLY ODLUM?

Anne Marie Forrest

POOLBEG

Published 2000
by Poolbeg Press Ltd
123 Baldoyle Industrial Estate
Dublin 13, Ireland

© Anne Marie Forrest 2000

The moral right of the author has been asserted.

A catalogue record for this book is available from the British
Library.

ISBN 1 85371 976 5

Cover design by Splash
Set by Poolbeg Group Services Ltd in Bembo 12/14.75
Reproduced by Intype.
Printed and bound in Great Britain by
Cox & Wyman Ltd, Reading, Berkshire

A NOTE ON THE AUTHOR

Anne Marie Forrest grew up in Blarney village, County Cork. Having spent time living in Dublin, Wicklow and Dundalk, she moved back to Cork where she works as a town-planner and co-runs a craft shop.

Right now she is taking time out to travel through Asia and Australia while working on her second book *Dancing Days*.

Who will Love Polly Odlum? is set in Cork City.

TO ROBERT

1

POLLY LOVES DAVY

WITH EYES closed and head flung back, Polly basked in the feel of his breath, breezing delicately across the V-neck of her bare skin as he slept soundly on her shoulder. Completely and utterly still she sat. Still, but for the smallest of slow, careful shifts she made with her other shoulder as she manoeuvred it into position. As, millimetre by millimetre, she hunched it up, so that her T-shirt gaped away, ever so slightly, so that his warm breath carried on, ever so gently. Carried on – on in between soft cloth and softer skin.

And she sighed.

Lazily she opened one eye, then the other

and gazed down at him. Then, yielding to temptation she brought her hand up to his hair and gently curled a jet-black lock around her finger. His long eyelashes fluttered, his breathing halted, she paused, but he didn't wake and she dared to brush away a stray lash from below his left eye, from his smooth sallow skin, which she then stroked delicately along the ridge of his perfectly sculpted cheekbone.

Dragging her eyes away from him, she glanced around the lecture hall at the rows and rows of students stretching out in front of her, all hunched low over pages, all writing furiously, all anxious to record the lecturer's every word, conscious perhaps – unlike Polly, who had more pleasurable things on hand, and on shoulder – of the likely need to regurgitate them at some point in the future. And seeing that no one was enviously watching them – *him and her* – she felt disappointed, but relieved too, that she could go on enjoying him unnoticed. For had anyone been watching they'd probably have wondered why she didn't nudge him awake and tell him to keep his distance. As one

2

would expect a person to do, when a stranger falls asleep on their shoulder.

For that's what he was – a stranger.

Not that he felt like one to Polly. How could he? When for months now, she'd spent her days staring at him over the heads of her fellow-students, pleading with him to notice her. Not that she *really* expected him to. When, for months she'd spent her nights imagining all sorts of convoluted scenarios: stuck lifts, capsizing ferries, raging infernos, which would throw them together and through which they'd survive, shaken but unharmed. All silly day-dreams she knew and she never *really* expected anything to happen. Not *really*.

But then, twenty minutes ago, Davy Long – for that was the sleeping beauty's name, ignorant of the perilous situations he and she survived each night, ignorant of her very existence, happened to sit down beside her. And she, once satisfied that he was unaware of the deafening thump-thump of her heart, began to enjoy this unexpected proximity. And even more when his head began to slump, then slump some more, until finally it fell sideways onto *her very own shoulder*. And although, still a long, long way off from happy-ever-after, it was closer to the beginning of it than she'd ever been before.

But Polly was human and greedily she was beginning to realise that there was still more pleasure within reach. That, after weeks and weeks of imagining what it would be like to kiss him, the opportunity was hers for the taking. And so, gently, she now began to trace his lips with her finger as oblivious and snug as a new-born babe he slept on, making little contented noises and nestling further into her neck. And ever so carefully she turned his head towards her, little by little, until his lips were in reach. And she paused, just before kissing him; to savour his smell – not clean exactly – but agreeably evocative of an old comfort sheet she'd had as a child, with all its scent of washing powder gone, replaced by a subtle mixture of sweat and breath and warmth and time. Then she leant towards him but, as she did, her elbow hit against her metal pencil-case and sent it clattering to the floor. *Crash. Bang.* Too late. Her chance was gone. Davy bolted upright and stared around with wide-open eyes. She looked away. Quickly. Guiltily. Knowing that she had been trying to take what wasn't hers to take and feeling very, very annoyed that she hadn't been quicker off the mark.

Oblivious to poor Polly's lost opportunity, Professor Kiely drew to a close.

"And I expect that between now and the submission date, at least five percent of you will experience the tragic and un-expected death of a very close and cherished relative," she was saying in her monotonous voice, responsible for sending more than just Davy to sleep. "And when that five percent come to me, I'll be sympathetic of course, but I won't take a balled-up sodden hanky and red-rimmed eyes as sufficient proof of a family death. I'll need to see the body. Alright?"

The rows of eighteen-year-olds before her gave a sluggish response of nods and grunts and shuffled in their seats, gathering up their things. Feeling more composed now, thinking she might salvage the situation with a smile or a light-hearted reference to their recent intimacy, Polly dared to turn to him, but he was gone. She looked around to catch a glimpse of him going out the door.

"Did I tell anyone to leave?" shouted the lecturer, but Davy didn't hear. "You," she called out, pointing at Polly. "Go call him back."

"Me?" asked Polly anxiously.

"Yes, you. Go on."

Polly got up and hurried out after him.

Seeing him standing by a pillar, she took a deep, deep breath. There wasn't any point in holding out for blazing infernos and capsizing ferries, for they were few and far between. And lifts terrified her so much that she never took them; unlikely then that she'd ever find herself stuck in one with him (deserted building, emergency line down, power cut, sub-zero temperatures, sleeping bag, bottle of champagne – yes, a sleeping bag and a bottle of champagne – he happened to be on his way to a party, you see – a lot of time and thought went into these scenarios). No, Polly realised that she had to take whatever opportunity presented itself. So now she took another deep breath and cleared her throat.

"Excuse me," she called, but too timidly

for him to hear. "Excuse me," she called again. Davy turned around and she walked towards him smiling a dimpled shy smile, wobbling on her usually comfortable, low, thick heels which nervousness had transformed into mere slivers of stilettos. She tried to steady herself – *right foot in front of the left, left foot in front of the right, slowly, no tripping* – until finally she reached him.

"Hello," he said and smiled.

She was distracted. By the beautiful way he'd said hello. By the beautiful way he'd smiled. By his beautiful eyes. Were they grey or blue? She peered a little closer, then realising he was staring back at her, she pulled herself together, stepped back out of his personal space and remembered the message.

"I was sent for you. You're to come back. We're waiting." Oh God, she could have wept. She sounded as if she'd come from Der Führer himself and that without further ado she was likely to catch a firm hold of him and frog-march him back to where the death-squad awaited. She tried again, to soften it a little.

"What I mean is that she sent me to ask

you to come back. That's if you want to. Well, that's not what she said exactly, she didn't say anything about coming back if you want to. In fact I think she wants you to come back even if you don't want to, if you know what I mean." He was staring. "Look, what I'm trying to say is that it's no business of mine whether you come back or not, I'm just passing on the message. Not because I want to particularly, but because she asked me. Asked me, to ask you to come back, that is. Told me really, told me rather than asked, I suppose." He was still staring, maybe she hadn't made herself clear, but how was a girl to think straight with all this staring with beautiful blue-grey eyes going on. "Do you understand me?" she finished weakly.

"I think so."

"So you're going to come back?"

"I think it's a bit late," he said, looking over her shoulder.

She turned around and caught glimpses of the lecturer's scarlet suit bobbing in the swell of student denim exiting the lecture hall.

"Well, just so as you know I passed on the message," she said.

And, having no desire to wait around to explain why she'd failed to return him, she hurried off.

Inside the ladies', her favourite refuge in times of crisis, Polly banged her head against the cubicle wall. Well, not banged exactly, for her resolve faltered every time her forehead neared the white tiles and instead she ended up hitting them softly. She just felt so mad, for, if she'd deliberately set out to, she couldn't have managed to sound so, so stupid. Why, oh why, had she bothered with the message anyway? Why hadn't she just gone up to him and teasingly asked him if he made a habit of falling asleep on strangers? Why? Because she was Polly, of course.

Realising that as much as she might like to, she couldn't spend the rest of her day, or life for that matter, in the sanctuary of the cubicle, reluctantly she opened the door, went to step out but then, catching a glimpse of Professor Kiely fixing her hair at the mirror before her, she hurriedly retreated. Leaning against the door she breathed a sigh of relief at not having been spotted, just as Professor Kiely on the far side of it, having witnessed Polly's look of horror and hasty turnabout in the mirror, wondered was it that she was getting older or was each year's intake of students really more peculiar than the last. And, as Polly listened out for Professor Kiely's departure, it struck her that she was complicating things as usual. Why hadn't she simply walked out and pretended not to notice the lecturer? Why? Because she was Polly.

She banged down the toilet seat, sat down and waited, thinking how very ridiculous she was. She really did complicate or make a mess of everything. Take the whole college thing. It seemed to her that within a day of starting, every other student, including her cousin Cliona, knew how it all worked; knew how to transform themselves into looking like students overnight; knew how to instantly surround themselves with a huge bunch of friends; even knew how to talk to boys, as if, well, as if they weren't members of the opposite sex. Both she and Cliona had started off knowing only each other yet now, any time Polly met Cliona, she was centre-stage of a huge gang (boys included) moving as one, as Polly came against them on her lonely ownsome. And just six months ago, the two of them could have been taken for twins – same brown uniform, same stocky white legs and same short dark hair, neatly tucked behind their ears. So how had Cliona managed to sprout dreadlocks which hung down to her bum when Polly's own hair hadn't grown more than an inch? Who'd explained to Cliona the knack of wearing clothes so that they looked like they might have come from some trendy second-hand shop, but obviously hadn't? Yet, no matter how hard Polly tried, her clothes always looked like they'd come from Marks and Spencer's end-of-season-sale, sensible, of good quality, and always, always, completely wrong. As for legs, well, she thought, raising her skirt to examine them, they were no less solid or white than they'd been in school but it wouldn't surprise her at all if, underneath the big and baggy khaki fatigues Cliona had taken to wearing, she now had legs to rival Naomi Campbell's.

Hearing the outer door bang shut and deciding that the coast was clear Polly emerged from the cubicle. She caught sight of her reflection in the mirror as she did so and stared at it and saw nothing that pleased her. When her mother said, "But lovey, you are pretty", in response to her daughter's frequent laments, wrongly Polly suspected that she really didn't mean it, since in the same breath she'd carry on to reassure her daughter that "Personality was far more important". But right now Polly felt her personality was about as engaging as that of a goldfish. And as for looks, well, if she and Woody Allen were the only contestants in a beauty pageant, it would be a close call as to who'd get to wear the crown.

Now Polly's attention had focused in on her eyebrows. As she stared at them in the mirror and wondered at their thickness, it struck her that Cliona's old joke about the two of them having eyebrows to rival Mr Burke's, their old science teacher, was no longer apt, not in relation to Cliona at least. For it suddenly dawned on Polly that Cliona's had disappeared and in their stead were two pencil-thin arches.

2

DAVY LOVES MICHAELA

AS POLLY was considering this new discovery, wondering when exactly it had happened and how she'd never noticed before, Davy was walking across campus.

He was still feeling a little sleepy. And annoyed. Anxious to keep a low profile around college, it bothered him that the lecturer had seen him leave for it meant he'd have to give her classes a miss from now on. He paused at the gates, yawned, and wondered what to do. He thought about going back to check on his squat but he was loath to; it was such a fine day and anyway, Bartley, an old street cleaner whose area included Cathedral View, had assured him that very morning that the terrace wouldn't be coming down for a while yet. Cathedral View was a terrace of derelict dwellings of near-playhouse dimensions, one of which Davy had made his home. Bartley, so he told Davy, got his information on "good authority" from City Hall, where he was well in with some of the "top boys". Spotting Davy on the street in the mornings, he'd beckon him over and, grasping him by the arm, he'd look around conspiratorially, then whisper at him, "You're all right for the while, I'll give you the nod when the builders are due". Bartley had taken it upon himself to keep an eye out for the "young fella" as he thought of Davy, ever since Davy, coming across the old man in a pub one lunch-time had stood him a pint, prompted by the tiredness on the old man's kindly face as much as by the fact that Bartley happened to be standing beside him as he was ordering. And although Davy had long forgotten about the pint, Bartley hadn't. A few mornings ago, as Davy was coming through his front door, literally crawling through a gap in his boarded-up front door, he thought he'd heard

Bartley, sweeping nearby, mutter, "Yes Sir, an Officer and a Gentleman". But Davy imagined he must be mistaken or, if that's what he had said, then he doubted it could be him the old man was referring to; his means of exit hardly befitted the manner a gentleman might be expected to leave his house of a morning.

But Davy really didn't set too much store on Bartley's inside knowledge, suspecting that the old man had no more idea than himself when the bulldozers were due to start clearing the way for the new road. No, Davy was more inclined to believe the new-age travellers, squatting in another of the cottages, who'd heard that the terrace would be coming down before the end of the month.

But it was such a fine day that in the end he decided to head to the bridge. In his pocket he had a copy of Kipling's *Plain Tales from the Hills*. It would be pleasant to sit in the crisp October sun and read, for the bridge would be quiet at this time of the day, being too early yet for most of the druggies and the drinkers who regularly congregated there to have stirred from their beds. And perhaps he'd catch a glimpse of her, "the girl with the hair", as he thought of her, passing by on her way back from lunch.

He walked down along College Street, along Abbey Street, across Gill's Street and around by Neilford Place. By Hot and Saucy – the takeaway – he turned into a cul-de-sac which served as an access to the few warehouses which ran along its length. These warehouses were under-utilised now and the dead-end stretch of road was used mainly for parking by the city's commuters and by its walkers on their way to the pedestrian bridge. At the point at which the road came to an abrupt end, the pedestrian bridge began and, suspended elegantly by a simple steel curve – swooping up, then down – it crossed over the dual carriageway built along what was once an old railway line some forty feet below. The cul-de-sac itself was a graffitied, littered area, but very quiet, except when the city's drop-outs congregated to drink and deal as they sometimes did. Now Davy stopped just short of the pedestrian bridge and climbed to the top of a flight of steps which led to a disused door at the back of the hospital. And he sat down on the top step. This was his favourite spot in all of the city, high over it with a bird's-eye view, from where he'd come to know Cork City as well as any Corkonian. On a clear day like today he could see right across the city. He could see the tops of the various historic buildings – Callanan's Tower, The Red Abbey, Elizabeth Fort; and he could see the spires of the churches, and there were many – St Nicholas's, St Vincent's, St Finbarr's, St Patrick's – a cautious lot these people of Cork, Davy often thought, hedging their bets and honouring all and sundry, but still cute enough to put double money, as it were, on the inner circle – St Mary's (Jesus' mother), St Anne's (his gran), St Mary's and St Anne's (mother and gran), St Peter's (his best friend), St Peter and Paul's (best friend and another of the lads). From the step, Davy could trace the line of the city's quays and recognise the buildings which fronted onto the River Lee, or rather River Lees for, as the river came into the west of the city it split in two but merged again at its eastern edge making an island of the city centre. A confusing geography for

Davy when he'd first arrived for, being unaware of the dual river flow, he'd been constantly perplexed at finding the Lee in front of him when he was certain he'd left it behind him. Beyond the city centre he could see the northside rising up steeply; to the right, the rows and rows of fine old houses, three and four-storied and brightly painted around St Luke's and Montenotte; and, to the left, the neat rows of corporation houses of Gurranabraher. Both the posh and the not-so-posh northside residences all looked down on the city centre and their inhabitants were as familiar with its happenings as they were with the affairs of their own immediate neighbourhood. The last thing Davy could see before the land fell away on into the countryside was the water-tower breaking the skyline at the city's edge.

Sometimes, sitting here on the steps he'd spot an interesting building, one he'd never seen up close and, having plotted his route, he'd head off towards it. He loved walking around the city, particularly in the early morning or late at night or on a Sunday – times when the city's shoppers and commuters had gone back to wherever it was they came from and left the city to its inhabitants. Sometimes, en route, he'd encounter a person and something about them would cause him to temporarily abandon the building and to follow them instead. He supposed it was weird to follow strangers and although he never really thought why he did, there were several reasons – boredom, plain nosiness, loneliness. Two types of people intrigued him enough to trail: odd people – those with mismatching runners or solitary mumblings – and beautiful women with just something about them. In *her* case it was her hair. It was soon after he had arrived in Cork and he'd been walking towards a bright blue building high up on Patrick's Hill when he'd first noticed her. He'd caught a glimpse of her hair first when she was still in the distance and, as she came towards him, he'd watched the sunlight play on its various colours, picking up one, then another, and there were many – gold, copper, red, mahogany and lots of others which he couldn't name in that mass of tumbling autumn. As she came closer, he studied her face, a beautiful elfin-shaped face with light clear green eyes and lips which hinted at a smile and promised laughter. Most people, Davy noticed, had a gloomy, vacant set to their face when they walked alone – who knows what they were thinking, if they were thinking at all. But she was different and Davy was fascinated to watch her expression which changed by the second as she came towards him; as if she was carrying on the most animated and contrary conversation in her head. As she passed him by, he caught the delicate scent of her perfume and heard her softly hum to herself. And he turned around and followed her. The route she took was the very one he had come from and she brought him back to where he'd set out, then passed by the hospital steps and on over the pedestrian bridge to the other side, to a yellow house in the middle of the terrace leading up from the bridge. Since then he'd seen her walking by many times as he sat on the steps and he had come to notice that she was as regular as clockwork. Five past one, home to the yellow house. Five to two, back to work. Five thirty-five, home again.

Occasionally he'd get an unexpected

bonus sighting. Once, passing a coffee shop on Washington Street, he'd glanced in through the window and saw her sitting there, head bent over a newspaper. He'd stopped, pretended to study the menu and watched her for a few moments. Then she'd looked up, stared straight at him and her face broke into the most wonderful smile. He smiled back. But then she picked up her pen to scribble in whatever crossword clue she'd managed to solve and which had pleased her and he realised that it wasn't him she was smiling at. Another time, seeing her going into HMV, he'd followed her inside and had watched her for ages as she flicked through the rows of CDs until finally she selected one and carried it around while she continued to browse. Then he watched as she stood in the centre of the shop, contemplating the CD in her hand. Would she? Wouldn't she? Finally she shook her head, dumped the CD and walked quickly out. He went to the door, searched the crowd for that mass of hair but she'd disappeared into the crowd of shoppers. He'd gone back inside, found the CD where she'd put it and bought it, although he didn't really have the money to spend on it, had never heard of the singer – Nick Cave – and didn't even have a CD player on which to listen to it.

Davy's timepieces were the city's clocks. Now he couldn't see any but thought it must be nearly two and figured that it was too late, that she wouldn't be passing by today. He saw a group of men coming up the road and recognised them as regular bridge drinkers.

"How's the Professor?" shouted one.

"Alright," Davy called back and watched them settle down, some on the bonnet of a parked car, others in a row along the footpath, each with his flagon of cider or couple of cans. One had a bull terrier with him, another a little girl – equally dirty and neglected-looking and left to amuse themselves as the drinking commenced. When Davy first started coming to the bridge, these fellows had given him hassle, mocked him for the book he had always with him and for his northern accent. But he'd known tougher types than these – his father and his brother Stephen for instance. Not to mention his mother – she'd have wiped the floor with them. They didn't intimidate Davy and since he'd taken their jibes good-humouredly they'd learned to leave him well enough alone. Once or twice, when he hadn't talked to anyone for days and they hadn't yet drunk themselves into a stupor, he'd even joined them for a while and had taken the can or bottle of cider they'd offered. And when they were on the serious batter, they'd touch him for a few bob and he'd give it to them if he had it on him.

He hadn't made much of a start on Kipling. He tried to get stuck in, but was beginning to suspect that this Kipling was an obnoxious old fart and instead he began to watch the girl sitting on the bottom step playing. She was aged five, maybe six, a little scrap of a thing, all knees and elbows and flimsily dressed for October. She'd collected a whole load of beer bottles and cans and had set them up in pairs on the step beside her. For the last ten minutes, she'd been talking quietly to them. Now it seemed that one bottle had displeased her for suddenly she grabbed it up, held it out in front of her and started wagging her finger at it crossly.

23

"You're a very bold boy," Davy heard her scold. "If you don't have your homework done tomorrow, you'll be in very big trouble. *Big trouble.* Are you listening to me?"

The beer bottle appeared to be a rather stubborn sort and she a very cross teacher.

"Billy, if you don't answer me, I'll give you a walloping. I'll wring your bloody neck," she threatened.

Davy laughed aloud and she looked up at him, then stared at him suspiciously. Eventually she asked, "What's your name?"

"Davy. What's yours?"

"Eva," she answered. Still staring at him she began to consider the possibility of having a real live student.

"Would you like to be in my school?" she asked him.

"I don't think so. You seem a bit cross."

"Only to bold boys." She studied him again for a moment or two more, then asked. "Are you a bold boy?"

"No."

"But you are a big boy?"

"Yes."

She climbed up the steps and stood before

him, looking closely at his black curls.

"Why have you got girl's hair so?" she asked and he shrugged. "So will you be in my school?" she asked again.

Davy glanced over at the crowd of drinkers and saw her father watching. On those occasions when the other drinkers were slagging Davy off, this man had never joined in, he'd just sat apart, silently staring at Davy, his gorilla's body all coiled up with tension and his palms permanently in fists as if he was perpetually ready for a fight. Davy had thought he'd only one expression, a nasty scowl, but now he realised he had a second – a viciously nasty scowl. He turned back to Eva.

"I think I'm probably too big for your school. Anyway, I have to do my own homework," he said, indicating his book. "You'd better go back, your class will be wondering where you are."

Her little face crumpled with disappointment.

"Will you play with me the next day?" she asked.

"We'll see."

While Davy had been talking to Eva, "the girl with the hair" had passed by and when he looked up he saw her hurrying down the road. He stared after her, disappointed to have missed seeing her face, but then she paused and he watched as she rooted around in her handbag, until she pulled out a Walkman, put it on, and continued walking, not realising that her wallet had fallen out.

"Hey," he shouted, but she was out of earshot. He quickly got to his feet and ran down the steps, taking two at a time.

"Aha, you knocked Billy over," moaned Eva.

"Sorry. Now there, Billy's fine again," said Davy setting the bottle upright. Then he ran down to where the wallet lay on the ground, picked it up and ran after the girl.

"Hey," he shouted.

Michaela looked behind and seeing Davy running towards her, she began to panic. She was going to be attacked and there was no one around to help, certainly not those other fellows, they were probably his friends; they'd probably join in. As he got closer she

26

began to run, but not quick enough for almost immediately she felt his hand on her shoulder. She yelled out.

"Calm down, for God's sake," shouted Davy.

"What do you want?" asked Michaela.

"Your wallet, you . . . "

"Here, here take it," said Michaela searching in her handbag.

"No, you dropped it."

He held out the wallet and she took it from him.

"I'm sorry, I thought that . . . " she stopped herself before she'd said it.

"You thought I was going to rob you."

"I'm really sorry, I was just a bit nervous. Look, thanks."

"And don't worry, there's nothing missing."

"I didn't think there was."

Davy left her standing there and began to walk back to the steps.

"Thanks," she shouted after him.

He shrugged and continued walking.

"Listen, hang on a second," she called.

Davy turned around.

"Can I give you something, you know, like a reward?" Immediately Michaela saw by the look on his face that she'd said the wrong thing.

"No thanks," he said.

3

MICHAELA LOVES COLIN

FROM THE fifth-floor office window Michaela looked down at the street below. Rush hour, as it was curiously called, had started and the South Mall was jammed solid; there was little of interest to watch. The pink-cloaked, pink-hatted crazy woman, whose craziness regularly prompted her to direct the traffic on the Mall – much to the confusion of uninitiated out-of-town drivers – hadn't been so prompted today. Nobody was blasting their horn and yelling at some sneaky driver for slipping into *their* car-parking space; no chance then of a blazing argument for Michaela to watch to pass the time. Nor were there any especially good-looking men

29

strolling along the pavement for her to gaze after and wonder about. Nothing at all exciting. Just lines of frustrated drivers, all listening to their car radio telling them what they'd no doubt worked out for themselves – that the South Mall had come to its usual Friday evening standstill. Michaela sighed, moved away from the window and sat back down at her desk. She glanced at her watch, saw that it was just gone five and wondered what to do; her basket was empty, her typing was finished, the post was gone, and there was still almost half an hour to go before home-time. For no reason other than that she couldn't think of anything better to do, she began swivelling her swivel-chair. Around and around she swivelled, oblivious to the sour stares directed at her from Denise across the room, until, feeling dizzy, she brought the chair to a stop. Noticing her colleague's sour face now, but supposing it was "the heartburn" from which Denise was "killed" or one of the other countless medical problems she was equally "killed from", Michaela convivially asked,

"So Dee, heading out tonight?"

"It's Friday," came the curt reply.

What kind of an answer was that, wondered Michaela. Did it mean she was or she wasn't going out?

"So are you heading out tonight, Dee?" she tried again.

"Denise. The name is Denise. Would you ever stop calling me Dee. And I told you, it's Friday. I never go out on a Friday."

"I see," said Michaela doubtfully. "Why?"

"I just don't. Now stop annoying me."

Michaela studied Denise. Everything about her screamed smug! Sitting there with her shoes kicked off, with her smug little sausage legs stretched out underneath the desk and her smug little piggy toes going wiggle-wiggle-wiggle. Smug. So smug, that Michaela now succumbed to the temptation to rise her.

"Maybe it's for religious reasons," she said thinking aloud.

"Ha?"

"I was just thinking that maybe you've some religious reason for not going out on a Friday. You know, the way Catholics don't eat meat on holy days or Muslim women don't

31

cook when they've their period because they're considered unclean."

"Michaela!" Denise's little nylon-clad toes stopped wiggling, such was her shock at such vulgar utterances. "You're *disgusting*!"

"So why don't you?" Michaela persisted

"Why don't I what?" asked Denise crossly.

"Go out on a Friday?"

"Look Michaela, can't you see some of us have work to do?"

"No you don't."

"Excuse me?"

"Denise, you're making out your shopping list."

In a huff Denise got up from her desk, removed her pink fluffy cardigan from the back of her chair where it habitually hung, draped it around her shoulders and went towards the door. Suddenly it struck Michaela that Denise always did this, always draped her cardigan around her shoulders before she went out to the toilet or to the photocopier, and she began to wonder why.

"Denise," she called. "Are you afraid of catching cold?"

"What?" asked Denise crossly, pausing by the door.

"Why do you always do that, you know, drape your cardigan around your shoulders? Is it the cold you're worried about or are you afraid that the sight of you in just your blouse will send the young solicitors wild with lust?"

"Of *all* the things to say!" said Denise outraged. "Michaela you really are *disgusting!*"

Ten minutes past five. Twelve minutes past five. Surely half past by now. No, only thirteen minutes past. Maybe her watch was slow. Michaela held it up to her ear. Well, it was ticking all right.

"What time is it, Muriel?"

Muriel, the other wicked witch, the second ugly sister, the third member of the happy crew, sighed, put her hand over the receiver, and said,

"Michaela, I'm on the phone!"

Five words, Michaela counted.

"It would have taken you less effort to tell me the time," she whispered at her loudly.

33

But Muriel just glared.

Why couldn't Muriel have just told her the time, Michaela wondered. But then, a lot of things about Muriel and Denise caused her to wonder. Sometimes, they'd all be sitting there, busily typing away when one of them would suddenly feel the need to volunteer the oddest piece of information. "Salt is the best thing for getting red wine stains out," Muriel would announce out of the blue causing Michaela to sit there puzzled, wondering had she missed something; but Denise wouldn't seem to think so. "Really?" she'd answer and later, ten minutes later, or maybe an hour later, or maybe even the next day, she'd carry on, "You're right, salt *is* good. But, pouring white wine on the stain is meant to be even *more* effective. It *neutralises* it." It would take Michaela a few minutes to figure out that they were back on the subject of red wine stains. And then later again, much later, when Michaela was sure that the topic was well and truly finished with, Muriel would pipe up, "Of course, salt would be a lot *cheaper* than white wine."

And they both seemed to have all these little rules to guide them through life. Like "allowing" themselves a cream cake at elevenses on Friday. Invariably one or other of them would announce, just as she took that first bite, "It's Friday, I deserve a treat", which always made Michaela wonder what she'd done on the other days of the week to make her feel so unworthy. Very little, Michaela imagined. They weren't exactly wild ones. No. It was a bit sad though, neither of them was more than twenty.

Denise came back into the room, threw Michaela a dirty look, carefully hung her cardigan on her chair again and settled herself down.

"Denise, have you got the time?" Michaela asked her. But there was no reply. "Denise, have you got the time?" she repeated. Still no response.

She got up, went over, and tapped Denise on the shoulder but her broad back didn't budge and Michaela decided on a different approach, a frontal attack, and went around, hopped up onto the desk and stretched out in front of Denise.

"Denise, switch on you hearing aid!" she shouted, pointing at her ear,

"Michaela, get off!"

"The batteries! Check the batteries, dear!"

"Get off, Michaela!"

"I was just wondering if you have the time."

"Mind your own business."

Defeated, Michaela went back to her own desk and dialled. "At the signal it will be seventeen nineteen and zero seconds," confirmed the friendliest voice she'd heard all day. Sadly, Michaela's watch had been right.

Finally, the minute hand dragged itself around to five twenty-five. That was close enough for Michaela. She grabbed her things, called out goodbye and bolted for the door.

Immediately Muriel and Denise checked their watches.

"Well," said Muriel. "It seems we can leave any time we want to now."

"And arrive in at any hour. Remember when I said to you that there was still no sign of her, it was at least ten past eight at that stage," said Denise.

"It was even later yesterday. Quarter past at least. And would you look at that? She's left her computer on. Look. Look. Who does she expect is going to turn it off? One of us?"

"Anyway, what business is it of hers why I don't go out on a Friday. Surely she should know by now that my night out is Saturday?" said Denise. "And lying across my desk and shouting at me like that. I've a good mind to complain her to Mr O'Neill, I really do."

"It wouldn't do any good. She wouldn't care. And anyway, he wouldn't say anything to her, I think he has a thing for her."

"No wonder he would, the way she carries on. You should have seen her coming up in the lift this lunchtime. You'd never think he was the boss the way she was chatting away to him. And laughing," she said disgustedly. "Out loud. At some *filthy* joke he told."

"Do you remember it?" asked Muriel, trying not to sound too interested.

"What?"

"The joke."

"No, not really. I didn't really get it. But I'm sure it was filthy. One of those *double-meaning* ones."

There was a pause as both of them tried to think of other things to say about Michaela.

"And vain," said Denise, getting in there first. "Thinks she's God's gift. God's gift. And that hair of hers! It just drives me mad. You'd think she'd tie it up, wouldn't you? But oh no, she sits there flicking it around the place, she's for ever at it. Have you noticed?"

"Have I what?"

Denise slipped back on her shoes and reached around for her cardigan and buttoned it up.

"Oh well, that's another day down," she said.

Michaela took the same route home every day. Reaching the corner by Hot and Saucy she paused and, peering up the road, she tried to make out if there was anyone hanging about by the pedestrian bridge. Now that winter was drawing in and the nights were getting darker, she supposed she should start going around the long way. This short-cut wasn't the safest, not with those drunks always hanging about. But it seemed quiet and, anxious to get home before Colin arrived back from Limerick, she decided to risk it. Hurrying along, she thought of her good luck at lunchtime, still amazed that the fellow who'd found her purse should be so honest, for he'd looked like he could have done with keeping it.

She arrived home to her house in the middle of the terrace. Straight away she took off her jacket and set to work. The place was a mess – clothes strewn all over the bathroom and bedroom floors, CDs, old newspapers and magazines scattered around the living-room, half-eaten meals all over the table, the sink piled high with three days of unwashed plates. She hated when Colin was away but that didn't stop her taking full advantage of these breaks from his obsessive neatness. In fact, it was a point of principle with her to absolutely wallow in her natural untidiness during his absences. He'd have gone berserk if he'd seen the state of the place. So, with the CD player on at full volume she rushed around – collecting up the cups, bundling dirty clothes into the washing-machine and putting everything either back in its place, in the bin, or shoving it under a cushion or behind the couch. Satisfied with her efforts, she finally made the bed. After a quick shower, she went to her wardrobe and tried on practically everything she owned and just as quickly discarded them. A long black dress – way, way over the top, she decided, looking at herself critically in the mirror. A simple cotton dress – she'd be freezing if he didn't arrive before long and, besides, he absolutely loathed simple cotton dresses. Her long silk skirt – shrunk in the wash, or maybe she'd had a few too many packets of crisps of late. Finally, when every decent thing she owned lay scattered across the bed, she settled for a short red dress and black high heels, considered underwear for a second but decided against it; it had no place in the kind of intimate evening she'd planned.

Her mother, a model wife with a store of 1950's how-to-be-a-prefect-wife books (*Always have a drink mixed for him when he arrives home – Take time to touch up your make-up – Change into something nice – Enquire about his day at the office*) would be very proud at what an exemplary wife her daughter was, Michaela thought wryly as she turned to the task of preparing dinner. But not so proud if she saw what Michaela did next. Marinating, boning, braising and steaming were all mysterious activities to Michaela; cooking to her meant sticking the requisite Marks and Spencer's cartons and packets in the microwave, waiting until it went PING, getting rid of all evidence of branded wrappings, then laying the food out prettily (Colin, who liked to think he was rather a connoisseur of fine foods, fortunately wasn't in the habit of frequenting supermarkets and so remained convinced, after six months of married life, that Michaela was an expert cook). With dinner – a Marks and Spencer's Chicken Masala and all its accompanying bits and bobs – going merrily around and around in the microwave, and the beer cooling in the fridge, she went into the living-room. There she set the fire, dimmed the lights and as she was searching through her CD collection for something suitable, she heard his car pull up outside.

"Hi," called Colin, coming in.

"Hi," she called back. "I'm in here."

Setting his bags down in the hallway, Colin came into the sitting-room. He flopped down on the couch, loosened his tie, rested his head back and closed his eyes.

"I'm wrecked," he said.

Michaela put a CD on to play, got up from where she was kneeling and came over to him. Sitting on the arm of the chair beside him she began to kiss him gently, little kisses along the side of his neck, and she stroked his hair. Eyes still closed, he smiled. She opened one of his shirt buttons and slid her hand inside.

"I've missed you," she said softly.

"I've only been gone a few days!" he laughed.

"I know, I know, but it seems like ages." As she was about to undo a second button, he opened his eyes and straightened up.

"I'm starving," he said.

"Well, there's some dinner ready," said Michaela, trying not to sound too disappointed but she'd hoped that food mightn't be foremost on his mind.

"But, Michaela, we're going out," said Colin.

"Going out?"

"Yes. Out."

"Out? Where?"

"To dinner."

"To dinner?"

"At Chez Zoe's."

"Chez Zoe's?"

"Michaela stop repeating everything I say. You're like a parrot, it's getting on my nerves. And there's no need to sound so surprised. Remember I told you I was going to book dinner at Chez Zoe's? That new place?" Then he realised that, although he'd meant to, he couldn't remember actually saying it to her, but he carried on regardless. "Remember? Before I went to Limerick?"

"Colin, you didn't tell me. Anyway, can't you cancel it? I'd much rather stay at home."

"Don't be ridiculous." Then he glared at the CD player, got up quickly, went over and turned it off. "That's better." He turned back to her and continued, "I thought you'd like to go out. You're always saying we don't go out enough. There's no pleasing you, Michaela, there really isn't. And anyway, this restaurant is supposed to be fantastic. Top class. They've a resident string quartet. Very romantic. You'll love it, I know you will. It's just your kind of place, all candlelight and atmosphere. Besides, it would be a shame to cancel it. It's

43

nearly impossible to get a table there."

"You're right, you're right," said Michaela. "We haven't gone out together for ages. And it is Friday. And maybe we could head out afterwards, to a disco."

"Well, I'm not so sure about that," he laughed. "I can't see Peg and Brenda being on for that."

"Peg and Brenda?" She stared at him but he wasn't paying her any attention. He was searching through the CD rack. "It's on the mantelpiece," she told him, knowing that he was searching for his Barry Manilow CD. It was the only thing he ever put on to play.

"Although Samantha might, she'd be on for anything," he said.

"Samantha?"

"And the two lads certainly will. They're mental when they get going."

"The two lads? Who the hell are the two lads? And Peg and Brenda, and Samantha? Am I supposed to know these people?"

"Sure you do. Ben Philips and Phil Brennan."

Michaela stared at him for a moment, puzzled. Then her face fell.

"Not those two fellows you work with?"

"Yeah, they're gas characters. Remember the last night we were out with them, that night of the office party. God, that was a wild night." And he started laughing. "Do you remember going home in the taxi afterwards, when Phil . . . "

"Yes, I do," she answered quickly, cutting him short. She'd no desire to dwell on the details of that awful taxi-ride home. To have gone through it once was enough.

"And Peg and Brenda – their wives. You got on great with them that night, didn't you?"

"I wouldn't say great exactly." But Colin wasn't listening, he was putting his Barry Manilow CD in the slot. The wrong way.

"You haven't met Samantha yet. She's the new rep – well, new to Cork. She was working out of our Galway office up to recently. It was her idea to go out tonight."

"So, let me see. There'll be you, me, Samantha, Peg, Brenda, Ben and Phil, all staring at each over a flickering candle, all being serenaded by this string quartet, in this lovely new atmospheric and romantic restaurant, that I'll love, that's just my kind of place. Are you sure there isn't anyone else coming? Anyone you've forgotten to mention?"

"No, that's it."

"What fun," she muttered, but he wasn't listening. He was busy trying to extract the CD having got it jammed. She might have helped him out if his choice of music had been anything else but she'd no desire to listen to Barry Manilow crooning, things were bad enough. "I know, why don't I ring Denise and Muriel from my office, ask them to come along? Make a real night out of it?" she asked.

"Well, I've only booked for seven, but maybe I can ring, see if they'll fit two more in. The more the merrier."

"Colin, if you ever listened to me talking about work, you'd realise I'm joking. I can't stand Muriel and Denise."

"So you don't want me to ring?"

"No."

"Anyway, we'll have a right laugh," he said.

"Yeah, a right laugh. So what are we

46

waiting for? Let's not waste any time. Let's get going! Why don't you pop old Barry into your pocket and, when we get tired of the string quartet, we can stick him on in the restaurant. For I think it's going to be that kind of a night."

Colin still couldn't figure out if Michaela was being sarcastic or not.

"But we have to change first," he said.

"What's wrong with the way I am?" asked Michaela, feeling a little annoyed, after all her effort.

"You look lovely. That dress is beautiful on you, it really is," he said, looking properly at her for the first time. "Maybe a little make-up."

"Thanks."

"Look, I'll go and get changed," he said. "I won't be long."

But Michaela knew he would, he always was. She put the guard in front of the fire and the dinner in the fridge, took out one of the bottles of beer and wandered upstairs. As he splashed and sprayed himself in the bathroom, she drank the beer, put on some make-up and played around with her hair.

And she put on a pair of knickers. So much for best-laid plans.

Polly's Friday nights required no planning. For Polly's Friday nights never varied.

Polly's family always had their tea that bit later than usual, for on Friday nights Mr Odlum went to collect Polly, his one and only, his darling daughter, his precious baby, his heart's delight – or his "pet" as he called her, not being given to sentimental verbosity – a simple term which belied the depth of his feeling, for she was all those things to him and more, almost everything you could say. And it was with a happy heart indeed that he made that weekly trip to the train station in Mallow to bring Polly home. Home, after her week in college.

And, as they did every Friday night, mother and grandmother waited in the Odlum kitchen, listening out for the sound of the car returning, for as soon as they'd hear it, they'd start frying the eggs and wetting the tea, tasks which needed to be left to the last minute if they were to be just right. Everything else was ready – the table was

48

laid, the rashers and sausages were set out on warm plates in the oven, home-made bread filled the basket. Every few minutes Granny went to the window and, peering out into the dark, she'd say, "You'd think they'd be here by now, wouldn't you, Margaret?" Then she'd turn around again, study the table critically and smoothen out an imaginary crease in the white linen cloth or select one of the heavy silver knives or forks, all equally shiny, for a bit of spit and polish.

Finally a car was heard.

"I hear them, Margaret. I hear the car. They're pulling into the yard, Margaret."

At this cue, Mrs Odlum cracked the eggs into the pan, saying, as she always did at this point,

"A fry will be a nice change for her. God knows what she eats up in Cork."

"Polly always loved a fry," said Granny giving her usual reply, as she went about wetting the tea. Then, pointing at the table, she remembered fondly, 'Even when she was only that high, she'd be robbing the rasher skins off of your plate. Wouldn't she, Margaret?"

"They're here. I hear the car," said Polly's Uncle Joe, arriving into the kitchen.

"Well, the tea is ready," said Granny.

"I'll just go out and give her a hand with the bags," said Uncle Joe.

Polly smelt the fry as she came into the house and her stomach turned. And, as always, she regretted not having told her mother, right from the start, that the last thing she wanted on a Friday night was a fry for, every single evening without fail, that's what she got served up to her at the hostel. But after all these months, it was too late to say anything. She couldn't bear to have her mother look at her, puzzled and hurt, wondering why on earth she hadn't said anything sooner.

"I'll just put the bags in your room, Polly," called Uncle Joe.

"Thanks, Uncle Joe," said Polly looking after him as he struggled up the stairs, thinking that the bags were far too heavy for him. But to tell him she'd take them up herself would be denying him his way of showing her that he was glad to have her home.

Her father went on into the kitchen before her.

"Will you look at what I bought home with me?" he was saying to Granny and Mrs Odlum as Polly arrived in after him.

In the rich farmlands of North Cork, the Odlums lived on their 150-acre farm situated half-way between Buttevant and Mallow. Like the neighbours around them, they were dairy farmers but, years ago, when Polly was two or three, taking advantage of the location of their farm which fronted onto the N20, the main Cork-Limerick Road, they'd set aside ten acres for market gardening and had opened a shop at the roadside to sell their produce. Over the years their range of merchandise had extended and now, in addition to their extensive array of vegetables and fruits, they sold other items – the concrete flower troughs and garden ornaments Uncle Joe had taken to making; the antiques Mr Odlum had started buying up; Mrs Odlum's seedlings and potted plants; and the tea-cosies, sweaters, home-made jam and other miscellaneous items Granny Odlum was forever beavering away at. The shop was no more than a shed really although, if Mrs Odlum had her way, which she didn't, it would have been flattened and a nice custom-made building put up instead, where they might sell tea and scones and the like to the passing tourists. So, over the years, as the range became too big for the building, the bulkier items were spread out along the grass margin and their operation had become something of a landmark to passing traffic.

Between the shop and the farm, the Odlums were a busy family and had a lot to tell Polly when she came home on a Friday night. As Polly supped her tea and played around with her fry, managing to make it look like she was eating it, she listened to the stories her family had stored up all week, for half the pleasure of their daily happenings lay in telling Polly.

"Polly, listen to what happened on Wednesday," began Gran now. "This lady came into the shop. Foreign she was. French, I'd say, by the accent." Although Granny was eighty-four now, serving in the shop was her job and she was never happier than talking to the people who stopped by. She'd keep them there for as long as she could, finding out all about them, and many a traveller's journey was delayed by an hour or more, when they came in for what they'd intended to be a quick look around. "Well, she left her husband in the car and came in," Granny was saying. "She hadn't much to say for herself, I couldn't get a word out of her. But the French are like that, aren't they? Kind of business-like in their manner," she said knowledgeably. "Anyway, she must have been twenty minutes looking around and I said to myself, I know her kind, she'll have a gawk at everything and buy nothing. But in the end, didn't she pick up a pot of jam, put a £10 note on the counter and, wait until I tell you this part Polly, before I had a chance to give her the change, hadn't she got back into the car and off they'd driven. Can you credit it? I figure she must have thought the jam was £10, not £1. Imagine thinking that a pot of jam cost £10!" hooted Granny.

"Polly, don't believe a word she says," said Uncle Joe. "Your grandmother is a crafty woman. She knew what she was doing alright when she pocketed that £10 note."

"Joe! Didn't I try to give her back the change? I ran out after her but she was gone."

"Of course she was. The only reason you ran out was to check that she *wasn't* coming back. Your grandmother is a swindler, Polly."

"Sure what's £10 to the likes of her?" asked Granny, not at all insulted. "She won't even miss it."

"Did I tell you I was over with your Auntie Deirdre on Tuesday, Polly?" Mrs Odlum asked, referring to her only sister, mother of Cliona of the dreadlocks and of her two younger and, as yet, dreadlock-less sisters, Ciara and Aileen. They lived on the outskirts of Mallow town in a six-bedroomed, four-bathroomed, detached house on its own extensive grounds. Although they didn't have a fraction of the money that the Odlums had, Deirdre certainly knew how to spend it, as Polly's mother was forever saying, with more than a hint of jealousy. A trip to her sister's always unsettled the hardworking Mrs Odlum. Coming home after listening to Deirdre's tales of shopping trips to Cork, of shows seen in Dublin, of foreign holidays taken with the "girls", as she always referred to the women she played golf with, Mrs Odlum would moan to deaf ears for the rest of the day. "What's the point in having money in the bank, if you can't enjoy it?" she could be heard muttering as she went about her jobs. "She was in Lanzarote," she was now telling Polly. "With Mrs Johnson and Mrs O'Toole, you know the lady who runs Fashion Fits. She showed me photos of the apartment they stayed in, fabulous it was. But really Polly, it was far too big for them – four bedrooms, all with double beds, a living-room, with another fold-down bed, a little kitchen – a galley kitchen I think she called it – and a balcony with a view of the beach. Mind you, Deirdre said they tended to stick to the pool, for the beach was a good twenty minutes' walk. But she got a great colour, although I don't think all that sun can be good, you'd never think she was younger than me. Still, she had a great holiday by all accounts. Do you know, Polly, it kills me to think that I'll probably die without so much as ever having been on a foreign holiday.

"Here it comes," said Mr Odlum, winking at Polly.

"What's the point of having money in the bank, if you can't enjoy it. Do you know, Polly, I've never even been abroad?"

"What are you talking about, didn't I take you to London on our honeymoon?" asked her husband.

"Sure that was years ago. Anyway it hardly counts. We went on the ferry. I'm talking about flying off to somewhere exotic, somewhere sunny. Do you know Polly, I've never even been on a plane?"

"I'll tell you what, Margaret," said Mr Odlum. "First thing in the morning, we'll take the car down to the long field. You can get up on the roof and I'll strap you down with some twine and give you a bit of a whizz around. Sure it'll be like flying, even better, you'll be able to feel the wind in your hair."

"Your father is useless, Polly, he won't go anywhere with me. When you're finished college, we'll go places together, won't we, Polly?"

Polly loved sitting there, listening to them all. Even if she'd already heard half of it already. Things that had happened two weeks ago, they'd tell her again, forgetting that they'd told her last week. Other stories she'd been hearing for as long as she could remember, like her Father's old joke about taking her mother down to the long field. Sometimes two of them, usually her mother and grandmother, would both talk to her at the one time, but she'd learnt the knack of letting both speakers believe it was really them she was listening to.

Her grandmother was eighty-four now, Uncle Joe was sixty-six, her father sixty-five and even her mother had turned sixty. All getting on she knew but found it hard to really appreciate, for she saw them at their best. She didn't hear her Granny's morning prayer said in thanks because she was alive for another day, or see her mother looking increasingly weary as she went about making the breakfast. Nor was she there in the quiet evenings during the week when her father and Uncle Joe sat by the fire after the day's hard work, feeling old and tired.

"Have you enough tea, Polly?" asked Uncle Joe.

"Loads, thanks, Uncle Joe," said Polly.

"There you are Polly," said Granny, slipping the rinds of her rashers onto Polly's plate. "I know how fond of them you are."

After the tea, Daddy settled down to watch the nine o'clock news and, as always, the comfort of a sated stomach and a roaring fire lulled him to sleep before the newscaster had even finished her summary of the stories of the day. Granny, as she always did at this time, had wandered off to her room to have a few squares of the chocolate bar which she knew Polly would have left under her pillow, and to do what she called her jobs, which meant getting her night-clothes ready and her teeth out before coming back to settle down for *The Late Late Show* (on, at the not very late-late time of nine-thirty. Polly supposed that when it had first started, like about a billion years ago, then nine-thirty must have been considered late-late). Joe had wandered outside for a smoke and to finish up on the farm before he too came back in for *The Late Late*. There was just her mother and herself sitting at the kitchen table now, and her father snoozing by the fire.

This was Polly's mother's special time

with her daughter, the only time they really got a chance to talk, so she always said. Their mother and daughter time, as she liked to put it, and the time Polly dreaded most in the whole week. For her mother wanted to hear stories of the wonderful time Polly was having in college, accounts of parties and of friends and of the kind of carry-on she liked to think she'd be getting up to if she was Polly's age. And there was no point in Polly telling her that she hadn't gone to a single party, hadn't made any friends, let alone boyfriends, and certainly no point in telling her that she was unhappy in college. She knew that if she did then, like everything to do with her, it would become a topic of general discussion with Granny, Daddy and Uncle Joe being brought in on it, all worrying about her and, their worry, and her unhappiness, becoming the constant topics of the household. It was easier to keep it private and keep her mother and everyone happy. So people Polly hardly knew became her friends for that half an hour and stories about parties she'd overheard became her own stories, and the family could rest happy that little Polly was having a great time up at the college. And when her mother, as she always did, came to that question which most interested her, "Anyone special?" which she'd ask offhandedly but with her eyes glued to her daughter, Polly would laugh and shrug and say "Mam, it's too early for that, I'm having too much fun," which sounded hollow to her but satisfied her mother who'd laugh and say, "Of course you are. Plenty of time yet for that sort of thing." So what had possessed Polly to say otherwise when her mother had posed that perennial question tonight? What had made her pause and answer hesitantly, "Well . . . "

"Yes?" said her mother encouragingly.

"Well, there is someone I like." It was the thought of Davy that made her waver so, the memory of the way he looked, and felt, as he slept on her shoulder that morning, for she had thought about little else since.

Just then her father grunted and stirred in his seat.

"Daddy, Polly has a boyfriend. Daddy!" called Mrs Odlum. "Are you listening? Polly has a boyfriend."

"Mam, don't go telling Daddy," pleaded Polly. "He's not a boyfriend exactly, just someone I like," she tried to explain.

But even in his slumber, Mr Odlum's ears had pricked up at the magic word.

"A boyfriend, Eh? Our little Polly has a boyfriend."

Just then Granny shuffled in and Mr Odlum lost no time in sharing this development on a much-speculated-upon topic.

"Granny, our Polly has gone and got herself a boyfriend," he shouted at his mother who suffered from partial hearing loss, as she settled herself down in her favourite seat by the fire to await *The Late Late Show*.

"I didn't say it was my boy—"

"Is he at the college as well, Polly?" asked Granny, who never missed hearing anything of interest – her hearing loss was only partial.

"Yes, he is Granny," answered Polly, for what was the point in saying otherwise?

"I expect he's in the same class, Granny. Going to be a teacher like Polly," said Mrs Odlum, who was very adept at filling in the blanks.

"Mammy, stop going on about him."

"What's his name? Is he a nice boy?" her mother asked.

"Mammy!"

"Joe, did you hear Polly has a boyfriend?" called out Mrs Odlum, hearing the back door bang shut.

"Ho ho! And when are we going to met the lucky fellow?" asked Uncle Joe coming into the room.

"Has Cliona met him?" asked Mrs Odlum, a little concerned.

"No, not yet."

"Probably just as well," she said relieved. "You don't want him thinking you're like her. I know she's my niece but I'd be the first to admit she's very wild. I'm all for young people having a good time, I was young myself once but, if half of what we hear about her is true, and I'm sure we don't hear the half of it, then that madam is going to come to a sticky end. It was the worse thing George and Deirdre could do, letting her move into a flat, she should have stayed in the hostel like you," said Mrs Odlum. "So pet, when will we get to meet him?"

"Mam, please!"

"Is he from Cork? We probably know his family."

"Sssh," said Granny. "It's starting." A hush descended over the room as the family turned towards the television and awaited the appearance of Gay Byrne – probably the only person in the world who could have stopped this inquisition – all except Polly who, conscious of the fact that there would be ad breaks, took herself off to bed to avoid having to answer any more questions. Like, what was his name?

4

COLIN LOVES MICHAELA
BUT SAMANTHA TOO

Davy had spent the rest of the day reading on the hospital steps by the bridge. Then, he'd returned to the squat to check that it was still standing. It was and, not feeling in the mood to stop in on his own for the night, he'd wandered back down to the bridge. The place was deserted when he arrived and he sat on the steps again, smoked a couple of cigarettes and enjoyed the quiet and the panorama of the lights of the city at night. After twenty minutes or so, one of the older of the regular bridge drinkers arrived; a shabby fellow of sixty, dressed, as always, in a green woolly hat pulled down over his ears and a long black coat which reached down to his dirty white runners and whatever lay underneath the coat, which nobody ever saw. The old man had spent most of the day drinking with a couple of other old fellows in the bars along the quays, but having been thrown out of all of these they'd split up to go in search of other sources of drink and had arranged to meet up again at the bridge. Seeing that his two friends hadn't arrived yet, the old man climbed up the steps and sat down beside Davy. Still drunk from the day's drinking he launched into tale after tale of the time he had worked as a porter in one of the city's finer hotels. Half-way through a convoluted account of how himself and one of Hollywood's biggest stars, who'd been staying at the hotel (and who Davy had never heard of), had drunk their way through the pubs of the city, his pals arrived with the drink. Settling down on the step below Davy and their friend, they began to drink and included Davy in the rounds the flagon of cider was making and in the conversation.

Their talk was just the foolish ramblings of drunks and Davy had made up his mind to go when he saw Michaela coming over the bridge. His first emotion was awe; under the street lights she looked absolutely gorgeous, with her hair loosely tied up, a little curl escaping here and there, a hint of make-up (although really she didn't need it, he thought), and a tight-fitting red dress which confirmed everything he had supposed about her figure. His second emotion was mortification; that she'd see him sitting here with this gang, swigging from a flagon of cider. He bent down low and edged over, trying to hide behind the fatter of the drunks on the step below. Unsuccessfully.

"Hi," she called out.

He kept his head down.

"Christ, she's a beauty," commented one of the two fellows on the step below Davy.

"It's not coming up to see us, she is!" said the other, turning around to poke Davy in the ribs as she climbed up the steps. "Doubt ya, Davy boy!" he said, clipping Davy across the back of the head.

Davy raised his head up.

"Listen, I hope I didn't offend you this lunch-time," she said, now standing on the

66

step just below the two old fellows and smiling up at Davy. Davy shook his head, he was utterly tongue-tied, he couldn't have said a word, not if his life depended upon it. And he wasn't the only one she'd made an impact on. Without realising it, the others were sitting that little bit straighter and they'd set the drink down. "I know it's stupid," she went on, completely oblivious to the impression she was making. "But when I saw you running after me I just panicked."

"No problem," Davy managed to say.

"I'm sorry I thought you were going to rob me."

"Hello, Miss. How are you?" interrupted the first old fellow, grinning widely and toothlessly at her. He'd taken off the green hat, a rare occurrence, something he didn't even do when going to bed, and was holding his hand out to her.

"Hello," she answered, smiled at him and shook the extended hand.

"We're friends of young Davy here," the old man went on, putting an arm around Davy's shoulder. "Cornelius O'Toole is my name," he introduced himself thus, though he'd been called nothing but Connie since the day of his christening.

"And I'm Michaela," she answered and then turned back to Davy. "I'd hate to have lost it. It has all my cards in it."

"No problem," Davy replied again.

"And I'm Francis O'Shea. I'm another friend of Davy's," said the one known to all as Francey and he too held out his hand, or what was left of it, for he'd lost a couple of his fingers one drunken night some years back but fortunately had no recollection of the event. She shook hands with him and, before she could pull away, he'd brought her hand to his lips, gave a damp kiss on the back of it, then winked at her and said, "I always do that to the pretty ones."

She smiled weakly at him, a little disgusted.

"Would you like a drink, miss?" he asked, offering her the flagon.

"No. Thanks all the same."

He pulled down his sleeve over his intact hand and used it to wipe the top of the bottle.

"There, go on now," he said offering it

to her again, glad he had thought to be courteous.

"No, really. I've a long night ahead of me," she answered not wanting to offend him but conscious that the only effect of wiping the bottle with his dirty sleeve was probably to dramatically increase the germ count. She turned back to Davy, "I'm sorry about mentioning a reward, I hope you didn't take it the wrong way, it's just that I was so grateful."

"Nugget Vickers," butted in the third fellow, annoyed to have momentarily forgotten his real name; he'd have liked to have used it so as not to be outdone by the other two, but for the life of him, he couldn't remember it, he hadn't heard it in over forty drink-sodden years. She turned to him and shook his outstretched hand.

"If I may be so bold, Miss, could I just say that you're a picture to look at," said Nugget, keeping a firm hold of her hand. "You're just like one of them old film stars."

"Mitch! Come on!" shouted Colin who was keeping his distance at the bottom of the steps and wondering had she taken leave of her senses – gabbing away with these drunks as if she was the best of friends with them. Only then did Davy notice him standing there in the dark and realise that this man, who'd come striding across the bridge ahead of her, at a speed which made it impossible for Michaela in her high heels and tight dress to keep up, was with her. And his heart sank. It wasn't that he'd assumed if she were available, she'd be available for him – it was just that he'd never pictured her with a boyfriend or husband, or whatever that fattish blond man was.

"Michaela, come down," shouted Colin more insistently.

"I better get going. Anyway thanks . . . Davy," she said, still trying to pull free from Nugget's firm hold of her hand.

"No problem," Davy said for the third time. "No problem at all . . . Michaela."

"My late wife was the spit of Gretta Garbo. Only better-looking," Nugget told her now, not ready to let go of her hand just yet.

"Is that right?"

"She'd the same type of hair as Gretta Garbo, you know, curling around the ears, shortish. The night I met her, I said, 'Joan', for that was her name, I said 'Joan' . . . "

"Michaela!"

"Yeah, I'm coming. I'm sorry, I'd better go," said Michaela, still trying to pull her hand free.

Nugget glanced down at Colin. "Yerra, don't mind that fellow," he said, not being in the least impressed by what he saw. "I'm telling you now, you'd be better off with Davy here. A very smart fellow indeed. Though you mightn't think it to look at him, he's read every book ever written. Sure, we call him the Professor, we do."

"Michaela!" called Colin.

"Look, I'm sorry but I really have to go. Goodbye," said Michaela and, finally managing to pull free, she hurried back down the steps to where Colin was waiting.

Davy and the three men watched as the couple walked on.

"Mitch, don't be drawing that sort on yourself," Davy overheard Colin say. Michaela shrugged and, conscious that Colin was speaking so loudly, she turned around, smiled and waved, then turned back again and struggled to keep up with Colin who'd gone striding on ahead of her.

As she disappeared around the corner, Davy considered the sound of her name. Michaela. Michaela. Beautiful. Exactly the right name. Imagine shortening it to Mitch! Only a pompous-looking ass like that fellow would be so ignorant, thought Davy, deciding that he wouldn't have liked Colin even if he wasn't with Michaela; that he looked far too full of self-love to have any left over for anyone, even for someone as perfect as her. A car sales rep for sure, he thought, but then, Davy always decided that people he didn't like were car sales reps. Though he couldn't say he really knew any as such.

The happy hubbub of the restaurant, with its sounds of clinking glasses, of dinner chat and laughter, of waiters bustling back and forth, was stilled for a split second in the aftermath of a most dreadful, high-pitched screech which pierced the air.

"Coonooll! Coonooll! Over heerree!"

"Samantha!" shouted Colin, and then raced across the room.

Michaela, walking across the restaurant at a more sedate pace, watched as Colin took hold of this Samantha's hand, examined her up and down and complimented her loudly, whilst she shook her head and protested equally loudly.

"This old thing, sure I've had it for years," Samantha was saying, or rather lying to Colin who was standing very, very close to her, his hand now stroking her velvet-clad shoulder. "I haven't had time to shop since I moved down. Staff welfare isn't exactly a priority with the big boys, is it? Slave drivers, the lot of them!"

"And how are we to compete with the likes of this? Eh, boys?" Colin turned and asked his other two colleagues, two men in their early forties who'd stood up to greet him. Their wives remained seated but were smiling up at Colin. Colin's hand had moved from Samantha's shoulder to bare arm and was still busy stroking it. "How many hours on the golf course do you think it takes us to bag the same business as this one manages with just a wiggle?" he asked the men, his hand now finding a resting place on

Samantha's bottom. Michaela was used to Colin flirting, it came as naturally to him as breathing, but even for Colin this was a bit too much, too soon. From shoulder to bottom in a matter of seconds! She coughed.

"Michaela, have you met Samantha? She worked with me in Galway. Another Compu2000 rep. She's just moved to Cork."

Michaela had come to realise that there was no point in taking umbrage with every girl Colin flirted with; it would be ridiculous to hold the dozens of girls responsible, so now she smiled and said,

"I don't think so. Hi, Samantha."

"Hi, Michaela. Nice to meet you."

"So you've moved to Cork lately?" Michaela asked.

"Been moved, more like," laughed Samantha. "Plucked from my happy little existence and cast out into the unknown."

"Michaela, you know the others – Ben Philips and Phil Brennan," Colin interjected, indicating the two men. Michaela did know them, or rather had met them once before at that office party, but she could hardly bring herself to smile as she shook hands with

74

them, foreseeing what the night held in store, if that last occasion was anything to go by. They looked very sedate and proper now, in their expensive neat grey suits, crisp white shirts, silk ties and shiny shoes; all polite smiles and handshakes, but Michaela, going by her last experience with them, feared that this veneer wouldn't last too long. As soon as they had a few too many, they'd shed their ties and jackets, and their beer bellies (now camouflaged under the jackets) would be bulging through gaps where their shirt buttons yielded to the pressure. But that was the least of it. As the night wore on, she'd probably have closer bodily contact with both of them than she'd like, as they'd take every opportunity to sidle up to her and tell her what a lucky man Colin was. And Ben, or Phil, or whatever the marginally more stout of the two was called, would probably whisper a variety of improper suggestions in her ear and explain what a bitch his wife was. The other, the marginally less stout, would probably lose a shoe, accost one of the waiting staff, fall asleep in the gents, get sick in the taxi on the way home and then proceed to pick a fight with the taxi-driver. At least that's what had happened the last time.

"And the girls – Peg, Ben's wife and Brenda, Phil's wife," Colin went on and Michaela smiled.

"Hello again," she said.

As on that last occasion "the girls", forty if a day, were wearing short dark dresses, pearl chokers, ruby-red nails and lips, big, big hair and high, high heels. They were both good-looking, but not attractive, and were obviously no strangers to the sun-beds and stair-climbers at their, no doubt exclusive, health club. Michaela's heart sank, as flashes of what she considered their stupendously boring conversation (professional versus home manicures, hairdressing tales of woes, the new Betty Barclay range) of that previous night came back to her. Oh dear, she thought.

"So, Mitch, why don't you sit there beside Peg," Colin was saying to her. "And I'll squeeze in here beside the lovely Samantha." And as he squeezed in beside the lovely Samantha, Michaela took her place at the edge of the table.

They ordered their meal.

"So Michaela, how's the legal world these days?" asked one of the men, Ben Brennan, or Phil Philips or Ben Philips or whatever, she didn't really care.

"As exciting as usual," she answered ambiguously, thinking how the hell was she supposed to know, she was a secretary, not a bloody barrister. Anyway, if she was to start on how she was really finding her little bit of the legal world, inside those four walls of the typing-pool, listening to the moans and inanities of Muriel and Denise, day after day after day after day, he'd soon regret having asked such an seemingly innocuous question and she'd be checking out the knives on the table in front of her to see were any sharp enough to slit her wrists with. Best change the subject.

"I expect if Colin is anything to go by, you're run off your feet, Brendan," she said.

"Ben," he corrected her and then launched into an interminable soliloquy on how very busy he was. Very busy indeed it appeared. He began to list out the names of dozens of client firms, seeming to think that this made for good dinner conversation; that for some reason Michaela would find this list of names and the size of each of his client's huge orders, right down to the very last little micro-chip, as fascinating as he did. It was going to be a very long night.

But not so for everyone else. Colin was in top form. Flirting with Samantha mainly, but being democratic enough to occasionally give Peg and Brenda a blast of his charm. And of course there was shop talk between Phil, Ben, Colin and Samantha which left Peg and Brenda free to discuss the good sense in not penny-pinching when it came to buying underwear – for a good bra will take you anywhere they agreed – and other such topics which their not-terribly-wide-range of interests covered. And Michaela stifled yawn after yawn, but nodded regularly enough so as to appear suitably interested and helped herself to the wine.

"You know John Williams," Ben, or Phil, or whichever was saying, "He used to be in business with Murray Jones, but Jones did the dirt on him. Although, they say John is doing very well on his own, that he's making an absolute fortune. Of course he made a killing on those houses he built out in Glanmire."

"That's right. He's just bought a Mercedes F-300, hasn't he?" said Colin. As Michaela listened to him go on, she wondered had he changed, or was it just that love had blinded her to this unbelievably pretentious side of him. "No, John's not short of a bob or two," he was saying, nodding knowledgeably at the others. "That's for sure. A great man for the golf, you know. I've played a round or two with him myself. Very, very sociable fellow. Marvellous house. Magnificent bathrooms. Absolutely magnificent. He imported the marble from Italy, you know."

Played golf with him, what a liar! The last time Colin's golf clubs had seen daylight was when he'd brought them home from the shop, thought Michaela. And the closest Colin had ever got to these Italian bathrooms, she guessed, was seeing their picture in the pages of a property supplement. But he was managing to make out that he knew this John Williams better than the others, so well in fact that he was a regular visitor to his house, therefore he was better connected and consequentially more important.

"My daddy's car is bigger than your daddy's car," she muttered.

"Pardon?" said Peg, thinking she mustn't have heard correctly. Michaela hadn't realised she was speaking aloud.

"Nothing. Just some lines of a song. Some more wine?"

"Yes, please. Anyway, as I was saying," Peg turned back to Brenda and continued. "If I limit myself to just a natural yoghurt, toast and black tea in the morning, a plain whole-wheat sandwich at lunch, maybe chicken or salmon with lettuce – no butter or dressing, then I'm still way under my calorie limit and I can afford to go a bit mad with my evening meal. You know, have a glass of wine and a piece of fruit for afters."

"Well, I'm the opposite. I tend to eat more at the start of the day and cut back later on. Of course . . ."

Once upon a time she'd have caught Colin's eye across the table and they'd both have had trouble stifling their laughter. Now he probably thought they were lovely women. Probably would have liked if she was a little more like them. If she tried to explain to him later why she didn't like them, she imagined he'd throw his eyes to heaven and wonder what she was going on about. She still loved him of course, but on nights like this she worried that things were changing, something was slipping away and she couldn't say she even liked him. It was easier when they were on their own, her love was surer then.

"I had him eating from the palm of my hand," Colin was saying now, leaning across the table towards the other two men but keeping one hand draped across the back of Samantha's chair. "He hadn't the slightest idea of what he was paying for, yet he was prepared to hand over £10,000! And was I going to dissuade him, tell him that it wasn't going to be of any use? That in six months' time, he'd have to upgrade his entire system in any case? Not on your life! Not if it meant losing out on my commission."

Watching him throw back his head with laughter and bang his fist on the table with the delight at how very cunning he was, an image of him in earlier times came to her. Just a little over a year ago, back in Galway, the two of them sitting in his father's car outside her parents house. They'd both grown up in Galway and were still living there back then. They'd only met four hours previously, at a party, but already she had begun to wonder if he might be the one for her – hasty, but not as hasty as Colin – within ten minutes of meeting her, he'd told her he knew for certain that she was the one. She remembered thinking how very beautiful he looked that night, staring out the front window of the car, glancing over at her every now and then, his eyes bright, his face all lit up, as he talked on and on until the dawn. She remembered him telling her about his plans for the future. How he had just started with Compu2000; that this job as a sales rep was just a means of getting money together; that he wanted to do things on his own; set up his own business; that really, he wasn't cut out for sales; that he was too soft. But, listening to him now, boasting proudly about how very clever he was, she thought that surely he had underestimated himself. Or overestimated.

Across the table, Samantha, feeling Colin's hand caress her knee, thought how very bizarre life was. Michaela wasn't the only one remembering that night. While Colin had chatted away until the dawn, not so far away Samantha had lain awake in bed crying because her boyfriend Colin had left the party before she'd arrived. Left with a beautiful girl with curly auburn hair, her friends had told her. "Samantha, you're such a silly," he had said to her the next day, kissing her tears away. "That was one of my sisters. She was sick. I had to take her home." And Samantha had laughed and cried at the same time and apologised for doubting him. And they'd kissed and made up and went on as before until she'd heard, but not from him, that he was getting married to a beautiful girl with curly auburn hair.

For months after, Samantha had felt that all she wanted to do was die, but now she was over him, well over him, and here she was sitting at the same table as the girl with the curly auburn hair, who, for so long she'd wished killed or at least tragically disfigured in an accident. And all she could feel for her was pity. Sitting there, ignorant to the fact that her husband's hand was inching up his-soon-to-be-again-lover's skirt. And Samantha was thankful for her lucky escape; that she wasn't his poor unsuspecting wife. Now that she was no longer in love with him, and was a great deal wiser and tougher because of him, she saw that as a lover he'd be fine, perfectly adequate. Not quite as thin or handsome as he'd been a year ago and in a couple of years he'd be positively fat, but she'd have moved on by then, found herself someone nice, someone who could be trusted. But he'd pass the time pleasantly for her in those first few lonely months on her own in Cork, until she'd settled in.

5

COLIN LOVES MICHAELA
BUT SAMANTHA AND
ANNA TOO

THERE WAS one thing Polly's mother refused to do and that was serve in the shop. "As long as I don't have to sit behind that counter, I'll turn my hand to anything," she'd say. Which she did. On the domestic side she took care of everything and everybody and she wasn't adverse to farm work either, being willing and able for any task, no matter how dirty or difficult. From her early rise at seven in the morning, until well after the tea it was all go-go with her. No, there wasn't an idle bone in her body, as Polly's father was often heard to say proudly. And even Granny

Odlum who'd been disappointed for at least the first ten years of her son's marriage that he had chosen a townie, had no choice but to overcome her prejudice and concede, to herself at any rate, that Margaret was some worker, better than many reared on a farm. Some worker, except when it came to the shop and so that task fell to Granny Odlum mainly and to Polly when she came home at the weekends.

A task which Polly didn't relish, although when she was growing up, the shop had seemed a most wondrous place. She could remember day after day, summer after summer, sitting outside the shop in the sun with her grandmother, watching the traffic go by, waiting for the occasional customer to pull over. Granny would knit and knit as she talked and talked, though her talking was just the verbalisation of some of the thoughts which flitted into her mind. There didn't seem to be much coherence or any real point to what she said, at least none that the young Polly could detect as she listened to her granny flit between the living and the dead, between relatives and strangers, hopping all over the decades and back and forth between the farm and the wider world.

"Polly", she might begin in those days long ago, as they sat together in the sun. "Did I ever tell you about the beautiful mink stole my mother always wore?" And as she described it to Polly – its lovely soft feel and how stylishly her mother used to wear it – her thoughts would have galloped on ahead. The stole would remind Granny of the day her mother had bought it which, coincidentally, was the very same day her sister Mary had upped and left home without a word to anyone. And whilst she talked on about the stole to Polly, her own thoughts would have wandered on to the very eventful life Mary had made for herself in America. "America," she'd say, abruptly changing the subject. "Now Polly there's the place anyone with sense would be. I often wonder what kind of life I'd have had if I'd gone myself." And Polly would look up at her puzzled, trying, but failing, to figure out the connection between America and the stole. But Granny's thoughts would be off again, racing way ahead of her words. And whilst Polly listened

87

to her opinion of that great land, Granny would be thinking of how, at seventeen, she'd have gone to Boston herself except she'd fallen in love, which would remind her of the great love she felt for her long dead husband, which would call to mind the regret she felt for Joe because he'd never married, which would prompt her to abandon the subject of America in favour of Uncle Joe. "Oh Polly, you should have seen Joe when he was a young fellow. God, he was so handsome. Why, he could have had any girl he wanted!" And Polly would puzzle for a while, trying to figure out what Uncle Joe had to do with America. And as she went on to describe the powerful body of him and the fine head of hair on the young Joe, Granny would be thinking of that lovely girl he'd nearly married, whose father had owned a pub in Mallow and, without thinking to tell Polly, she'd switch to Mallow town of today. "You'd hardly recognise the place now with all the new housing going up and the new road and all that," she'd say and Polly would wonder where? Somewhere in America? But surely Granny had never been there, how could she know what it looked like? So for much of those afternoons, Polly had struggled to make sense of what her grandmother was talking about. Or half struggled, for it didn't really matter to a little girl sitting in the sun with her darling grandmother.

Every summer, Cliona, Ciara and Aileen, would come to stay with the Odlums for a few weeks. Her three cousins thought that Polly was the luckiest girl in the world. To children who had just their own garden and the gardens of their friends to play in, to have a whole farm of your own seemed about as good as it got. And although the farm never seemed much fun to Polly when she was on her own, for those few weeks it was a different place. When her Auntie Deirdre drove away from the farm, she left behind three spotless little girls, all bows, ringlets, white ankle-socks, manicured nails and frilly dresses. And when she came to collect them a few weeks later they looked no different, except for the odd tell-tale plaster and a healthy colour. But the interim was a different story. Unlike their own mother who went spare at the sight of a grass stain, Polly's mother expected them to be filthy before long and so dressed them in Polly's oldest clothes each morning. And for those few weeks they went around in torn and muddied T-shirts and shorts; and their nails became dirt-encrusted, their hair tangled, their elbows grazed and their faces grimy and freckled. For how could it be any other way when they passed the time riding high on trailers of hay, playing at cabby house in the lofts, hiding and seeking amongst the bales in the barn, swinging on tyres roped to the rafters, rolling down the fields, picking blackberries, minding the young farm animals and wading through the stream in search of minnows or "collies" as they called them. Whew! And that was just the mornings. And, in the late afternoons, when they were tired out, the girls would bring stools out from the kitchen and go and sit with Polly's Granny outside the shop (a farm *and* a shop *and* a Granny!) and listen to her stories. Often Cliona would recall those times to Polly, laughing at how they must have looked like right little raggedy roadside urchins.

And therein lay the problem. There was,

thought Polly, now sitting behind the counter on the Saturday morning, something so very hucksterish about having this kind of a higgledy-piggledy shop at the side of the road. When she was younger, Polly had thought her mother's reluctance to work in the shop stemmed from the fact she was just too busy otherwise. Now, with the heightened sensibilities of a teenager, since she too was beginning to feel the same way, Polly was beginning to understand her mother's real reservations. The problem with the shop, she felt, was that it was so public. So desperate. So undignified. So very greedy in a way that no other shop could be, peddling a few antiques or old junk to be more accurate, and some home-made bits and pieces, at the side of the road. And Polly was beginning to understand that no matter how dirty a job her mother was doing on the farm, at least she could do it without risk of the public in general, or their neighbours, seeing her.

Outside, the October sun was shining brightly, but inside the shop it was dark. And freezing cold. Dismissive of Polly's efforts to convince her that an open shop-door wasn't likely to prompt anyone to suddenly grind to a halt, Granny Odlum still insisted that it be kept open at all times and now the little bar heater at Polly's feet was providing little comfort from the cold. At times like this, she wished she had a proper part-time job, like Cliona, who worked in a pub. Once, she'd said as much to her parents, but they'd looked at her as if she was completely crazy. "Why," her father had asked, genuinely perplexed, "go work for others when there's so much to be done at home?" The only way to keep warm, Polly had learned, was to engage in some running on the spot, so now she climbed down from her high stool, came out from behind the counter, went to the middle of the floor and began to run. Gradually she began to warm up slightly but then, pausing to catch her breath, she happened to notice Granny's coat hanging on the back of the door, or rather Uncle Joe's coat which had been commandeered by the old woman. Polly took it down and put it on, feeling for once grateful for Granny's annoying habit of taking possession of any item of clothing she fancied, no matter who in the family it belonged to. Last year she'd taken to wearing Polly's school coat so regularly that Polly's mother, fed up of the squabbles each morning, had bought Polly a second one. If her grandmother had stuck to wearing the coat around the farm, Polly wouldn't have minded as much. But she hadn't. Walking down the main street in Mallow one day with some girls from school, Polly had been mortified to see her coming towards them in what was obviously a St Patrick's coat, as the sniggers of the girls testified, even though she'd taken the trouble to dolly it with her best scarf and favourite brooch.

Now, the Joe/Granny coat completely swamped Polly and, wondering how Granny, inches shorter than herself, managed to keep her balance under the weight of it, Polly gathered up the ends to prevent herself tripping and walked across the shop, went back behind the counter and climbed up on the stool once again. At last she was comfy. She dug her hands deep into the substantial pockets to complete the effect then, feeling one of her grandmother's rosary beads in the left pocket, she smiled to herself. When there were no customers in the shop, Polly knew her grandmother often sat here, lips moving ceaselessly as she fingered the beads. Decades and decades and decades of the rosary she said. Most, Polly knew, were said for her; that the train she was travelling on wouldn't crash; that she wouldn't be sucked into the drug scene – fat chance, she could have told her; or, that the man who'd killed a student in Galway wouldn't make his way down to Cork and seek Polly out from the thousands of students. The rest of the prayers were divided between her other relatives, long dead or likely, in Granny's opinion, soon to be dead.

This morning, Polly had brought down two books with her to the shop – Chaucer's *Canterbury Tales* and John Irving's *Cider House Rules*. And now that she was warm at last she turned her attention to them. The first was prescribed reading for her course in "Old and Middle English" and she had to hand in an essay on it by Monday. She fully intended to do the essay first and so, diligently, she tried to made a start on it. But Polly was weak-willed when it came to study and, after trying for all of forty seconds, she decided to treat herself to just twenty pages of Irving first, already knowing, though not caring to admit it, that she'd spend the day reading just twenty more pages of Irving and her essay, like nearly all her college assignments, would be another Sunday-night-rush job. And so she sat there, waiting for customers, feeling nice and warm and alternating between reading John Irving and watching the shapes her breath made in the cold air as she day dreamed of Davy.

An hour had gone by when Polly heard the car. Looking up, she saw a black BMW soft-top pulling up outside. In love though she might be, she was also an eighteen-year-old girl and now she watched keenly, eagerly waiting to get a better look at the driver, hoping that he'd provide some excitement on an otherwise boring Saturday morning by being as handsome and dashing as his car suggested. As he got out, Polly noted and approved of his broad build and his head of blond-white hair and at first thought him to be appropriately handsome. But, as he walked around to the passenger's door, she saw that he was just a little too plump for her liking and decided that there was definitely something shifty in his expression. He opened the passenger's door and a woman stepped out. Her clothes, jewellery and figure were the most distinctive things about her. She was wearing a simple plain dark suit, so simple and understated that it had to be very, very expensive; masses of heavy gold jewellery to counteract the subtlety of the suit; and she was whippet-thin – like an undernourished world-class model. But her gaunt face was border-line plain, noted Polly with a degree of bitchy satisfaction, glad that the woman didn't have good looks on top of her certain wealth, marvellous figure and BMW-driving boyfriend, who, despite Polly's reservations was, she had to admit, conventionally handsome in a bland day-time TV soap sort of way.

"All right, you win," laughed the man. "I've pulled over, but I'm begging you please, please, please don't spend all morning in there!"

"As if I'd be so naughty," said the woman

and she lowered her head, put it to one side and smiled at him, coquettishly, Princess Diana style. Inches taller than him, she bent to kiss him. One small kiss, then she pulled away.

"Yes, you would, you know you would," he laughed, keeping his eyes closed, waiting for more. The girl leaned forward to give him another kiss, another small one for her mind was on shopping, but this time he reacted quickly and pulled her in to him and he began to kiss her hard, pressing her up against the car. Soon he was dug into her, as Polly's cousin Cliona might have said had she been watching. But only Polly was watching, a little disgusted, feeling voyeuristic but incapable of turning away as he continued to eat the face off of her, as Cliona might have indelicately put it.

"Colin!" the girl said eventually. "Stop!"

"Ann," said Colin softly, taking no notice of her half-hearted protests. And now, having explored her mouth as thoroughly as is possible without the aid of medical instruments, he moved on to her ear and proceeded to give it an equally thorough examination with his tongue, while his hand travelled up her skirt. Polly watched on, feeling herself blushing, thankful that it was herself who was minding the shop and not her grandmother, who, whenever they showed any of what she called smut on RTE, was so scandalised that she wrote to complain and since her definition was very wide, she was one of the most prolific writers to RTE, Donnybrook, Dublin 4. She'd have been out with a bucket of water or a stick by this stage, thought Polly. As Colin's lips moved down to the hollow of Anna's neck and she stood there with her head thrown back, Polly was beginning to think they wouldn't stop until they'd went the whole way, there and then, on the side of the road, in broad daylight! But Anna suddenly broke free of his roving hands and his probing tongue and his pressing body.

"Colin, we have to be at Mummy's by twelve."

"Well, what are we going in here for so?" moaned Colin.

"Come on, I won't be long. The kind who run these places haven't a clue. You could easily pick up something really valuable for next to nothing. You know the set of chairs Mummy has in her dining-room, well, she got them in the most God-awful place in Athlone, almost worse than this. For an absolute song! Guess how much she found out they were worth when she got them valued?"

Colin shrugged.

"Go on, guess."

"How the hell would I know?" asked Colin feeling cross. He'd a splitting headache from all the wine of the night before and the way she was forever making him guess the price of things really annoyed him. This day wasn't turning out the way he'd planned at all, at all. He'd expected to spend it cocooned with Anna in her apartment in Limerick, not visiting mothers and junk shops. He'd annoyed Michaela by telling her he had to go to work on a Saturday and he'd annoyed Samantha by turning down her whispered suggestion, as they left the restaurant last night, to call around to her today.

"Guess," demanded Anna.

"I don't know."

"Four thousand pounds for the set! Can you believe that? Of course, they're probably worth more now, that was years ago. She has an eye for a good thing, like myself. Come on, just a quick look around," she said and gave him a coaxing kiss. "Who knows, some day I might marry, move out of my little apartment and have a house of my own." And then she giggled. "It's never too early to start on a bottom drawer, you know."

Thinking that it would of little use to her if she was depending on him, Colin followed in after her.

"Hi," said Polly as they came. "Nice morning," she managed to say with professional politeness, though she didn't feel much like it having heard every word the woman had said. Colin didn't bother to acknowledge her, he just looked around in disgust and Anna just about managed a faint snotty smile.

Anna proceeded to walk around the shop, studying everything with her eye for a good thing, Polly supposed. Every now and then, she paused to examine something closely, but not daring to touch, presumably to avoid catching some terminal disease from the dust. She didn't seem to notice the hand that constantly stroked her bottom as, again and again, she called out, "How much?" And each time Polly told her, she snorted in disbelief, "For that old thing?"

Getting a little tired of all her snorting, Polly resumed reading.

Spotting a chair which took her fancy, once again Anna demanded to know "How much?" But Polly didn't hear her, nor did she see Colin nudge Anna, but she couldn't fail to hear his loud stage whisper which followed.

"She can't hear you, Anna. She's having trouble with her book. Watch closely and you'll see her lips moving."

Anna left out a shriek of laughter.

"Sorry, sir, did you say something?" asked Polly, annoyed now. This couple were really obnoxious.

"Yes, I did actually," said Colin. "I can see that you're obviously extremely busy reading your book but my girlfriend would like to know how much this chair is. If that's not too much to ask."

Polly banged the book down on the counter and stared at him. For an instant, she thought about telling him that she wasn't in the mood for this kind of crap right now. But instead she smiled.

"I'm fierce sorry, sir," she said. "I didn't hear you. "'Twas an awful big word I was stuck on. Sometimes they do be hard and I don't be so good at the reading. I finds the long words terrible hard. You look now like you'd be educated, you might be able to help me with this word I'm stuck on, for 'tis a new word to me and terrible complicated. Will I spell it out for you?" She smiled up at him and then began to spell, "I.G.N.O.R.A.M.U.S."

"Ignoramus," Anna called out eagerly, proud to display her learning, a display that would have surprised her old teachers.

"And would you know what it means like?" Polly asked, addressing Colin. "Here, I'll read out the sentence: 'When he opened his mouth he sounded like the great big ignoramus that he was.' Did I say it right, sir?"

Colin stared. She looked like a bit of a "God help us" swaddled in her big black old coat, hunched up on her stool behind the counter. But a "God help us" or not, he was almost certain she was mocking him.

"'Tis the reading I find hard, sir, I do better at the writing. Anyway, you were asking about the chair. Well 'tis a funny thing that, for you're the second one this morning. And, as I told that other fellow, it's priced at twenty-five pound, cheaper than what we bought it for, but it's been sitting there that long we just want rid of it. Me ma says that the fella what did sell it to her was a dirty scoundrel trying to make out that it was fierce valuable like, that it came from Park House. But sure, me ma felt sorry for him, she's like that and the poor fellow was a bit of a misfortune. Drink, I suppose. But as she says herself, she was done. Look at the state of it, he wasn't telling a lie when he said it was over two hundred years old."

"Did you say Park House?" asked Anna.

"Yeah, that's right, Sir Coulter's house."

"Sir Andrew Coulter?"

"Yeah. But I'm telling you now if it came out of Park House, then it was whipped. Mind you, it wouldn't be the first thing that fellow stole. Anyway, as I was saying, I promised that man I'd hold it for him. He's just gone into Mallow to get money. You see we don't do those visa yokes. Queer fish he was too, this fella, with his little dickey bow and his fancy hankie hanging out of his pocket. English, I'd say. Sotherby, I think he said his name was, or maybe that was his boss's name. Anyway, he gave me his card to show me he meant business. Wait there and I'll get it, it's worth having a gawk at; beautiful it is, all gold writing." Polly bent down and pretended to search. "It's here somewhere," she called out from under the counter, well aware of the furious whispering going on between the two.

"Look," said Colin to Polly. "My girlfriend is just crazy about it and I'm a soft touch. I know I'm foolish, but I'll give you thirty for it."

"Oh Jaysus," said Polly, still poking about. "I don't know. That other fellow would go mad if I sold it to ya."

"Thirty-five," said Anna.

"Oh I don't know, he'd be hopping."

"Forty, we'll give you forty," said Anna.

"Where could I have put it?" said Polly finally emerging and looking around on top of the counter.

"Fifty," shouted Anna.

"Sixty," shouted Anna.

"Look, look," said Colin quickly, fearful that Anna would keep on bidding against herself, "He could well have decided that it's not worth the effort to come back for. In fact, he's probably halfway to Cork by now."

Polly hummed and hawed.

"Seventy. And that's our final offer," said Colin, looking warningly at Anna.

"Deal," said Polly. She spat on her hand and then held it out to Colin, just to see the look of disgust on his face as he felt obliged to shake it to close the deal.

Polly watched as Colin carried the chair out to the car.

"Careful," said Anna. "Don't damage it."

And it was all Polly could do to stop herself laughing out loud. Since the chair had survived years of misuse around the farm as a stepladder and latterly as a block in the hedge, nothing they were going to do was likely to damage it. What a kick Granny would get when she told her, she thought, as she watched them drive away. Polly wasn't her Granny's granddaughter for nothing; she could play the huckster when she wanted.

6

MICHAELA AND DAVY

"What will it be, love?" asked Noreen, the canteen lady.

"Steak and kidney pie with chips, please," Davy replied and, as he watched Noreen pile the food onto his plate, he wondered why more people like himself didn't come to the University to avail of the food. It wasn't exactly cordon bleu, the opposite really, whatever the culinary term for that was. But it was very cheap and the helpings were enormous.

"Have you enough in that, dear?" Noreen asked him, showing him the plate. He was tempted to say no, just to see where she proposed to put the extra, for the chips were stacked high on the plate, balancing as precariously as a house of cards.

"Yes, that's loads, thanks," he answered, but she ignored him and, with the skill of a practised magician, managed to add a few extra chips. Noreen's idea of portion control differed to her manager's, being based on what she thought the customer needed. From the very first day she'd seen Davy in the queue, she'd determined to fatten him up and only he, and a few other scrawny fellows, who looked like they were in need of looking after, were the recipients of such generous helpings.

"Thanks," he said, taking the plate from her.

He moved along to the cash register.

"Next," called Noreen.

"A salad plate, please," said Polly

Polly was a little calmer now. When she'd arrived into the canteen and saw Davy at the end of the queue, she'd got into a nervous flap, turned and hurried back out again. Then she'd stood outside the door, looking in at him through the little glass panel, trying to decide what to do. After her performance last week outside the lecture hall, she didn't think she could bear it if he recognised her. But if he didn't, well that would be even worse. The prefect scenario, she decided, would be for him to remember meeting her but to be uncertain as to when and where. In the end, a combination of optimistic belief that this third scenario might materialise, together with her stomach-turning revulsion at the thought of yet another fry at the hostel, drove her back in. She was beginning to fear that if she kept eating frys at her current rate then she'd end being one of those people, occasionally featured in the papers, who were so obese that the fire brigade had to be called out to rescue them when they got stuck in their bath. She still had quite a long way to go before that happened, but her skin had begun to break out. Which is why she now ordered the salad.

Noreen handed her the salad plate. Polly looked at it in disgust. The half tomato, the two roles of plastic ham, the limp lettuce leaves and the sad decorative sprig of parsley, all tightly wrapped and flattened under the cling film, looked pitiful and tasteless compared to the delicious-smelling mound on Davy's plate. And more expensive, which was a serious consideration since her parents gave her what they thought was more than enough money to meet her living costs but which fell far short – a fact Polly could never bring herself to tell them. What to do, what to do, Polly deliberated; puny, cold salad versus hot, delicious, better-value steak and kidney pie. The salad would certainly be a good start to her new regime, plus she liked the idea that Davy would see she was the kind who looked after herself, that she was a healthy, salad-eating sort of girl.

"Could you move along, please," said Noreen. "You're holding up the queue."

"Sorry," said Polly. She turned around and smiled apologetically at the people behind her and moved quickly along. But just as Noreen was taking the next order she came back again.

"Excuse me, but I've changed my mind. Could I have a steak and kidney pie with chips instead, please?" asked Polly.

Noreen sighed and grabbed the plate back; generous though she was to her few favourites, service with a smile was a commodity she was frugal with. She handed Polly a plate with a helping a third of the size of Davy's. Polly looked at it and considered complaining but then, she looked up to see Noreen glowering at her, daring her to, and she changed her mind. She moved along.

Davy was waiting to pay while the cashier emptied bags of change into the register. As Polly approached he turned around, looked at her, smiled vaguely but without so much as a glimmer of recognition and turned back again. Polly's heart sank. To her, falling in love was all about feelings of having known one another since time began, of matching souls, of instant bonding, of being two halves of a sphere. And the like. But, just before she'd come down to the canteen, she'd found a more academic theory of love in a psychology book which she'd come across, (well, scoured the library for actually) which purported that basically three things – proximity, similarity and familiarity – were responsible for making people fall in love. On her way from the library to the canteen, Polly had mulled over this bit of information.

Though she'd have preferred her own more romantic version, she realised that her impact on Davy didn't quite match his on her and she'd decided that she was going to work on the familiarity and proximity bits of this trinity. She resolved that each time she saw him, she'd say a few words to him, nothing earth-shattering but enough for him to gradually begin to feel he knew her. All this had been fine in theory but she hadn't expected to see him quite so soon; she'd been thinking of putting her plan into action over the following weeks, not immediately. But now that she was feeling more composed, she decided it was time to say a few words to him. But what about? She considered several subjects but dismissed them just as quickly; the weather – that would be a bit sad really; the inequity in their respective portions of steak and kidney pie too – he might think she was angling for a share of his; other things in the world that were precisely the same shade of grey-blue as his eyes – a bit forward perhaps. It had to be about something they had in common. Like what? Like nothing! Unless she counted their one previous meeting. This was as good as she was going to come up under such pressure.

"Well, I hope you haven't left any other classes early," she said in what she intended to be a slagging tone of voice but nervousness made it sound like she was scolding him.

"What?"

"The lecturer," she explained. "She sent me out to call you back the other day, remember?"

"Oh right," he smiled. "Of course. I'm sorry, I didn't recognise you for a moment."

No kidding, thought Polly.

"Or fallen asleep. You were sound to the world in her class."

"Pardon?"

"In Professor Kiely's class."

Davy wondered if she was a class prefect or something. Maybe she was charged with keeping an eye on things since the classes were so big. Why else would she be reprimanding him like this?

"I wasn't actually asleep," he said cautiously, bearing her possible role as some sort of prefect in mind. "I just had my eyes closed."

"That'll be £2.45 when you're ready," said the cashier.

Davy paid her and took his tray and went to find somewhere to sit down. Polly paid and then looked around to see where he was sitting. Take things slowly, she told herself, no point in rushing over and asking if she could join him. No, just follow the new strategy, work on the proximity bit and sit directly in his line of vision.

Davy couldn't enjoy his steak and kidney pie. Not with the constant feeling of being watched. Again and again he quickly looked over, trying to catch her at it, but she was too sharp and all he saw was a girl staring at the plate in front of her with inordinate interest. But he was convinced that she was watching him and it was beginning to really bug him. He usually enjoyed sitting here in the canteen, eating his food, surveying all that was going on and he didn't like the idea that he was the one under scrutiny for a change. He began to eat hurriedly, determined to leave quickly.

After he'd taken a few bites, the door to the canteen swung open and a grungy, wild-looking girl burst in. He looked up, saw her glance around and noticed her look of recognition when she spotted Polly. He watched her stride across the room making a bee-line for Polly, wondered what she could possibly have to do with this quiet-looking one and decided that, maybe in her capacity as prefect, the quiet one had reported the grungy one for some misdemeanour and now the grungy one was coming to get her. He expected Polly to be alarmed when she looked up and saw the girl. Instead she smiled.

"Hiya, Cliona!" she said.

"Hi, Polly. How's it going?"

"Fine. Nice addition to your facial jewellery," remarked Polly.

Cliona's hand went up to her left eyebrow and she twiddled with one of the three rings newly pierced into it.

"Do you think?"

"Not really. But I'd say your mother really likes them."

"She went absolutely mental. How come you're not eating at the hostel as usual?" asked Cliona, sitting down.

"Don't talk to me, I'm sick of it. Do you know how many eggs I had last week?"

"Well, it's not something I give a lot of thought to."

"Nineteen!"

"Now, I know you, Polly, and I *eggs*-pect you're probably *eggs*-aggerating. I wouldn't say you're telling me the truth *eggs*-actly.

Polly looked at her blankly. "Why would I lie about a thing like that?" she asked.

Cliona sighed, "*Eggs*-pecting? *Eggs*-aggerating? Oh, forget it."

"Very funny," said Polly, the penny finally dropping. "But I did, I had nineteen eggs. I had five frys, all with two eggs, a boiled egg each morning from Monday to Friday and, if that wasn't enough, before I came back up last evening my mother gave me a four-egg omelette to keep my strength up." Just then she looked over and saw that Davy was listening. Marvellous, just what any man would desire she thought, an nineteen-egg-a-week-girl, very sexy altogether.

"I never knew you liked eggs," said Cliona.

"That's the point. I hate them."

The girls continued on talking, but their voices had lowered and Davy couldn't hear them any more. But he studied them, thinking that they made very unlikely friends; one with her neat skirt and jumper, the other with her grunge clothes, rings pierced into every projecting part of her face and a mane of dreadlocks. But at least the sensible-looking one had forgotten her surveillance operation and he could relax.

The thought that Polly might be interested in him hadn't crossed Davy's mind. He'd never had a girlfriend, he'd never really had anything to do with girls at all, unless he counted his brother Stephen's wife Lynda and by no stretch of the imagination could she be called his girlfriend. She'd been thirty for a start and he'd been fifteen. And to him, the term girlfriend suggested something innocent and mutual, which was not at all what their "relationship" had been.

But he wasn't thinking of Lynda now as he sipped his coffee and looked around. He was remembering that first time he'd come to the canteen. He'd been so nervous, afraid that someone would come over to him and tell him to get out; that he'd no right to be here. It was hard to believe that it was less than two months ago when, passing the gates of UCC on the Western Road, he'd first decided to wander in and have a look around. That first day he hadn't dared to go into any of the buildings; he just walked about the grounds looking at them from the outside and at all the students milling around until, eventually, he sat down against the trunk of one of the trees in front of the library and watched the students going in and out. It was a real Indian summer day and the students had just returned from the break and he looked on as they all met up again. All around he heard yells and screams as they rushed over to one another, so excited at meeting up again after the long summer break. He listened to snatches of their conversation. How brilliant the summer in Cape Cod had been. What a mad time they'd all had. He heard them exclaim over this one's fantastic new clothes or that one's fabulous tan; heard one laugh and say her father was going to kill her because she hadn't saved a penny; another fret about the complications the summer had brought to her love life. It was really a very strange place, he thought, full of young people bursting with life's possibilities, all carefree with not a single real worry. So different to him when he'd been their age. It seemed unbelievable to him that he was just a few years older.

The weather had been fine all that week and he'd come back again and, gradually, realising that nobody was taking any notice of him, he became a little bolder. First he started using the canteen, then the library and finally he ventured into the lectures. Now he liked to think that he was making more use of the university than any of the real students. They chose one course of study and stuck to it whereas he sat in on any lecture he fancied and browsed through library books right across the disciplines. Law, Commerce and Arts were the lectures he went to most, for the classes were bigger and more impersonal in these faculties so that neither the lecturers, nor the students themselves, knew everyone in the classes. It didn't matter what class he went to really, it was all new to him, except some of the English lectures.

The main reason, he supposed, for coming to the college so often was that he had nothing much else to do. Without employment, people needed some escapism. Some people found it by watching telly, but he didn't have one – anyway he hated it. The ambience of the university and the opportunities to learn new things were his escapism. Another reason was that he already had a degree in English without ever setting foot in an university. He'd studied through an open university programme while in prison, so now he wanted to get the feel of what it was like to be a normal student. He'd begun to realise that the actual degree was only part of what these students would graduate with, equally important was the confidence they developed during their time in college. The cheap food was another reason he came. And being able to watch all the beautiful girls wasn't the least of them.

As he finished his steak and kidney pie, a bunch of students came to the door of the canteen. Without coming any further, one of them called out.

"Come on, Cliona! We're going now to get some off-licence before heading into town."

"Right," called Cliona getting up. "See you, Polly."

"See you," replied Polly and watched her go. Then she looked over and saw that Davy was gone and she picked up her tray and carried it back to the counter. She still felt hungry. Cliona had nibbled away at her food as she went on about her plans for that evening, though she'd neglected to invite her along, Polly noted. Not that she'd have gone but still, it would have been nice to have been asked. After buying a bar of chocolate to fill her up, Polly headed back to the hostel.

At about the same time Polly had been staring in at Davy through the glass in the canteen door, Michaela was putting on her coat and getting ready to leave the office. The phone rang. It was Colin.

"Hi, honey, I'm glad you're still there. I wanted to catch you before you left," he said.

"Why, what's up? Are you back in Cork already?"

"No, that's why I'm ringing. I haven't left Limerick yet and this meeting is going to run on for ages," he lied, being in fact only ten minutes away from her as he spoke, stretched out on a couch in the living-room of Samantha's apartment on Washington Street. Samantha was in the kitchen preparing a candle-lit dinner for the two of them.

"Ah Colin, you said you'd be home early."

"I know, I know, but there's nothing I can do about it."

"What time will you be home so?"

"Well, I've decided to stay here tonight and travel on to Galway in the morning. It'll save me a trip later on in the week," said Colin, having made up his mind that he'd be sleeping in Samantha's bed tonight, confident that the candle-lit dinner would be just a prelude to better things.

"Ah Colin!"

"Now, Michaela, don't start harping on."

"I wasn't harping on. I'm just disappointed. I've hardly seen you all week, just yesterday, and you were so tired then that you slept for most of the day."

"Well, it's worse for me. Remember I'm the

one who has to work all hours, and the one who has to spend yet another night in a lonely hotel room."

"I know, I'm sorry. Listen, why don't I give you a ring later, to cheer you up? What hotel are you staying in?"

"No, no, don't bother. I could be tied up here for hours yet."

"Well, why don't you ring me when you're finished so?"

"I don't know, Michaela, it could be very late. But I'll try, OK?"

"What time will you be back tomorrow?"

"Look, Michaela, I don't know. I'll ring you as soon as I'm on my way, OK?"

"Yeah, OK," she said in a subdued tone.

"Come on, Michaela, don't be getting into a sulk."

"I'm not getting in a sulk, Colin. It's just that I was looking forward to seeing you."

"Listen, I have to get back to the meeting. Ring you tomorrow. Love you. Bye."

The phone went dead and Michaela sighed.

She walked out of the office feeling down-hearted and, not wanting to go back to an empty house, she headed aimlessly towards the city centre. Dawdling along, she wished there was someone she could ask to come for a drink. But there wasn't. Muriel and Denise would have thought her mad if, on the spur of the moment, she suggested anything of the sort; they'd have wanted at least a month's notice. And that probably in writing. Not that she'd have asked them; she couldn't think of anything more depressing than sitting in a pub looking across at their sour faces, trying to think of things to say which would be boring enough to hold their interest. But, given that she'd moved to Cork over six months ago, it was a pathetic state of affairs, she thought – not to have a single person to go for a drink with. Having friends was always something she'd taken so much for granted back home in Galway; there'd always been someone to head out with or to call over to and the only time the concept of loneliness crossed her mind, and then only fleetingly, was when the television ads at Christmas advised people to look in on their elderly neighbours living alone. When they'd first come to live in Cork, she'd been so wrapped up in a state of newly married bliss that she hadn't noticed her lack of friends or really cared. But now that Colin was so busy, it was different. She seemed to be always on her own. But what could she do about it? If only adults could go up to one another in the same way children in the playground could and ask, 'Will you be my friend?" things would be far simpler, she thought. She supposed she could start going to night-classes or join a gym, for that's what a problem page would surely advise her, if she was desperate enough to write in. But both activities held zero appeal which probably meant any friendship forged would be done so under false pretences and, forevermore, she would have to pretend to her new-found friends that she too just loved step aerobics or found first-aid really, really exciting. But if only she had someone to whom she could moan to, about her job, about Colin and how she never saw him these days, about the vague feelings of sadness and disappointment which she so often felt lately, then perhaps things mightn't seem too bad. There was little point in talking to Colin about how she felt, for any time she'd tried, he'd either switched off, finding it all too uninteresting, or else got angry, suspecting that she was getting at him.

She found herself on Patrick Street just as the shop assistants were locking up after their day's trading and she walked along, pausing every now and then to study the clothes on the mannequins in the windows. But that just made her feel dissatisfied with her own dull old wardrobe. For over three months now, she hadn't bought a stitch of new clothes, ever since she'd got in a right panic over her future and decided something must change, for all she could see looming before her were dull, dull, dull, oh so very very dull, dark, dismal, dreary – another few dulls for good measure – depressing years in her present job or in some other equally boring one. She began to fear that she'd start turning into Denise and Muriel if she didn't make a change soon; that she'd start finding their conversation scintillating. And it would be all downhill from there. In July, she'd start planning the Christmas night out and in no time at all, she'd find herself counting the years as they flew by, looking forward to the day she'd receive her retirement clock. It was all enough to make her break out in a cold sweat whenever she thought about it.

So, she'd decided to start saving with a vague notion of going to college or of opening her own business, of doing something to save her from this terrible future. She'd stopped buying clothes and CDs, her two big indulgences and began to scrimp and save, spending money only on such necessities as the bills and food. Whenever she felt inclined to splash out, she just made herself think of Muriel or Denise, which fortified her determination. But it was a very slow process for whenever she'd got a few hundred pounds together, some bill would plop through the letterbox and she'd be back to square one. And trying to get Colin to pay his fair share was a losing battle. He always promised he would, but he never remembered and so, to keep the ESB, the Telecom and the Bórd Gais people from gathering at the door, Michaela always eventually ended up trooping down to their offices on the payment-way-overdue-tomorrow-we're-cutting-you-off-day. Saving was a slow process indeed and she was beginning to think that by the time she finally got the money together, at least she'd be spared the expense of travelling to and from this new occupation of hers for, by then, she'd probably be eligible for the free travel. What annoyed her most of all was that she was sure Colin must be earning far more than she.

She came to Dunnes Stores and, noticing that it was still open, she came to an involuntary halt. She stared in at the racks of clothes and even from the doorway she could see a lovely green top and a long grey skirt which would go beautifully together. She wondered what other treasures lay within. Maybe she should go in. Just to see. Not to buy anything, of course. Unless it was reasonable. Very reasonable. Maybe something small, like those dangling earrings. To cheer herself up. No, no, no, she told herself and she tried to move but her legs proved less resolute than the rest of her. She summoned up the faces of Muriel and Denise to alarm her legs into running away from this temptation, but even that scary picture hadn't the usual effect and she let herself be carried into the shop. She picked up the earrings, the top and the skirt and then walked around checking to see if there was anything else she might try on, and, surprise, surprise, there was, quite a few things in fact. Laden down with a sizeable bundle (oh, how she loved shopping) she joined the long queue outside the dressing-rooms. She waited. And she waited. For over fifteen minutes, but there was little movement. A voice came over the loudspeaker and announced that the store would be closing in five minutes. Michaela made a mental calculation. If there are four people waiting in the queue for a dressing-room, and spaces are becoming available at the rate of one every three minutes, how long will it take before she gets to try on the clothes? Not within the next five minutes, that's for sure. She dumped the lot on the nearest rack and left the shop.

But she still wasn't ready to go home. Having failed in her attempt to spend money on herself, she was dammed now if she was going home without succeeding. She came to a restaurant and went inside. Having been shown to her table, she studied the menu and then parsimoniously ordered a glass of wine and a seven-inch pizza. But then she reconsidered and, thinking to hell with it, she changed her order, switching the pizza for a twelve-ounce steak and the glass for a bottle of wine.

Promptly, the waitress came down with the wine and poured Michaela a glass. She started to sip, but, as she looked around her, she began to realise she'd made a terrible mistake. The restaurant was full of young couples gazing into each other's eyes, and groups of friends laughing and chatting. The only other person on his own was an old man who looked about as depressed as she felt. She began to think that she must look pathetic and ridiculous sitting here on her own, with a big gloomy face on her, a thought which made her feel even more gloomy and she could feel the tears welling up.

After his fine helping of steak and kidney pie, Davy left the canteen and headed for the college library. He climbed the stairs and headed straight to the section on Algerian Art. Searching through the shelves he found the book on Criminal Law where he'd left it earlier that day, safe in the knowledge that nobody was likely to look for it here. Because he wasn't a student, he couldn't take books home and the only way to ensure that the book he was currently reading wasn't withdrawn by someone else was to misfile it. Now, with his book under his arm he found a seat, settled down, and began to read. Two hours passed and so engrossed did he become in the book that he was surprised to suddenly find that the lights were being dimmed. He looked up and saw that the students around him were packing up to go. After returning the book to its hiding place, he left the library.

On his way home to Cathedral View, two boys, aged about ten, came against him. One had a tyre hanging around his neck and was rolling another tyre along in front of him. The other was dragging an old car seat along.

"What are you smirking at, mister?" asked the boy with the car seat.

"Nothing," laughed Davy.

"Hey, are you laughing at us or something?" asked the other.

"No, I was just thinking that I've never

seen anyone robbing a car by instalments before."

"We're robbing nothing. These are for our bonfire." They glared at him.

"Ya looney, ya," said one and they walked on.

When Davy was young, Halloween had been up there with Christmas for all the kids on his housing estate. They'd spend weeks collecting material for their bonfire and it had always been the best in the area. When the other fires had burnt themselves out, all the other kids came down to see theirs still blazing away. Now Davy turned and headed towards the bridge thinking it would be a good vantage point from which to see all the fires on the hills of the northside of the city. But when he reached it he saw that there was one even closer than that, on a derelict site, earmarked for a filling station which opened onto the motorway running under the pedestrian bridge. He took up his customary position on the top step at the back of the hospital and watched the activities down below.

*   *   *

The cheek of him, thought Michaela, as she wavered from side to side on her way home, hiccuping. Who did he think he was? With his "Darling, there's no need for the two of us to be eating alone". When he'd first looked over at her and smiled, she had smiled back, feeling sorry for the other solitary eater, but she'd certainly never meant it as an invitation for him to come join her. God, he was obnoxious, he really was, the way he'd ignored her protests and pretended not to hear her say that she preferred to eat on her own. And then telling the waiter to bring his dinner over, that he was eating with the lovely lady! He was disgusting, he really was – why he was old enough to be her father! And then that thing he'd started doing with his foot, rubbing it up against her leg. Ugh! To think that she had spent twenty-five pounds for a few mushrooms and two bites of steak, for after that foot thing, she knew she couldn't bear to stay a minute longer. Well, at least she'd managed to finish quite a lot of the wine before he'd descended upon her. It was probably just as well she hadn't had anymore, she was feeling a bit drunk as it was.

Deciding to hell with taking the long way around, she turned up by the corner by Hot and Saucy, thinking that if anybody dared try to mug her, it would be him and not her who'd end up sorry. She hurried along until she came to the steps and then she stopped. Davy was sitting on the very top step, sound asleep. She stood there for a while looking up at him, thinking how cold he looked and wondering if he'd anywhere else to spend the night. She considered waking him up to ask, but there was little point, she wasn't going to invite him to come home with her if he'd no place else to go. She left him sleeping and staggered on. On the bridge she spotted the bonfire below and she leant over the side and watched the kids. One of them spotted her.

"Hello, Missus," he shouted.

"Hello," she shouted back.

"Come on down," he called.

"I don't think so."

"Go on, jump, I'll catch you!"

She laughed, then walked on.

She went straight to bed, thinking that after the wine she'd drunk she'd be asleep as soon as her head hit the pillow. But not so.

She lay there for ages and ages, wide awake. She was still starving and she couldn't get the image of Davy asleep out in the cold from her mind. What if someone came along and attacked him? What if he died of hypothermia? She turned and tossed. Eventually, deciding that she might be better able to sleep on a full stomach, she got up and went down to the kitchen. She looked into the fridge but there was nothing, only a pound of sausages. She took them out and as she was about to put them on to fry, a crazy idea struck her and without giving herself a chance to think herself out of it, she ran upstairs and dressed. Then she collected some things together and left the house.

"Davy," called Michaela softly. But Davy went on sleeping and, working the smell of frying sausages into his dream, he smacked his lips.

"Davy," Michaela called again.

She shook him gently until he half-opened his eyes. He saw Michaela peering at him, smiling, and he sighed contentedly and closed his eyes again. What a lovely dream,

ANNE MARIE FORREST

he thought. Michaela gathered some of the
sausages from the pan, put them on the paper
plate and held them under his nose and called
his name again. He opened his eyes.

"Hello there, Davy. Have some food."

Michaela was kneeling beside a little
primus stove on the step below him. With
one hand she was turning the rest of the
sausages in the pan, with the other she was
holding out the plate to him. He sat up,
thinking that this just had to be a weird
dream. Even so, he took the plate from her.
She sat down beside him.

"Can I have part of the blanket?" she
asked.

Davy looked down and saw an unfamiliar
blanket draped around his lap.

"Of course," he mumbled. She sat in closer
to him and covered her legs with the blanket,
then she opened a flask and offered it to him,

"Hot whiskey, without the cloves and
lemon. And sorry, I forgot the glasses."

She smiled at him as he took it from her.
She picked up a sausage from the plate and
began to eat.

"I saw you asleep as I passed by earlier. So

I had to come back and do something in case you died of hypothermia. I couldn't have that on my conscience."

Davy couldn't think of anything to say – how could he tell her that this was the nicest thing anyone had ever done for him?

"It's Halloween, you know," she said, not noticing how moved he was.

"I know, I was watching the kids down below and I fell asleep."

They sat in silence, eating the sausages and taking turns at the whiskey. He didn't know what to say. There was nothing much to say. She was here, the fat blondy bloke wasn't. They sat close together, their sides touching, he could feel her hip against his. If he started talking, he thought he'd never stop, he was afraid he'd blurt out something stupid like she had most wonderful face in the world or, worse still, that he loved her and thought about her a hundred times a day. Or that this was the nicest thing that had ever happened to him. It was the most perfect night in his life – sitting here in the dark, save for light of the bonfire down below, the little flame of the primus stove and the coloured light coming through the stain-glass windows of the hospital church above them; with the smell and taste of the sausages and the hot whiskey, and the sounds of the last few children around the fire below. And, above all, the closeness of her.

Michaela was content to sit there in the dark and silence. It was a comfortable silence. There didn't seem to be any need to talk.

And they stayed like that until the sausages were all gone and the last of the whiskey was drained. Finally the lights of the church were switched off, the youngsters had gone home and the blazing bonfire had become just a heap of smouldering embers.

"Do you have somewhere to sleep?" she asked him.

"Yes."

"Well, I'd better get going." She leaned over and kissed him on the cheek, then got up. "Goodnight, Davy."

"Goodnight, Michaela," he said as she walked away. "Michaela!" he called after her and when she stopped and turned around, he said, "Your blanket. And the stove."

"I'll get them from you some other time,"

she answered, thinking that he might have more use for them than her.

"Thanks," he called.

Davy wasn't the only person to get an unexpected awakening that night. After the candle-lit dinner, and just as Colin had hoped, Samantha had taken him by the hand and led him to her bedroom. But, after they'd made love and as he was drifting off to contented sleep, she began to shake him.

"Colin, it's nearly eleven, you'd better go home."

"No, I'm fine here," he mumbled.

"Colin, I'm asking you to go home."

"No, I'm fine. I'll stay the night."

"But I don't want you to."

"Course you do."

"I don't. Now get up."

"*Sssh*, go back to sleep," he mumbled.

Suddenly, she pushed him away, got out of bed and went and called a taxi. When she came back into the room she gathered up his clothes and dumped them on him.

"Colin, I've called a taxi for you. I want you to go now. Alright!"

"I don't understand," said Colin, as he fumbled with his socks.

And he didn't, for this time they were playing by Samantha's rules which were aimed at making Colin want her more than she wanted him.

By the time Michaela arrived home, Colin was sitting at the kitchen table, waiting for her.

"Where were you?" he asked as soon as she came into the kitchen.

"Oh hi ,Colin, you're home! I thought you were staying in Limerick. I didn't expect you."

"Obviously. So where were you?"

"I went for something to eat."

"With who?"

"No one."

"I don't believe you.'

"Who do you think I went with, Colin? I don't have any friends in Cork."

He smelt the whiskey on her breath.

"Were you drinking?"

"Yes."

"You went to a restaurant on your own and got sloshed."

"Yes, I went to a restaurant on my own and got sloshed."

"That's really sad, Michaela."

"Yes. I know it is," she agreed. Then she sighed. "Colin, I'm not in the mood for this. I'm going to bed. Goodnight."

"Is that what I get when I've driven all the way from Galway just to be with you?" he shouted after her, in his anger forgetting that he hadn't actually.

"I'm tired, Colin," she called back.

"Aren't you even interested in how I got on today?"

"I'm sure I know." She came back into the kitchen and stood by the door. "No doubt, you got on very well. You met lots of clients, had lots of important meetings and clinched some really important accounts. You always get on very well, it's just a pity you never bring any money home. I can't even remember the last time you paid a bill or bought a single thing for the house. But then, I don't really want to get into that right now."

141

She walked out, but seconds later came back in again. "Do you want to know how I got on at work today, Colin? Do you ever ask me Colin? No. And really, I can't ever be bothered telling you because you wouldn't be interested and anyway, it would be just too boring to have to talk about it. It's bad enough having to go through it even once. Good night, Colin."

"Michaela, I don't think you should drink so much," said Colin the next morning.

Michaela nearly choked on her cornflakes.

"Pardon?"

"Well, I don't think it does you any good. It puts you in very strange form, you were very rude to me last night."

"Oh, for crying out loud. One night you decide that I come home with a little too much to drink and you go on like this. I can't believe it. When I think of all the times I've had to put up with you."

"Michaela, I really don't know what's come over you lately, you've changed."

"I've changed? What about you?" she said, slamming her spoon down on the table.

142

"You see. You see. You're just so confrontational."

"Oh shut up!"

"See, see what I mean! You've a real attitude problem, Michaela."

Michaela wasn't listening any more. She got up, picked up her coat and bag and left the house and headed down to work.

Passing by the steps where she and Davy had sat last night, she smiled, thinking how strange it had been sitting there with him. Strange, but lovely really.

7

COLIN LOVES MICHAELA –
BUT SAMANTHA AND ANNA
AND NOW CLIONA?

Davy had never known much kind-
ness. Certainly not in prison. But even before
that. For Davy hadn't had Polly's good
fortune to grow up in a loving family such as
hers. No. His family was the kind which often
prompts people to wonder why a licence is
needed for a dog, but not for a child. For
Davy's story is like that of so many children
to be read each day in *The Irish Times* or in *The
Examiner*, in reports of parents who treat their
children in a manner most people, no matter
how malevolent their mood, wouldn't even
dream of treating the scrawniest, mangiest,

most flea-infested stray cur they chanced upon. Let alone treat a little boy.

But once Davy had known kindness. For there had been an exception in this "dysfunctional family", as families such as Davy's are called. And that had been his grandmother.

Her love for, and kindness to the young Davy had matched that of Polly's grandmother. Up until the age of eight, he had lived with her here in Cork. And a beautiful, happy boy he'd been too, such a joy to the ageing woman. Even if he'd been a handful for her at times. Even if she had to hobble down to the school on arthritic legs to bring him home day after day. Even if she had to go out at night searching for him; for happy and beautiful though he was, he was sometimes bold, as eight-year-olds very often are. Why, Davy's grandmother wouldn't have given him up for the world! Unless she had to. Which, as it happened, she did – when his parents wrote to say that they had returned from England to settle in Belfast and, now that things were more sorted, they wanted Davy home. Home? Where's home? Home was with his

145

grandmother surely. But what could she do? She'd only been taking care of him. And it was then all kindness, and taking care of, had ended for the young Davy.

The very last time Davy had seen his grandmother was on the day he'd been sent back to Belfast, all those years before. She had travelled with him by bus as far as Dublin to see him safely onto the Belfast bus, for the second half of his journey. He could still recall the details of that day. He could remember looking out at her through the window as he waited for the bus to leave; could remember her waving in at him through a mixture of unrestrained tears and brave smiles; and, he could remember the sense of shock he felt, even at that young age, when he realised for the first time that his Granny was old; that the woman he'd always thought of as a live-wire – to use one of her own expressions; had thought of as powerful and strong, forever laughing or scolding, was in fact a nervous old lady. He would never forget the sight of her standing on the forecourt of the bus station clutching onto her handbag, for fear it would be snatched from her up in Dublin, or of her hurriedly stepping out of people's way as they snapped "Excuse me" and pushed past her as she stood there waiting for the bus to depart and take away her grandson. And he'd never forget how small she looked that day. A nervous, small, old lady. And that was the last time he had seen her.

He had written to her over the years. As soon as he received a letter from her, which was very often – at least once a fortnight, he sat down and promptly replied to it, filling her in on the kinds of things that are important to a boy – goals he'd stored, how well Liverpool were doing, how tall he was getting. And although he'd never mentioned anything of the misery at home, he felt she knew. Just as he knew that, if she'd been up to it, she'd have come to visit him, for she never ended a letter without telling him so. Just as he knew that she always hoped he'd come and see her soon in Cork, for she always said so in her letters. But at first he was too young to travel down to her; besides, he had no means of getting the money necessary for the fare. And then, it was too late. For at fifteen he'd been sent away, locked up. And then she stopped replying to his letters, many letters, in which he tried to explain things to her. But he never heard from her again. And that was the hardest thing of all to take. Of all people, he thought she'd be on his side.

And that's why he'd decided to come to Cork after being released, rather than return to Belfast. He'd come to Cork because he wanted to explain to her, face to face, what had happened, to explain why he had been sent to prison and to stop her thinking badly of him. And he'd come to Cork because it was the only place he ever remembered being happy. Since his arrival he'd only been up to her house once, on that very first day. Now, this morning, after leaving his house, his head muddled with thoughts of Michaela, with no definite idea of where he was going to go, he found himself making his way to his grandmother's house for the second time. Michaela's closeness and kindness of the night before had stirred in him memories of his grandmother and he felt a sudden need to see her house again. To feel close to her. To remember her.

Now, as he walked towards her house, he

recalled his visit to it on that very first day back in Cork. Coming by bus, he'd arrived into the station in Parnell Place and immediately he'd started walking, thinking he'd be sure to know the way to her house and the only home he had known; sure that instinct would guide him. But he'd ended up walking around in circles. So, although he was loath to, being still shy from his long stay inside, he'd stopped to ask passers-by the way but could make no sense of what any of them were saying in their up-and-down Cork accents, only managing to catch the profusion of "likes" and "boys" which dotted their speech, as it had once done his. Eventually, without even realising he was anywhere near it, he just happened upon her little, red brick-terraced house on Friar's Walk. But it had changed completely. And it was only then he understood why his letters to her from prison had remained unanswered. It wasn't because she didn't want to have anything to do with him. But because she had died and nobody had bothered to tell him.

And now for the second time, Davy stood outside the house. The house that was no longer hers. A house all gentrified now, lived in by new people who knew nothing of the old woman who'd been born and who'd died in it, who'd slept under its roof every single night of her eighty years, bar a handful. But Davy didn't see the little neatly clipped ornamental shrub in the middle of the paved area to the front of his house – that puny hot-house shrub was invisible to him. What he was seeing was the grand old outsized chestnut tree it replaced; a tree which had once stood proudly, rising up from the foot-high weeds and grass, with its branches stretching out over the footpath. He was seeing himself dangling from the tree. Hearing her cry, "Come down off that, Davy, or you'll break your skull!" And hearing himself call, "Come and get me so, Granny!" And her shouting false threats, "You'll be in hot water if I catch a hold of you. I'll leather the bejaysus out of ya! I will. I swear. You'll be a sorry boy, Davy Long!" And then seeing himself edging his way along the branches until he was out over the footpath, then jumping down and running off up the road with her hobbling along behind him, calling out "Davy! Davy!" as she chased after him. Davy. Davy. A sometimes bold boy.

"Catch me if you can, Granny!"

Now, standing there, he realised that he was the only person who ever thought of her fondly. Otherwise she was no more. And who would think of him fondly, he wondered, when he was gone? Who was there to think of him fondly even while he was alive? The events of the night before – Michaela's actions – were just those of a stranger with her own life to lead, not something for him to build hopes and dreams upon. Sadly he turned away from his grandmother's house thinking that having no one meant that no one witnessed his life, that it didn't mean anything to anybody. That it didn't mean anything at all and, if he were to die right now, Michaela would never know the way he felt about her.

"Hey mister, are you crying?" asked a little boy staring up at Davy.

And he walked slowly down Friar's Walk where once he'd ran. With no one chasing after him.

For the rest of the day he couldn't settle, he didn't know what to do with himself. He hadn't the concentration to sit through a lecture or read in the library, so there was little point in going to the college. He didn't think he could bear the silence of the squat and he most certainly didn't want to go to the bridge, for he felt he'd be incapable of acting appropriately as the grateful "down and out" with Michaela, if he met her, which he presumed was how she saw him, if she stopped to talk to him, that was. Which she mightn't, now that her good deed for the week was done. So he walked around all day. Thinking. Trying not to think.

All day he tramped around the northside. Up and down steep steps, through the warrens of narrow lanes, through corporation estates, through waste lands, along stretches of sick river. He walked head down, oblivious to the litter underfoot. Oblivious to the smell of the brewery. To the dog that followed him for an hour. To the children whose territory he walked through; to their footballs which skimmed past his head. To the old women, white-haired and leather-faced, clad in nylon housecoats, sitting on kitchen chairs on the pavement outside their front doors, enjoying the unexpected fine day, who called out hello as he passed by. To the old and young men gathered at corners, whose eyes followed him as he walked past and who didn't call out hello. Then, finally, down the steep incline of Patrick's Hill he came, so steep it made it almost impossible for him not to run. Back to the city centre again.

Passing by the cinema on the Grand Parade he noticed the crowd moving inside. Checking his pockets for the price of a ticket, he joined the end of the queue, thinking that a movie might serve as a break from his forlorn reflections. But almost as soon as he'd settled down, he knew that this was not to be for his mind still buzzed and buzzed with thoughts of Michaela and the film played on, unseen by him.

How could Michaela have known that her actions of the previous night, made on the spur of a drunken moment, would have had such an effect on Davy? Before last night, had anyone cared to ask – not that there was anyone to care to ask – did he love Michaela, Davy would have answered, "Yes". And, if asked why, and coaxed enough, he might have said that it was the way she looked in her red dress, or mentioned the colour of her hair. If coaxed a little, he might have pinpointed the liveliness in her expression which made him think that life with her could never be dull or, he might have said it was her eyes; that the owner of such clear eyes could never be unkind or devious. To an attentive listener he might have carried on and said that it was the way she stood politely listening to drunks, when most people wouldn't have given them the time of day. He might have mentioned any number of little things about her. But, after last night, he wouldn't have been able to pick out any single thing, or even a combination of things, to explain why he felt the way he did. He just did. It was just her. What is it that changes *fancying* or even being *in love* with someone into actually loving them? Who knows? Did one single second mark that change in Davy, as they sat together in the dark last night, sides touching, not a word being spoken? The outcome of Michaela's kindness was that it had changed the way Davy felt about her forever. He just knew that he loved her and that this feeling would never change. He knew that he would never, ever feel the same way about anyone else. He knew that he would do anything to help her, to protect her, that he would do absolutely anything for her. Platitudes – cynics might be inclined to think, those who've heard it all before and have found that such proclamations usually mean nothing. But such cynics can never have known the love of someone like Davy. For if Davy believed that he'd always love Michaela, then he would.

So, unseen by Davy, the film played on. But had he been trying to concentrate, he'd have found it very difficult, for the couple sitting in front of him were driving everyone else around them crazy. For most of the film they chatted together as loudly and as freely as if they were sitting in a bar or café, only falling silent when they were snogging one another, silences which all but the persons sitting on either side of them welcomed, for then these unfortunates were subjected to elbows and legs being flung this way and that, as the couple got dug into each other.

But Davy noticed none of this; he was miles away, still wondering as he was about the relationship between Michaela and Colin, wondering did she love him, and if she did, then why?

Someone who wasn't physically miles away was Colin and, if Davy had leaned forward, prodded one half of the snogging couple, for it was Colin, and posed such questions to him, it is certain that Colin would have told him where to go.

So without taking in so much as a single word, lost in his own world, Davy sat through the film until finally the credits came up and the lights went on. But only when the people around him started moving, did Davy realise that the movie was over. He put his jacket on and, still lost in his own unhappy world, he stood waiting for the man beside him to start moving along to the end of the row, oblivious to the distress of the girl in the row in front, the second half of that snogging couple.

"Colin, I've lost my earring, help me find it," a very tousled-looking Samantha was pleading.

"Oh Samantha, it could be anywhere. Come on."

"No, I have to find it. It was my mother's."

The man beside Davy started edging his way along the row and so too did Davy until his hand brushed against something stuck in the top part of one of the seats in the row in front. He looked down and, seeing something glittering, he picked it up. It was the lost earring. He looked around for an owner. He didn't see Samantha; she was down on the ground, on all fours, running her hands over the sticky floor.

"Are you looking for this?" Davy asked Colin who was studying the ground in front of him, not putting too much effort into the search. It would have taken more than one of Samantha's mother's earrings to get Colin crawling around on the spilled crisps, the discarded chewing-gum and the sticky coke patches. Something belonging to himself, perhaps. Colin looked up at him and, not recognising him from their one brief encounter on the bridge the Friday night before, he took the earring from Davy, nodded, and muttered his thanks. But

157

although he'd only seen him once before, Davy recognised him instantly.

"I can't find it anywhere, Colin," came a voice from underneath the seat.

"You can get up, I have it," said Colin.

"Well, thanks for telling me," came the irritated response.

Davy's stomach lurched. He didn't think he could bear meeting Michaela again so soon. Not here. Not now. And not with him.

Samantha got up. Davy stared at her. Then at Colin. It was definitely Colin, no doubt about that. But who was the woman with him? Where was Michaela? He stared at one face, then the other, then back again, so intensely that Samantha and Colin exchanged worried glances and, deciding that Davy was obviously some weirdo, they both quickly turned and hurried along to the end of the row.

Davy too edged his way along and fell into the crowd of people waiting to leave the auditorium. As he waited, he watched Samantha and Colin ahead of him. He watched as they stood there giggling, arms wrapped around one another, and he watched as Colin stooped to kiss her. Never had Davy felt such hatred for anyone as he did for Colin at that moment. What should he do, he wondered? He tried to calm himself. He tried to think. What was the best thing to do for Michaela?

As the crowd moved forward Davy saw Colin affectionately slap the girl's behind and he wondered what in God's name the fool was doing in a cinema, behaving like this, when he had the most perfect person as his own? And, what on earth did Michaela see in him anyway, he wondered as he noticed, with some repulsion, that Colin was now licking this girl's ear. Well might he wonder. And Davy didn't know the half of it. How much madder would Davy feel if he knew about Anna. And how much madder still would he have felt if he knew that, whenever Colin was out of a night, unaccompanied by Michaela, Samantha, or Anna, he wasn't slow to chat up any woman he took a fancy to – practically every woman – and that he rarely ended a night out alone. Maybe – but probably not – Davy might have had some comfort if he knew that, despite his philandering, Colin adored Michaela and had from the moment he'd seen her, just like Davy, and still thought of her as the most beautiful woman he'd ever met, thought of her as his true love. Going off with other woman was just something he couldn't help, as he'd explained to an envious Ben Philips just the other day. Not that he'd ever leave Michaela, he'd hastened to add, in case Ben Philips got any ideas.

The crowd spilled out onto the street. Keeping his distance, Davy began to follow the couple. Across the Grand Parade and down along Washington Street. Then, still not having had enough of each other for one afternoon, Samantha and Colin stopped in a doorway to kiss again. Davy stepped into another doorway and watched. And seethed. Everything about Colin was beginning to really bug him.

"Pig," he muttered. Two passers-by turned and stared at him, then hurried past but, not even noticing their stares, he muttered on. "Obese, fat . . . pig." More than a slight exaggeration as it happens. But who can blame him? Although Colin was heavier than he'd been just a year previously and a far less critical observer than Davy would have noticed the slight double chin he was developing and that little bit of a belly.

"And ugly," Davy muttered following them across the road, feeling madder and madder. Downright inaccurate this time, but then Davy could hardly be expected to like the look of him. But most people would have considered him a handsome man. Polly hadn't, that day he'd come into the shop with Anna. But amongst women she was one of the few exceptions.

"Blond dyed sissy-head," he muttered, becoming more and more childish. One might have thought he'd have been able to come up with more hard-hitting insults after his long spell inside but, unknowingly, this time he spoke the truth. For Colin did dye his hair. And had done so since his teens. As a child, aunties had *oohed* and *ahhed* over his hair and his four sisters had complained that the blondest hair in the family was wasted on a boy. But the young Colin didn't think so, he knew the advantages of being blond; knew that a blond angelic-looking boy got away with a lot more than say, a mousy-haired boy, and later, that a blond teenage boy made teenage girls go *"hmmm"* when they first saw him, then *"yes"* to whatever he proposed far quicker than they would to his duller-haired rivals. Which is why, when his own hair was beginning to darken, coincidentally around the same time he noticed his eldest sister's hair was getting lighter, it didn't take him long to find out her secret – *Sun In* – and it too became his secret. Nobody in the world knew about it, not even Michaela. Except the lady in Congdon's chemist. And she had just suspicions and only after his repeated and unasked-for assurances that the bottle was for his sister.

"Poncey salesman suit," said Davy still muttering childishly, still shadowing them, still wondering how Michaela could love him. A salesman Colin was, and a excellent one at that – a persuasive talker and a chameleon – adaptable skills, those ones which make a good salesman and very useful in the love game. Now noticing Colin glance at his own appearance in a shop window, admiring himself laugh at Samantha's joke, Davy struggled for more insults,

"Bimbo," he managed weakly. No, Davy definitely hadn't paid enough attention to his cellmates. Nevertheless it was accurate enough. A bimbo, or a himbo, he was, lacking as he did a certain depth of character. Michaela had come to realise this. Samantha had come to realise this. Ninety-five percent of the women he met came to realise this. Anna, not being exactly the deepest herself, hadn't. But his salesman's skills, his knowledge of women – divined from his four older sisters together with his looks, went a long, long way. Which is why, to answer one of Davy's questions, Michaela, and indeed other bright women, such as Samantha, and the not so bright, such as Anna, fell for him in the first place.

The couple reached an apartment block. At the front door Samantha fiddled around in her bag for keys while Colin nuzzled into the back of her neck. Finding her key, she opened the door, took hold of Colin's hand and they both stepped inside. But as she turned to close the door, Samantha noticed Davy standing across the street, glaring over at them and, recognising him as the man who'd been staring at them in the cinema, nervously she nudged Colin.

"Clear off, you weirdo," shouted Colin before slamming shut the door.

Davy stared at the building. After a minute or two a light went on in the top floor and he saw Colin come to a window and draw the curtains.

"Dye-head blondy, fat, poncey suit-wearing bimbo salesman," he muttered.

A man and woman passing by, stared at him, then hurried on.

"I'm not drunk," Davy called after them.

"Sure you're not, pal," shouted back the man. "If you say so."

Davy realised he was being ridiculous. He had to stop thinking about Colin and of how much he hated him. This was about Michaela, what he should do for her. He considered going straight to her house to tell her what he'd seen. But would she believe him? Probably not. And would it do any good? And anyway, he'd end up being the despised messenger. He needed to think things out before doing anything.

"Hello."

Davy glanced away from the window and saw a girl, vaguely familiar, standing beside him, looking up at him.

Polly saw by his face that he didn't recognise her, she'd expected as much; she usually had to introduce herself to people half a dozen of times before they finally came to recognise her without any hints from her. But it would've been nice if it had been different with him.

"Hi," he answered politely.

"You probably don't remember me. I spoke to you the other evening in the canteen," she told him.

He looked at her again.

"Oh right. I do. The head-girl."

"Pardon?"

"You ordered me back into the class last week."

Another light went on in the apartment. The bedroom, no doubt, thought Davy.

"Well, I wouldn't have said I ordered you exactly," Polly was saying, feeling a little irritated. Never mind, she told herself, at least he recognised that she wasn't a total stranger; that was something.

"Do you want to come to a party?" asked Polly. So surprised was she at her own words that she almost looked around to see who'd spoken them.

"Well, I don't think so, I . . . "

"It's just across the road," she said, realising that now she'd started, there was no point in pulling back. "It's my cousin Cliona, she's having a party. I'm just on my way in." She nodded towards the apartment block.

"In there?" asked Davy

"Yes."

Davy thought about it. There was nothing he could do from out here. It seemed wiser to do a Horse of Troy on it.

"OK so."

They walked across the road. Polly rang the doorbell and they waited. She felt elated. For a few seconds. Then the worrying began.

"It's not a big party or anything," she said. "At least I don't think it is. Well, I don't know, really, I suppose it could be. Cliona has a lot of friends. Lots. Some of them are a bit wild, at least that's my impression of them, but you can never tell. I mean Cliona looks wild, but she's not. At least I don't think she is, but

166

other people would. But then, she probably wants them to – you know, part of the image." He really was a quiet sort, Polly thought, glancing up a him. "To be honest, I've no idea whether the party will be wild or not. I've no idea what kind it will be. But you can leave whenever you want. But there'll be free drink at it. And food. Though I'm not suggesting that that's why you're coming, though you're quite welcome to take as much as you want. It's a party after all. That's what parties are about, isn't it? Though, I have to say I haven't been to many. Well, I mean I've been to a few, of course I have, more than a few. And you don't have to spend the night just talking to me. If you stay, that is. Because you can leave whenever you want. No, you can talk to anyone you like. But you don't need me to tell you that, that's what parties are about after all – meeting people. As well as the food and drink." She looked up at him again and it seemed to her, even in her state of babblement, that he just might not be giving her one hundred percent attention. "And music. They're about music too . . . ," she came to a faltering end, deciding that he wasn't exactly the best person in the world to keep up his side of the conversation.

The door opened.

"Pollywolly! Hey, hey, hey!" screeched Cliona and, being in effusive party mode, she gave her cousin a great big bear hug; then letting her go, she looked at Davy.

"So Pollywollywonder, this is the him! I was beginning to think that your mother was making things up." Davy smiled at Cliona, waiting for Polly to set her straight. Polly couldn't bring herself to. She screwed up her face, closed her eyes tight and waited for Davy to tell her.

Since it seemed Polly wasn't going to say anything, Davy began,

"Well, I'm Davy. I'm not actually who . . . "

"And I'm Cliona, Polly's cousin. But we're more like twins. Only fourteen days between us. I'm sure Polly has told you all about me."

Polly opened her eyes. Cliona had taken Davy by the arm and was bringing him inside.

A bemused Davy looked back at her,

"Come on, Pollywollywonder," he called, smirking.

"You call her that too!" shrieked Cliona with delight.

The only light was the 40-watt bulb hanging from the centre of the ceiling which had been covered in red cloth to give the room atmosphere. So much atmosphere that Polly couldn't see where she was going. And all the smoke didn't help. And it wasn't just cigarette smoke either, she thought, nodding sagely to herself.

"Watch it," came a shout as Polly tripped over the entwined legs of a couple stretched out on a beanbag on the floor.

"Sorry, I didn't see you there," she said and stooped down to ask solicitously, "Are you all right?"

"Fuck off!"

There was a crowd of about thirty packed into the small sitting-room and, apart from a few snogging couples, everyone was standing around in groups talking over the loud music. Polly hurried on after Cliona and Davy and, as they were passing by one such group, a hand suddenly stretched out and caught a hold of Cliona's arm.

"Squealer! Hang on a tick, I'll be back,"

said Cliona as she pulled away but not before Polly had studied the hand; the long, skeletal, bloodless fingers, the raw red protuberant knuckles and the jutting wrist bone, exposed where the sleeve stopped short. And then she looked up, then up a bit more, for its owner was tall, very tall, over seven foot, up to his impossibly long neck with its enormous Adam's apple, practically the size of a real Granny Smith, and then up, up some more to his face with its cadaverous aspect, which, in keeping with rest of him, suggested that he just might not be getting all the vitamins he needed on his strict vegan diet; that a little red meat wouldn't go astray.

"I'm just getting my cousin and her boyfriend a drink, Squealer, I'll be back," said Cliona, as the seven-footer-something bent down to kiss her, but it was a long way down and Cliona was well gone by the time he got there. Davy and Polly followed on after her as she weaved her way through the crowd, smiling, waving, laughing and dispersing kisses and "Hi!"s and "Alright?"s to all along the way until finally she reached the marginally less crowded kitchen where she handed them each a can from the beer-packed fridge. "Now Pollywolly and Davywavy!" she said, then paused and smiled at them both sweetly, albeit drunkenly. "Ah, isn't that cute, the way your names go so well together." Then she continued. "Now, even though I know you lovers would prefer to hide yourselves away in a quiet corner for the night, I can't let you, not at my party. You're going to have to mingle." She caught each of them by the hand and towing them along behind her, she began pushing her way through the crowd, back over to Squealer and his group.

"OK, everyone this is my cousin Polly and her boyfriend Davy. Davy, Polly, this is Squealer and Neiler and Fi and Ollie and Toris. Oh, oh, the doorbell! Be back in a minute," she giggled, and disappeared back into the throng.

At the edge of this little group, Polly and Davy looked at one another, smiled awkwardly, then opened their cans. Polly hated beer but, watching Davy take a long slug she followed suit, trying not to taste it, but thinking it would be good to get some inside her; to relax her a bit. But it didn't, it went down the wrong way and she started spluttering and coughing, like some old codger on forty a day. She doubled over, whooped great coughs and struggled to catch her breath. Davy, trying to help, took the can from her and began to hit her on the back, which was of no help and the effort of trying to tell him to stop only made her worse. She pushed him away, straightened up and yanked the can back.

"What are you trying to do, kill me?" she asked crossly.

Squealer had stopped mid-sentence and he, and the others, had turned to stare at the red-faced Polly. She coughed again, a little cough that then turned into a great rasping one and when it was over, she managed an embarrassed smile, for this Squealer fellow looked like he had beer for breakfast, cans and all, and wouldn't be too well-disposed to someone who couldn't hold their beer, not to mind someone who couldn't even swallow it.

"A peanut, went down the wrong way," she gasped, patting her chest, unaware that not five minutes ago, Toris had been bemoaning the lack of any titbits in the room.

"I'm fine now," Polly wheezed. "Carry on."

And they did.

"It's you who should be paying me for it, mate, I said to him," Squealer resumed.

"I'm sorry for pushing you away," whispered Polly to Davy. "I just got a bit of a fright."

"That's OK," said Davy. "Are you alright now?"

She nodded, then thinking it would be easier to listen to these people than to try and think of things to say to Davy, she turned into the circle. Davy did likewise.

"And I meant it," Squealer was saying. "He should have, shouldn't he?" Polly stared up at him, fascinated by his Adam's apple and the way it bobbed up and down as he spoke. It was going like the clappers.

"Course he should. Too bloody right," said Fi. Polly looked down now, to Fi, she was tiny, hardly up to Squealer's waist. "I mean it's art, isn't it?"

"Well, that's what I said to him," replied Squealer and Polly looked up again. "He owed me. Not the other way around. You saw it didn't you, Fi?" he asked.

And Polly looked down again, waiting for her to reply.

"Yeah. It covered the entire ceiling. It was something else. It was really amazing," she said. "Like really . . . well, like really amazing. Sort of . . . what was it you said again, Squealer?"

"I don't know. That it was like, ah, Picassoesque?"

"Yeah, it was just like one of Picassoesque's," agreed Fi, who was not too knowledgeable when it came to the subject of art.

"Would that be like something from Picassoesque's or, as I'm sure you actually mean, Picasso's blue period or from his pink?" asked Davy. "Or perhaps you're referring to a cubism influence in his work?"

All heads, including Polly's, moving as one, as if directed by an invisible baton, turned to Davy.

"What I'm really wondering, I suppose," Davy explained. "Is whether it reflected the gloom and despair of his blue period, or the life-affirming quality of his later pink period?"

Davy did sometimes remember what he read and, if they were all going to be so pretentious, well, why not join them; at least he knew what he was talking about.

"Well, it had everything in it," said Squealer, and Polly managed to stop gaping at Davy and craned her neck up once more. "I put my soul into it, didn't I? I mean, who knows, it could be worth a fortune in years to come. And the worst thing is, he's like, like, going to paint over it. Graffiti, that's what he called it. His sort really, really get to me, you know what I mean like? Bloody philistine! Like what is he anyway?" He paused and happened to look down at Polly. And then he stared at her and wondered could Cliona have actually said this little Miss Muppet was her cousin. Polly didn't notice him staring at first, she was waiting for his Adam's apple to get going again, but when it didn't, she glanced up to his face and, surprised to see him looking at her, she wondered if he was waiting for her to answer.

"A philistine?" she hazarded when he kept

on staring, for it seemed a reasonable guess.

"Exactly," he replied, so emphatically that it seemed to be the first time such a thought had struck him; as if Polly had come up with an amazingly new and very astute insight into the man's character. "A philistine, that's exactly what he is. And a bloody parasite! Living off my rent! And what's it to him anyway, what I did with my room? I was paying him for it, wasn't I?" He took a slug from his beer and so did each of the others, all comfortable with the momentary pause in the conversation. Except Polly, who always felt a desperate need to fill such pauses, and never more so than with Davy standing beside her.

"Does it hurt much?" she asked, turning to the girl called Toris.

"Eh?"

"Your nose ring?"

"No, it's all right, you don't even notice it after a while."

"Really?" Another pause. "I mean it must be awkward, especially when you've a cold." The girl looked at her and wondered if Polly was being deliberately rude. But Polly wasn't, she was genuinely curious about the matter and she continued on.

"You know, when you blow it." Toris stared disdainfully, but Polly didn't notice. Not at all. On she went, delighted to have found something to talk about. "I don't think I'd like one myself, I have to say. Whatever about one in your belly button or in your eyebrow. I mean they're fairly odd and all, but they're not quite as bad as one in your nose. They haven't the same hygiene implications." Digging deeper and deeper, ignoring that little voice in her head warning her to stop, *right now*. "I don't mean that they're unhygienic or anything, just kind of awkward. It just seems that it would be pretty disgus . . . awkward, not being able to blow properly." Deeper and deeper. "You know, when you have a cold like." It became obvious, even to Polly, that her opinion wasn't being warmly received. "Although, I'm only speaking personally of course. I just mean I wouldn't like one personally. With my nose being so small I think I'd have problems. Not like most people. Not like you. I'm sure you'd be fine."

Toris turned away.

"Is she really Cliona's cousin?" she asked the others with disdainful incredulity. And the group closed in and Polly and Davy found themselves completely excluded.

This is a nightmare, thought Polly. Never in her life had she felt so out of place. She looked around the room. Everyone, bar herself and Davy, was dressed "alternatively". Uniformly alternative. With as much variety amongst them as a group of Bank of Ireland girls in uniform. Their clothes looked as if they had been washed over and over again, all together in some giant washing-machine until the original colours had merged to become this nondescript charcoal/grey/green that they were all dressed in from head to foot. The only splashes of colour, apart of Davy's red sweater and her Laura Ashley flowery skirt, were the heads of those who were dreadlock-less and instead had spiky red or yellow hair; the originality and shock value of which was somewhat lost in its multiplicity. This was the dopiest thing she had ever done in her life, thought Polly, coming to this stupid party and dragging

Davy along. Then she looked over at him. She was surprised to see him grinning at her.

"What's so funny?" she asked.

"You're not exactly diplomatic, are you?"

"I don't know why she got so odd. I was only making conversation. I was only telling her what I think. And it would be horrible wearing one when you've a cold. Well, wouldn't it? Would you like it?"

"No, but maybe you should have stuck to the weather."

"And what about you so?" she snorted. "Showing off with all that stuff about Picasso."

"Showing off?"

"Yeah." And then she laughed. "But it was well done!"

He took a drink. She sociably put her can to her lips.

"People have them in even more peculiar places than their noses, you know," said Davy, watching her closely.

"What?"

"Rings. Some men have their penises pierced," he told her, waiting to see her reaction. And it worked.

"No!" said Polly, her eyes nearly popping out of her head, as she stared at him in disbelief.

"I bet he has," said Davy, nodding towards Squealer. Polly looked over at him and stared for a few seconds, then turned back to Davy and in a considered voice said,

"That's probably why he's called Squealer so."

Davy let out a roar of laughter causing everyone in the room to turn to them and Polly wondered what she'd said that was so funny.

"And women get it done down there as well," said Davy.

"Now I know you're lying to me!"

Davy briefly forgot his reason for being here, he forgot about Colin and his girlfriend, and whatever they were up to, and even forgot about Michaela. He decided he liked this Polly. She was a funny one really. He could imagine being friends with her. Polly looked back at him again. He was smiling at her.

"So, have you decided if Toris has?" he asked.

"How did you know what I was thinking?" she asked, astonished.

He realised that she was probably feeling as out of place as he was, she certainly looked it. Maybe that's why she'd dragged him along when she'd spotted him hanging around outside; because she knew the kind of people that were going to be here, and the night that lay ahead. And for the first time, he began to think about her.

"So, Polly wolly wonder."

"That stupid name! Nobody but Cliona calls me that. I haven't heard it for years. I think she must be drunk."

"You don't exactly look like cousins."

"I think that's an understatement. But we used to, when we were younger. Cliona's always giving out to me, she says that I'll be forty by the time my clothes catch up with my age. I suppose she's right. And about the boyfriend thing, I'm sorry, I'll clear it up with her later. Heaven knows how she got that idea."

"So tell me, Polly what are you going to be when you grow up? When you finish college?"

"I don't know really," answered Polly and she shrugged. "Teach, I suppose. Well, that's what my parents think I'm going to do. But I'm not sure. I probably won't even get my exams. So far my marks have been awful. I never seem to be able to stick to the point in my assignments. At least that's what was written on the last one I got back from Professor Kiely. But I thought I was being clever, you know, taking it from a different angle than everyone else. But obviously I strayed too far. *Please read the question carefully and stick to answering it!*"

Suddenly she felt self-conscious and she stopped talking. For a while they watched the crowd around. Someone had switched the music to reggae and a lone couple in the middle of the floor gyrated to it. The pubs had cleared by now and the flat was absolutely jointed.

"And what about you?" Polly asked.

"What about me?"

"You're in First Arts as well?" she said quizzically.

"Well, not exactly," answered Davy.

"But you come to our lectures. Are you an exchange student from Queens or something?"

"No."

"I just thought you might be, you know, with your northern accent. What are you doing? You look a bit old to be an undergraduate. Are you doing a Master's?"

"Yes, sort of," he answered vaguely.

"I see. You're not exactly in first year and you're sort of doing a Master's. Ah yes. It's all very clear to me now. You don't give very much away, do you?"

She looked at him, waiting for him to explain. For a moment Davy almost did, but he wasn't used to telling people about himself. And if he told her he wasn't really a student, it would lead to a whole lot of explaining. Instead he answered,

"You're right, I'm doing a Master's."

"In?"

"Well, in English."

"I see. I kind of figured that out. But what are you doing your thesis on?"

God, she didn't half ask a lot of questions, he thought.

"Well, in English literature," he said, stalling.

"You're doing a thesis on English Literature for your Master's degree in English. How very novel, if you'll excuse the pun. Still, it doesn't leave an awful lot for the other postgraduates though, does it? Nobody could fault you for picking too specialised a topic, that's for sure. Has it got a title?"

He stared at her blankly, trying to think of something.

"Light and Darkness: The Racial Divide in Twentieth Century American Poetry," he said eventually. It was the name of a book he'd come across in the library earlier that day and he thought it sounded aptly earnest and boring enough to be a thesis.

"Interesting," said Polly doubtfully.

"I suppose," he answered non-committally, praying she wouldn't start quizzing him about it.

"But why do you sit in on our lectures?"

"Well, you know, I like to take a break from my research and, since I want to lecture eventually, I like to see them at it." He felt mean lying to her like this, but she wasn't giving him much choice.

Colin came down the stairs fuming. Samantha was really acting the bitch, he thought. Sending him off home, like a little boy. How long was she going to keep this up? So certain had he been that she'd let him stay the night, he'd rung Michaela only hours ago to say that he'd be stuck in Sligo for the night. Of all places! Why hadn't he picked somewhere nearer? Even she wouldn't believe that he'd managed to have dinner with some clients and then driven back to Cork in under three hours. "That's not my problem," he muttered in a girlie voice, mimicking Samantha's response when he'd told her as much. He turned the corner and almost collided with a couple who'd just come from the party. They'd left the door to Cliona's apartment open and, hearing the music and party sounds, Colin realised that he just might have found a place to pass a couple of hours before going home at a hour he could reasonably explain.

He wandered in and, presuming that the layout of all parties was the same, he made for the fridge in the kitchen. A few curious glances were thrown in his direction – he looked more than a little out of place, but he was right in supposing that people would assume that he was a friend of a friend of a friend or dismiss him as someone's weird brother in a suit. With a drink in his hand he went into the sitting-room and leaned against a wall, just behind Davy and Polly who didn't notice him for Polly was busy quizzing Davy, trying to establish the hypotheses of his thesis. Colin sipped his beer. Weird bunch he thought, real save-the-whale types. The girls were probably all lesbians and vegetarians with hairy armpits. Except the one in the flowery skirt, now she was pretty, he thought, although she could do something about those eyebrows, a little plucking wouldn't be any harm. He wondered if he'd met her before, she looked familiar. But she didn't count anyway, she was obviously with someone; the weirdo from the cinema, he realised, and thought, small world indeed. He decided that there was nothing worth hanging around for here, meaning there was no one he wanted to hit on, and he began to drink quickly having made up his mind to go to a night-club, where he'd meet some normal-looking women.

He left the room and on his way out of the apartment he passed one of the bedrooms. The door was wide open and he saw a girl lying on top of the bed. At every party there was one, he thought, always some girl smashed out of her head. Still, he wasn't exactly choosy and it had worked for him before. He wandered in. "Oh God," he muttered, thinking that he should have known it would be another bloody hippie. "No, thank you," he said to the sleeping form and was about to leave when Cliona stirred.

"Hello," she said, opening her eyes just a bit. In the first nervous hour of her party, when she was convinced that nobody, except Squealer who'd taken up residence after his brush(!) with the Philistine, was going to show, she'd drunk three double vodkas, three beers and had a few joints. One minute she'd been in flying form, all "Davywavys" and

"Pollywollys" and racing off to get the door, and the next, she thought she was going to get sick or pass out and had taken to her bed.

"You've come to my party," she said, trying to focus on Colin.

"Yes."

"Welcome to Cliona's party. Great party," she muttered. "Isn't it?" Then her eyes closed again. She was scuttered, he thought, but not bad-looking, for a hippie. Her top had risen up, exposing her flat stomach with its little gold belly-button ring. He wasn't gone on the ring, but besides that, she wasn't bad, not bad at all. She opened her eyes again and tried to make out who he was.

"I don't know you. Who are you? Polly's friend I expect," she said getting a hazy impression of neat dress. "Are you Polly-wolly's friend? Pollywolly's friend in a suit?"

"Yes," he said. He closed the bedroom door and sat down on the bed beside her.

"I s'pected as much. Her friend but not her boyfriend. Her boyfriend has different clothes on. And a different face. Unless she has two. Two boyfriends. Not a boyfriend with two faces. Nobody has two faces. Only monsters. Does Polly have two boyfriends? Two Mr Pollywollywonders?"

"No, I'm just her friend."

"I think I'm probably drunk," she told him with her eyes closed. "In fact I s'pect I'm plastered. Would you say I'm plastered?"

"Maybe a little."

"Maybe a little. I'm afraid you'll have to get yourself a drink because I'm maybe a little plastered even though it is my party. Because it is my party. I'm indisposed because I'm maybe a little plastered, because it is my party."

"Would you like me to get you one?"

"No, I've had enough. I must get back to my party."

These hippies were all into free love, Colin imagined. He'd never done it with someone like her before. She'd probably be into all sort of weird things, especially when she was stoned. He reached out and touched the belly-button-ring. She didn't seem to mind. He began to stroke her stomach.

"Don't do that," she mumbled.

"But it's nice, isn't it?"

"Yeah, but I don't know you, Pollywolly's friend."

He kept on stroking her.

"Stop."

"Why? You said you liked it."

"Can you hear someone screaming?" Polly asked Davy.

"No."

"Listen. There. Do you hear it?

"Yeah," he answered doubtfully.

"It's Cliona, I'd know her scream anywhere."

"Polly, if it is her, she's probably just messing."

"Squealer, do you know where Cliona is?" asked Polly, then not waiting for a reply, she turned back to Davy.

"I'm going to check."

She shoved her way through the crowd of people and Davy came after her. She glanced around the kitchen but Cliona wasn't there so she hurried out into the hallway and asked each of the people in the long queue to the one toilet had they seen her, but nobody had;

many hadn't even heard of her. She hurried to Cliona's bedroom and put her ear to the door.

"I think she's in there," said Polly turning the handle.

"Polly, you can't." Davy caught a hold of her. "No Polly, she's not a little girl. You can't barge in."

There was another scream. Davy burst in. Colin was lying on top of Cliona and she was trying to push him off. Seeing that it was Colin and, quickly realising that this was no mutual love thing going on between him and Cliona, Davy caught him by the arm and pulled him off of her.

"Get off," said Colin. "How dare you come barging in when we're . . . "

He didn't get a chance to say another word. Davy dragged him out of the bedroom, out of the flat and down the stairs, and out onto the road. Then he held him up against the wall and stared at him. Colin was terrified, Davy's face was inches from his own and he'd never seen anyone looking so angry in his life.

"Take it easy, man. She was crying out for it."

Davy knew that he should just walk away
"Not the face, man, come on."

Davy punched him hard in the stomach
three times. Once for Cliona. Once for the girl
in the cinema. And once for Michaela.

8

DAVY

DAVY'S SLIGHT build belied his strength. His first punch knocked the wind out of Colin, his second caused him to double over, groaning loudly in pain, and the impact of the third and the most powerful punch – it being for Michaela – into Colin's soft and yielding belly brought him to the ground.

And as Colin lay there whimpering, Davy walked away. He made it as far as the corner, then his legs began to give and he had to stop. Leaning against the wall he began to vomit. He felt absolutely dreadful. He was sweating all over. He vomited, again and again, until there was nothing left. Eventually, he straightened up, wiped the sweat from the back of his neck, and went to move on but immediately he felt the sick rising up again. He leant forward and empty-retched.

Davy had been in fights before, many, many times and far, far more vicious than this one but, they'd never been of his own volition and, having being the target of so much pointless violence he'd learnt to detest it. Davy had known as a child that his alleged misdemeanours were just excuses for his father to indulge himself in the sadistic pleasure he got from whipping his son; just as he'd known in prison that the other men's accusations that he'd "looked funny" at them, or whatever, were also excuses to vent some of their own anger. And now Davy felt he was no better, and suspected that really he'd only used Cliona as an excuse for hitting Michaela's husband, simply because that's who he was – Michaela's husband. For he knew that his and Polly's timely interruption would have been enough to prevent Colin from harming Cliona any further.

He began to walk home slowly. When he reached Cathedral View, he got down on his belly and wriggled his way in through the gap in his front door. Then, not having the heart to change out of his clothes, he crawled into bed, in under the dirty old blankets – left by the previous occupants who'd be lying there now had they not been re-housed in preparation for the advent of the new road. And in the bed's sagging hollow – another legacy from these unknown people – he lay all that night and for most of the following day and night. He didn't sleep much, just lay there, staring up at the ceiling, with not even the mind to read. A few times he got up to the bathroom, then moped around and thought about leaving the house, but he couldn't be bothered and each time he returned to bed. For finally, the optimism which had buoyed him up since his release from prison and which had begun to slip over the last few days, had come crashing down.

The incident with Colin had nothing to do with it, not really, it was just a trigger. His misery stemmed from the events of months, of a lifetime even. So he lay there thinking. Mainly he thought about how stupid he'd been, stupid not to know that fresh starts belonged in fairy tales and not in a sorry real life such as his; stupid not to realise that his attempt to leave all the crap behind and start afresh had been doomed from the outset; and, stupid to be so cock-sure of his ability to sort himself out and to think that his savings of £300 would last until he found himself a job to keep him going while he set about procuring what he really, really wanted.

And what Davy had really, really wanted was a job in a library. So impressed had he been by the quietness, the dignity, the whole atmosphere of the prison library on his first visit to it – though it was a pretty pathetic library – that he'd decided this was the life he wanted. A life that was as different as possible from that of his family. Many a night in prison he imagined himself as a librarian, had imagined for himself a life spent sitting behind a library counter tapping away on his computer in a tweed jacket and wearing little round glasses with silver frames (curiously – for he didn't wear glasses now). He imagined himself impressing young girls with the depth of his knowledge on all matters literary and holding the door open for old ladies as they carried away their week's supply of big-print romances. To be a librarian was Davy's greatest ambition, or greatest real ambition – to have Michaela fall in love with him was just daydreaming nonsense.

But so far, Davy hadn't done anything about this library idea; he hadn't yet felt ready to present himself for what he considered a very exalted position. He'd wanted to get settled first, find somewhere proper to live, find another job to keep him going in the meantime. But, despite his considerable efforts, no work of any kind had materialised even though he'd confined himself to applying for jobs which didn't require much in the way of skills, experience or self-esteem, and after each rejection, the jobs he sought required less and less of all these three. Only a week before, he'd applied to an insalubrious skin and hide business, tucked away in one of the lanes of the city. Cleaning the pelts of dead animals destined for export and transformation into fine leather luggage was a job only for the truly desperate, thought Davy and, with its lack of mass appeal, figured that he might stand a chance. A fat chance, as it turned out. Even though he'd wised up and had learned by now to keep the unsavoury detail of his criminal past to himself, the unexplained and suspicious gap between the ages of fifteen and twenty-three was equally damning. Even though he'd learned not to bother showing his one reference for, glowing though it was, it *still* came from a Prisoner Governor.

His one stroke of luck had been finding this place to live. It was reasonably dry and the previous owners had left behind many things. Besides their blankets and the imprint of their old bodies, they'd left behind the bed itself, a cooker, some pots and pans – things they'd deemed too shabby for their brand-new home. That the electricity had never been disconnected was the biggest bonus. And so Davy had been able to get by from week to week spending very little. He had two sets of clothes and these served him adequately. He passed most of his time reading in the city and college libraries,which didn't cost him a lot; but since he couldn't take books out from either, he also bought books, one at a time, from a second-hand shop and, when he'd finished them, he brought them back again and got fifty percent of the cost back which he reinvested in another book. He spent about six pounds a week on food. Being wary of the effect that it had had on the rest of his family, he didn't drink much, just occasionally, with the men on the bridge, and now and then in a pub, but only as an excuse for sitting there. So thus far he had managed to survive on that few hundred pounds. He'd even managed to splash out on occasion. Like the time he'd bought the Nick Cave CD Michaela had been carrying around when he'd spotted her in HMV. And that hadn't been a waste. True, his lack of a CD player meant that he'd never heard it but he'd spend hours poring over the lyrics and knew them off by heart and, curiously it seemed to him, they all could have been written with Michaela in mind. But now his money was running out.

Finally, on the second morning after the fight, he stirred himself, climbed out of the bed, left his house and walked into town. Out of the £300 he'd earned in the prison library, he counted that he had £29.45 left, a sum that wasn't going to last forever no matter how careful he was, so now he went into a café and decided to blow as much as it took on a grand big fry. He ordered, then sat waiting, thinking what a crap place the world was. When the waitress put the fry in front of him, he looked at it and, savouring the sight and smell of it, thought that, although the world was a crap place, it had its compensations. Starving, he tucked in and made very short work of it.

Less than fifteen minutes later, he left the café. A good fry and a strong pot of tea knocks the socks off all the self-help books and counselling sessions in the world to get the body and soul back on track again and now he felt full of vigour, felt better than he had for ages and began to see things clearly. He saw that the image of himself as a young gurrier unworthy of a job in a library was never going to change and there was no point in waiting for it to. He made up his mind that, for once and for all, he was going to find out whether or not he had a hope in hell of ever becoming a librarian. He had a degree in English after all and maybe the college would be more open-minded about his past than the owners of Healy's Skin and Hide. Maybe not, but he was going to do what he should have done on the very first morning he'd arrived in Cork. And if he hadn't a hope, then he wouldn't waste another second day-dreaming, he'd take himself straight down to the dole office and to hell with dreams.

The grand old three-storied terraces along College Road had originally been build as private residences but, over the decades the nearby university, in its efforts to accommo-date an ever-spiralling student population, had gradually purchased almost all of them as their elderly owners passed away. In this second role as some of the college's smaller academic departments or offices, the houses soon lost that well-tended look of affluent homes and their genteel owners would have turned in their graves if they could see the ensuing deterioration of their pride and joy; the crooked and yellowing blinds behind dirty windows, the peeling paint, the weeds; and above all, the students who trooped in and out of these once gracious homes discarding their cigarette butts on beautiful tiled floors and filling the rooms, up to the fine ceilings, with talk so different to what these rooms had once been used to, talk about whom they'd shifted and of the copious pints they'd drunk the previous night.

Full of resolve, Davy, remembering having noticed that one of these housed the college Career's Office, and thinking that this would be a good place to start on his quest, came directly from the café to College Road. Now he walked along reading the little plaques mounted by each of the front doors, looking for the one which indicated the Career's Office. Finally he came to it and stood on the footpath outside for several minutes, gathering up courage. It occurred to him that he must look a sight, not having had the motivation to wash or change since before the fight. He licked the palm of his hand and tried to flatten down his curly hair with spit but with little effect. Glancing down at his clothes he saw that they were pretty grubby and guessed that he probably didn't smell too agreeable, but couldn't be sure; it was a hard thing to know about oneself. He knew he should return home to Cathedral View and clean himself up, but he was loath to, fearing that he might never find the nerve to come back again. Instead he went inside. He called out *hello*, but nobody responded and he passed in through the hall and into what had once been the sitting-room. The room was lined with shelves crammed full of book and pamphlets. At one end, behind a desk, sat two women. It was coffee-break time and each had a cup in one hand and a partially-eaten cream cake in the other. Davy smiled at them. The older woman, about sixty, with a kind face, smiled back and appeared to be about to address him but the younger one, having decided after a cursory examination that Davy wasn't worth interrupting her elevenses for, didn't give her a chance.

"Rose, is there enough hot water in the kettle for a second cup?" she asked the older woman who hadn't as yet taken so much as a sip from her own. Not that Rose's companion noticed or cared, holding out her cup she went on, "And mind, it was a bit strong the last time."

Relieved that they didn't question his right to be here, Davy walked around the room looking at the contents of the crowded shelves. He hadn't a clue where to start. To look purposeful he picked up a book lying on a table. It was a careers directory for computer graduates and scanning through it he saw that it was all double-Dutch to him, that he'd never even heard of the jobs it listed in computer-speak. What was Java and what would a person need to know to be employed as a developer of same, he wondered. What did it mean by Packaging Technician, hardly a fancy name for someone skilled in the art of doing up parcels. And what on earth was a Small Talk Developer? A person who thought up new and interesting responses to the question, "Isn't the weather dreadful?" He put the book down and picked up another, an engineering one this time. At least he had some idea of what an engineer was, or so he thought. Now he discovered that in fact, according to this book, it meant dozens of things depending on which word it was used in conjunction with – chemical, mechanical, civil, electrical, electronic, industrial, all vaguely comprehensible, but other types had him baffled – what could a localisation engineer possibly do? The idea that maybe, "librarian" was just a generic term for many more specialised careers suddenly struck him. He felt very ignorant and realised that he was going to have to ask one of the women for assistance. He glanced over at them and saw that they were watching his every move; that he'd become the coffee-break floorshow so to speak.

"Can I help you?" asked the younger woman, though her voice and expression made it clear that it was absolutely *the* very last thing in the world she cared to do. She was in her late twenties and could have been attractive except for her sour expression and the thick make-up. The heavy foundation she wore was shades too dark with an orangish tinge and looked like a mask, stopping short as it did of her deathly pale neck, in a neat line around her jaw.

"Maybe," answered Davy approaching the desk. "You see, I'm interested in becoming a librarian and I was wondering if you'd have information on any courses I could take."

The young woman sniffed the air, then stared pointedly at Davy, and, with a pained look on her face, she addressed her colleague,

"Rose, open the window will you and let some air in." Mortified that he did so obviously smell, Davy stepped back from the desk a little. "Are you currently a student here?" she asked him.

"Well no, but . . ."

Her expression confirmed that this was just what she suspected.

"Our service is for current or prospective UCC students, you understand?"

"Well, I thought UCC might run a course I could take."

"I'm afraid not," she said and turned away.

"I see. Maybe you have some information on courses in other colleges," suggested Davy, not ready to give up just yet.

The young woman sighed.

"Possibly," she answered. "But they'd all be post-graduate courses." And, in case he didn't know what that meant, she went on to explain, "You'd have to have a degree already to be considered for them."

"Well, I have a degree," said Davy with some satisfaction.

"Really?" she said, looking him up and down sceptically. "Well I suggest then that you contact your Alma Mater, they might be able to help you."

"My what?"

"Your Alma Mater."

Davy looked at her blankly, not knowing what she meant. She rolled her eyes to heaven.

"Where did you gain your degree from?" she asked impatiently.

"It was an Open University course," said Davy.

"I see." Again her expression confirmed that this was no more than she expected. "Are you sure it was a degree? It wasn't a certificate or a diploma?"

He was sorely tempted to tell her what a miserable condescending cow he thought she was and walk out, but he'd only be cutting off his nose and she, no doubt, would be smugly satisfied to be proven right in her estimation of him. Instead he nodded wordlessly.

"Well I'm quite sure we have nothing of relevance," she was saying. "But if you want, you can try the shelves by the door. If we have anything, then it will be over there."

"Bernie," interrupted her colleague nervously.

"What is it, Rose?" asked Bernie crossly

"I believe that . . ."

"Have you made us some more coffee yet?"

"No, I'm just about to. But I think that UCC now . . ."

"Go on then, before the water goes off the boil."

Davy walked over to the shelves where this Bernie woman had pointed and began going through the titles of the directories on the shelves. These were filed without any order – legal, commercial, medical, and many others, all lumped in together. There seemed to be something for everyone bar him. The woman was right, he was wasting his time.

Bernie didn't see him go. Having finished "dealing" with him, her own term for the service she provided, all her attention was now focused elsewhere, all on her left wrist as it happened. She was holding it out in front of her, staring at it, trying to decide if her newly acquired gold bracelet looked best worn with her watch, as she had it now, or on it's own.

Rose, having obediently got up to make Bernie's coffee, had her back turned so she didn't see Davy slouch away either. Making the coffee was about as exciting as it had got so far in this new job of hers, which wasn't really a job at all but a four-week placement, the final part of the "back to work" course she was taking. Before she'd started she'd hoped so much that, if she proved herself competent, then she just might be kept on. Now, after one week she was beginning to wonder how she'd stand another hour and was seriously considering just chucking it in. Her recent decision to join the work force was born entirely out of financial reasons caused by her sudden change in circumstances. Given a choice, she'd still be at home looking after her husband Gerard, waving him off to work each morning, as she'd happily done for the last thirty years. But seemingly, this wasn't what Gerard had wanted and, sadly, she'd only found out when it was too late, on the night he told her he was leaving her for one of their friend's daughters.

After so many years at home, going back to work had Rose terrified, she was sure she wouldn't be up to it. It was perfectly clear that Bernie thought she wasn't. From the outset she made it obvious that she felt she was dealing with some antediluvian creature who wasn't playing with quite the full deck. Maybe she was right. After all Gerard held similar views and he should know, Rose supposed, having lived with her for so long. He wouldn't be leaving her, so he'd explained on that dreadful night, if she wasn't so slow and stupid and unexciting and old.

So the younger woman treated Rose like she would an imbecile. Rose resented this, but suspected it was justified, her confidence being at the all-time low that it was. Something else however had begun to bother her far more and that was the inequitable way she noticed Bernie treated the students. Bernie viewed them as a nasty interruption in her day except, that is, for her chosen few – handsome, affluent-looking young men who were well, to put it bluntly, white – for whom nothing was too much trouble. To attract one of these white handsome, affluent-looking young men was, after all, Bernie's reason for taking the job ten years ago, although thus far she'd had absolutely no success. But her ambition held fast although her chances were growing slimmer as the age gap widened, her make-up thickened and her expression grew ever more sour by the day. Anybody else, males who were either ugly, dark-hued or who looked like their stay in college was a financial struggle and all females, got short shift from Bernie and usually left without information which she might easily have given them had she felt so inclined. Up until now Rose had felt powerless to do anything about it, she wasn't sufficiently *au-fait* with the career opportunities open to these students to help them herself and was more than a little scared of Bernie to dare question the advice she gave out. Or, as more usually was the case, didn't give out. But earlier that morning a fax had come in from one of the Arts Faculty lecturers informing them that a new post-graduate course in library technology was due to commence in the coming academic year, which was exactly what this boy was looking for. She had taken the fax from the machine herself, had handed it to Bernie and had seen her read it and she knew that it was now stuck in the bundle of papers on the desk in front of Bernie. Rose was as soft as a ball of butter; the sight of Davy as he'd arrived in looking so uncertain, so vulnerable and neglected, had caused a lump to rise in her throat and now, she was thinking that if she let him leave without telling him, she'd never be able to forgive herself. But her stomach was churning at the thought of confronting Bernie.

"Rose, my coffee? I've been waiting for bloody ages," barked Bernie, unaware of her colleague's inner turmoil.

"Stuff you and your coffee."

There was a silence. It was hard to know who was more taken aback, Rose or Bernie. Rose had never before been so rude to anyone in her life. In fact, she was never rude to anyone ever; if someone bumped into her in town or skipped a queue, it was always Rose who ended up apologising. But things were hard enough for young people without the likes of Bernie being so unhelpful, it was time to take a stand.

"Excuse me but I believe I'm paid, not a lot, but paid nonetheless to do a job and that isn't to make your coffee," she said.

Pushing a gaping Bernie aside she began flicking though the bundle of papers on the desk.

"I beg your pardon. How dare you? That's my private correspondence!"

"No, it's not," said Rose, still rooting. If she did nothing else in her time here, she was going to make sure this fellow knew about the course. She found the fax she was looking for, scanned through it, then picked up the phone and dialled. Only then did she look round and realise that Davy had left. She shoved the receiver into Bernie's hand and said, "When Professor Thompson comes on the line, hold him, tell him that I want to speak to him." She ran out of the building, ran along College Road until she caught up with Davy who was miserably making his way to the dole office. Without a word of explanation she grabbed a bemused Davy by the hand and hurried back to the office, dragging him along behind her.

"Have you got Professor Thompson on the line?" she asked Bernie.

Bernie nodded.

"He's not very happy to have been kept waiting," she whined.

"What's your name?" Rose asked Davy, taking the phone from Bernie.

"Davy, Davy Long."

"Hello, is that Professor Thompson? Hello, Professor Thompson, this is Rose O'Rourke from the Career's Office. I'm ringing you on behalf of a Davy Long who's here with me at the moment. He's very interested in this new library technology course due to start next autumn, you know the one you sent us details of this morning. Well, I'd like to send him straight over to you if I may. Oh, I see. Well what about this afternoon then? No? Tomorrow?" she suggested. "No? Well later in the week then? No?" Her face was turning red with anger. "Well, I must say Professor, I'm very disappointed. This is very poor form indeed. I'd have expected more from the university's academic staff. Do you not want to get the students interested? What was the point of sending us over the fax if you're not prepared to meet them?" Then she listened for a moment. "All right, I'll see if that suits him. Three o'clock this afternoon?" she asked, looking up at Davy and before he got a chance to respond, she went on, "Yes, that's fine with him. Thank you very much indeed, Professor." She put down the phone, amazed at her own audacity, even more than Bernie who was staring at her open-mouthed. "Well that's settled, you're to meet him at three o'clock."

She got up and photocopied the fax and handed it to Davy. "Now, there's all the details you need. Be sure to bring a copy of your CV along with you. Don't be intimidated by Professor Thompson, he sounds like a grumpy old fool. Speak up and make eye contact. Remember that everyone has to start somewhere. Now," she said looking him up and down. "I suggest you go home and change first, OK?"

Davy nodded, intimidated by this bossy woman

"And I want you to come back here sometime over the next few days and tell me how you get on, alright?"

Again Davy nodded. Rose wasn't convinced.

"Promise me," she demanded.

"Yes," said Davy

"Say it," demanded Rose.

"I promise," said Davy.

"Good luck," Rose called as he left.

He almost collided with a young Asian girl on her way in.

"How can I help you?" Rose asked as the girl approached the desk.

This was way too fast for Davy. He'd hoped to come away with an idea of his chances and maybe a contact number and name to follow up on in his own time. Not a bloody appointment with some Professor. No, it was way, way too fast. He'd have been quite happy to call this fellow. Might well have done so this very afternoon. If he was ready. But he hated being put under such pressure. He marched along the road, his quick pace reflecting his agitation. Blast her anyway, he thought, kicking a can in his path and crushing a cigarette pack under foot. No matter what he'd promised, he decided, there was no way he was coming back to tell her about the interview. Because he wouldn't have anything to tell her. Because he just wasn't going to go.

Without even realising he was heading in its direction he suddenly found that he was almost at the bridge. This was the last place in the world he wanted to be. Even though he'd made up his mind to tell Michaela about Colin, he still hadn't worked out exactly how he was going to put it. What could he say? "Oh hi there, Michaela. You'll never guess who I met at a party the other night. Your husband Colin ! Imagine! Small world isn't it? And you'll never believe what he was up to? Trying to rape a poor defenceless girl as she lay passed out on her bed! Can you credit that? Who'd have thought it, eh? Oh and by the way, there's more – he has a girlfriend as well. Yeah, I happened to be sitting behind them in the cinema. God, you should have seen the pair of them! Snogging non-stop all the way through the film. All over each other they were." No, he couldn't bear meeting her right now. The clock in the distance told him that it was five past one, precisely the time he usually spotted her on the bridge, so he quickly turned around and started heading back towards town. But poor Davy, he just wasn't thinking straight, for Michaela didn't just drop from the sky at this time each day but got there via a more terrestrial route and, as he turned the corner by Hot and Saucy, he ran smack into her.

"Hello there Davy," she said. "I haven't seen you around for a while."

"Hi Michaela. How are things?"

"Fine," she lied. She didn't look fine at all, but awfully, awfully unhappy. Her smile travelled no further than her mouth. Her beautiful green eyes had none of their usual animation and even her hair seemed depressed, seemed to have lost some of its curl. And he thought how much sadder she'd look if he were to tell her about Colin. He imagined her eyes filling up with tears and the bottom half of that prefect heart-shaped mouth trembling at the news. And for a second he let himself imagine the pleasure he'd have in steadying it with a kiss.

"Davy?"

Miles away, savouring the pleasure of this imaginary gesture of comfort, he didn't hear her.

"Davy."

"Sorry, what did you say?" He wondered had he been very obviously staring at her mouth.

"I was just asking if you've been to any good bonfires lately?"

He shook his head, wishing that she hadn't brought that up for it forced him to remember her kindness to him; the sausages, the blanket, the whiskey, but more especially her coming out to sit with him in the cold when she could have been cosily tucked up in bed. And he knew he had to tell her right now. He owed it to her. She had been so good to him and now it was his turn. He couldn't let her go on not knowing what her husband was really like. He needn't tell her everything, just enough to warn her, even if it meant that she'd never talk to him again. Because she probably wouldn't.

"Michaela."

"Yes?"

"There's something I need to tell you."

"Yeah?"

"You see . . ." She was staring at him, sadly. God, happy or sad, she was just so lovely. "You see . . ."

"Yes? You look very serious, Davy."

"Well, what I have to tell you is serious."

"Oh."

"What I have to tell you," he started. "Is that . . . is that . . . is that . . . " Over and over like a scratched CD. He thought of hitting himself in the chest to dislodge the words. He started afresh.

"What I have to tell you is that . . . is-that-I-have-an-interview-this-afternoon-at-three-o-clock." God, where had all that come gushing from? It seemed he'd hit the fast-forward button. What had happened to the words he'd meant to use? So, he hadn't the guts to tell her about Colin, but why couldn't a nice harmless comment about the weather have come spewing out instead?

"Is that it? Is that your exciting news?" She burst out laughing.

"Yeah," he answered, then added peevishly. "I don't see what's so funny." He was annoyed that his great disclosure, even if it had been unintended, evoked such a mirthful response.

"I'm sorry. I'm not laughing, really I'm not. I just thought you were going to tell me some-

thing awful, something about . . . Oh, forget it.
So you have an interview this afternoon?
What for?"

"For a post-graduate course in library technology," he said, trying not to sound too
proud, but realising that he was pleased she
should know and, even if he wasn't going to
go, there was no need to complicate things by
telling her that.

She looked at him, her face showing
surprise for just a split second, but long
enough for Davy to notice.

"So I'd better get going," he said huffily
and Michaela realised he was offended by her
reaction.

"So are you all set for it?" she asked, trying
to make amends.

"Yeah," he answered sourly, he was not to
be won over that easily.

"Got your CV ready?"

"Yeah."

"And your suit pressed?"

He hesitated.

"Oh my God, I bet you haven't! I bet
you haven't even thought about what
you're going to wear!" She stared at him

suspiciously. Then she asked, "Davy, do you have something to wear?"

Bull's-eye. His lack of suitable attire wasn't the least of his reasons for not wanting to go the interview.

"I . . ."

His hesitation was answer enough for her.

"Right," she said, stretching out her hand to him. "Come on."

"Where?"

"You're coming with me. I'll sort you out." She grabbed hold of his hand and began pulling him along, "Come on."

She dragged him along the road, over the bridge and back up to the yellow house. She unlocked the door, pushed him in, then up the stairs and into the bathroom, ignoring his protests all the way.

"What time did you say the interview was on?"

"Three o'clock."

"Plenty of time." She turned on the shower. "OK, in you go."

He stood staring at her.

"What?" she asked looking at him. "What's the problem?"

"I was just waiting for you to go before I, well, before I take off my clothes."

"What? You think I'll find you so irres-istible that I'll jump you the minute I see a flash of your willie?"

"No, but . . . "

"Alright. I'm going. You'd better lock the door to make sure you're safe!"

He stepped in under the gushing hot water. This was the first shower Davy'd had in ages and it felt marvellous. Especially after months of enduring bath time at No. 7 Cathedral View, the bathroom there being an unheated galvanised extension to the rear of house, and the hot-water supply being insuf-ficient to fill the sink let alone the bath. Sitting in a puddle, scooping up tepid water and pouring it over oneself whilst the wind whistled in through holes in the galvanised roof wasn't conducive to luxuriating. So now he just stood for ages under the steaming water. Five, ten, fifteen minutes passed before he looked around for the shampoo. He saw that there were two bottles, a male-looking black one and another pink feminine one – *Summer Bouquet*. He uncapped this second one, sniffed it – a Michaela smell – and helped himself, thinking that he'd have a scent of her on his pillow that night. Another ten minutes passed, then he became aware of a banging on the door. He turned off the water.

"Davy, are you all right in there?"

"Yeah. Just finished." He stepped out of the shower and looked around for a towel, there was none. Only a small hand-towel, a scrap of a thing. "Michaela," he shouted. "Michaela," No answer.

He wrapped the scrap around him as best he could.

"Davy, come in here," shouted Michaela from the bedroom.

He sidled in along by the wall trying not to draw attention to his near-nakedness. The lack of towels was not by chance and covertly Michaela studied him and approved of what she saw; his body was perhaps just a little too thin, yet very fine – it was well-defined, well-proportioned and nicely brown.

"OK, I've gone through Colin's wardrobe," she was saying. "Unfortunately he takes his cue in clothes from Barry Manilow or the like, so there's not exactly anything suitable for an aspiring librarian. But we'll find something for you. OK, let's start with the suit. Here," she said. "Try this one on for size."

"But it's cream!"

"So? There's nothing to say librarians can't wear cream."

"Michaela, I don't mean to sound ungrateful, but look at the lapels. They're a little on the big size, don't you think?"

"Davy, for someone who'd nothing to wear not so long ago, you're very fussy all of a sudden."

"Barry Manilow? Joe Dolan more like!" he grumbled, taking the suit from her. He waited for her to leave the room. After a while he realised that she hadn't a notion of going. She was busy poking around in the wardrobe. Trusting that she wouldn't look around, he dropped the towel and as quickly as he could he slipped on the suit.

"Can I turn around now?" asked Michaela, craftily watching him in the wardrobe mirror.

"I suppose."

At the sight of him, she tried to compose her face, but she couldn't. He looked completely ridiculous. His lack of shirt accentuated the impact of the lapels. And they were enormous! Catching sight of the smirk on her face, he looked down at himself, then back at her, and the two of them burst out laughing.

"With a strong wind behind you, you'd clear the Atlantic," laughed Michaela.

Davy saw a hairbrush on the dresser, picked it up, then hopped up onto the bed. With his "microphone" in one hand and with his other hand outstretched to Michaela – his audience – he started to sing, hips gyrating,

"I write the songs that make the young ones sing,

I write the songs of love and sp-ec-cial thinn-ngs"

Michaela laughed and Davy sang on, delighted that she was finding his Barry Manilow impersonation so entertaining. He intensified the vigour of his pelvic thrusts unaware that his too-loose trousers were gradually being dislodged by his energetic gyrations and, since the first *"I write"* he'd warbled, Michaela had been watching, waiting for them to drop, for it was only a matter of time. But unaware, he sang on, putting his heart and soul into it. Tears were streaming down Michaela's face, she tried to warn him about his trousers, but the words wouldn't come out, she was choking with laughter. Too weak to stand, she slumped to her knees, still laughing.

"La la, la la, la la, la-a-a aaaa laa-aa . . . " he sang. Not until he felt a peculiar chill did he glance down.

"Oh God," he muttered. Mortified, he stooped down to pull up the pants, but stumbled and fell off the bed.

Wiping the tears from her eyes, Michaela finally managed to get up off her knees and help him up.

"Alright, maybe the cream suit isn't the one."

"Where are my own clothes? I'm going home."

"Ah come on Davy, I'm sorry I laughed."

But Davy wasn't listening, holding the waist of the baggy pants in a fist he tripped towards the door.

She quickly pulled a green suit out of the wardrobe and begged,

"Please Davy, just try this one on, please."

"No."

"Please."

"No."

"Please."

Realising that maybe he was overreacting, he grabbed it from her and trying to muster some dignity he asked, "Would you mind leaving the room while I change, please?"

"Davy, I've seen everything already!"

He pushed her out of the bedroom.

A few minutes passed.

"Davy, can I come in?"

"No."

"Please?"

"No, this one's even worse."

"I'm coming in."

He was standing in the middle of the room. This suit seemed even bigger on him, his hands were halfway up the sleeves and the ends of the trousers crinkled around his feet. He looked like a little boy dressed up in his father's suit.

"Well, at least the lapels look OK," she said, doubtfully studying him.

"There is that, but it would be handy if I could walk in it."

"Stand up on the bed.

"I've done that trick already."

"No, I'm going to pin up the legs and arms."

"That's not going to work."

"Sure it is. Go on, up on the bed."

Reluctantly he obeyed her and she searched around in a drawer until she found a tub of pins.

"This is never going to work," he said.

"Sure it is. Hold still."

"Excuse me missus, it's my special day, my Holy Communion. I'm saving for a bike," he said with his hand stretched out for money.

"Stop messing. And stop wriggling."

She worked away for five minutes. The end result was passable. Just about. Then Michaela handed Davy a tie, shirt, socks and shoes to go with the suit. He carefully removed the pinned suit, and realising that there was no point in asking her to leave, he gave a wiggle each time he caught her looking at him. He put on the whole ensemble.

"Now you're all set," said Michaela. "You look very nice indeed. Very handsome," she said and she meant it. "Now," she went on, "There's no point in bringing your own clothes with you. "Come back and collect them after the interview. I'll be here from about five onwards. Anyway, I'll be dying to hear how you got on."

It was twenty past two when Davy left. Past the time Michaela should have been back at work. But first she went upstairs again to put Colin's things back in order. Colin was very particular about the way he kept his clothes and if, by chance, he were to come home from work before her and find them strewn all over the floor, she knew he'd go ballistic. Particularly given the rotten mood he was in lately. Over the last two days he'd hardly said a word to her, apart from snapping irritably whenever she spoke to him. At first she'd put his bad humour down to the stomach cramps he'd complained of two nights previously when he'd returned from Sligo early; they'd been bad enough to cause him to stay in bed all the following day. But he'd got over these and his mood hadn't improved any. She now thought that the likely source of his mood lay in the mysterious phone calls he'd been receiving. He hadn't told her about them but twice, once when he'd been in the shower, once when he'd nipped out to the shop, she'd answered his mobile-phone and the caller had hung up immediately, without saying a word. Several times since, she'd noticed that Colin didn't answer his phone in his usual gregariously loud phone voice, instead he'd hurried from the room when his mobile rang and then she'd heard him talking in hushed tones in the hall outside.

She gathered up Colin's cream suit and replaced it on its hanger, smirking as she remembered Davy's mortification. As she continued to tidy up, she considered how attractive he was, she hadn't really noticed before, not until he'd come out of the shower all freshly washed.

Then she stopped and listened; she thought she heard a floor board creak downstairs but, dismissing it as just one of the mysterious sounds old houses are full of, she resumed tidying. She went into the bathroom, picked up Davy's clothes, and, as she considered how very dirty they were, she heard the kitchen door squeak. The hairs on the back of her neck rose. There was definitely someone downstairs in the kitchen. It couldn't be Colin, he was so busy that he'd hardly time to come home at night, not to mind during the day. She tried to remember if she'd left her keys in the front door, it wouldn't be the first time. She listened, wondering where the intruder was now but couldn't hear anything, just the loud beat of her heart. Stealthily she inched her way back into the bedroom and over to the phone by the bed. As she was reaching out to pick up the receiver, she heard someone bounding up the stairs. She looked around for a weapon. She grabbed up a wire clothes hanger. The door was flung open wide. She charged.

"*Michaela!*" shouted Colin.

"*Colin!*" screamed Michaela at the same time, but it was too late, she'd already dragged the sharp edge of the hook of the hanger down his cheek.

"*Aagghhh!*" screeched Colin.

"*Oh God!*" cried Michaela.

Colin's hand went up to his face. He rushed over to the dressing-table mirror.

"My eye, Michaela, you could have got my eye!"

"Oh Colin, I'm sorry, I thought you were a burglar."

"What have you done to me?" He stared at his face in the mirror, at the narrow red welt, three inches long.

"I'll sorry Colin. I didn't know it was you. Look, I'll get some ice." She hurried downstairs. Seconds later, she came back with a bag of ice.

"Here, put this up to you face. Is it sore?

"Of course it's sore."

"I'm sorry."

"What the hell are you doing here anyway?" he asked crossly.

"I'm taking a late lunch," she explained. Then seeing him glance curiously at the bundle of his clothes on the bed, she added, "I just thought I'd go through your clothes, you know, see if anything needed washing."

"I see," he said. He was studying his wound again and didn't consider the implausibility of her explanation; for it was implausible, it was the last thing in the world she'd think of doing of a lunchtime.

"Anyway, what are you doing here?" she asked.

"I just came home to pick up some things before heading to Limerick, though I'm not sure I'll be able to go now," he said. Then, still fingering his superficial wound, he added peevishly, 'You could have blinded me, Michaela."

"Limerick?"

"Yeah. Remember, I told you this morning."

Hardly, thought Michaela, he hadn't said as much as "Good morning," to her.

"Is it still sore?" she asked him.

He nodded, then asked, "Do you think I need a doctor?"

"Nah, a kiss will make it better." She went to kiss him.

"Don't be so flippant. You could have blinded me," he said, pushing her away. "I'm going to call the doctor."

"Better tell him to bring a plastic surgeon with him."

"Oh God, you don't think I'll have a scar?"

"Probably not. Anyway, scars can be very sexy," she teased but relented when she saw him staring at his face with such concern. "In fairness, Colin, I don't think you need a doctor. Look, keep the ice up to your face and I'll go and make you a cup of tea."

"Yeah, a cup of tea would be good for the shock."

Michaela went downstairs.

"And maybe a sandwich," he called after her.

A little later she heard him call,

"Michaela, have you seen my green suit?"

"Which green suit?"

"I only have one. And my new silk tie, you know the one with the bluey-green fish pattern?"

"Yeah, I loaned them both to a friend of mine," she called from the kitchen. "He was going to an interview and I told him you wouldn't mind if he borrowed a few things of yours."

"*You what?*" he roared.

"Calm down, I'm only joking. How do I know where they are? Don't you have some convoluted classification system going? Haven't you got everything filed away by designer, then by price, then colour?"

"What?"

"Nothing," she said, coming back up the stairs with the tray of tea and sandwiches. "Why don't you take the tie with the yellow flowers instead?"

"God no, that's fierce gaudy-looking."

"Do you think?" She'd bought it for him at Christmas.

"Yeah, it's a bit cheap-looking. Christ, this is ridiculous, I can't find anything."

Michaela sat on the bed, eating her sandwich, watching him.

"That tie cost Ann . . . *ahm* me a fortune, it's hand-painted. I'd really like to find it," he moaned.

"So how long are you going to be away?"

"I'll be back tomorrow afternoon."

"I see. Well, that's good to know, saves me the embarrassment of making an unnecessary trip down to the Garda Station to report you missing."

"Michaela, I'm certain I told you. Anyway, I'd have left a note."

"Extraordinarily considerate indeed," she said.

"So what time are you due back at work?" he asked.

"I should be gone back. I'll be going shortly."

"I thought you'd be swanning around town, out lunching with your friends from the office."

"No, I usually come home," Michaela said, thinking that he really didn't have a clue. Friends from the office! Yeah right!

"Is it not a bit of a walk up to the house at lunchtime?"

"No, not really, five minutes. Anyway I like the walk."

"What time did you say you're going back?"

"As soon as I've finished my sandwich."

"Why don't I run you down?" he asked.

"OK, that'd be great," she replied, surprised that he was being so considerate all of a sudden.

Davy took deep breaths. In out. In out. In out. He tried to stay calm. He paced the corridor – up down – feeling sick with fear – up down – his stomach in bits – up down – his shirt clinging – up down – his palms horribly sticky. Up down. Up down. Up down.

His moist palms bothered him. He wished he'd something to wipe them with in case this Professor shook hands with him when they met. He'd already rummaged through Colin's pockets in search of a tissue but all he'd found was an empty condom wrapper; an unwelcome reminder of Colin's sordid sex life. Though he tried not to dwell on such an unpleasant subject, unbidden his thoughts kept drifting back. It seemed odd that Colin had put the wrapper back in his pocket; to Davy it implied that he'd been wearing the jacket when he'd used the condom, which suggested some fairly sleazy scenario; it hinted at hastiness, fugitiveness, of back-of-the-car kind of sex with the wrong person. Someone other than Michaela.

Each time he paced by the bin and saw the wrapper lying where he'd thrown it, he winced. Purple and distinctive, it lay in solitary splendour and Davy was worried that the Professor might see it and suppose it was Davy's since he was the only person around, bar the secretary. He knew he was being a bit paranoid but he just didn't want the Professor to think he was the sort who'd have used condom wrappers to dispose of wherever he went. Eventually he stooped down to retrieve it.

"Davy," called the young secretary, looking at him through the little hole in a glass panel and, though bemused to see him stooping down with his right hand deep inside the bin, she carried on, "The Professor will see you now."

"Thanks," he said. He straightened up and quickly stuffed the condom wrapper back into his pocket.

"It's the first door on the right," she told him.

He went over to the door she'd pointed at and knocked. No answer. He knocked again. Still no answer. He considered walking straight in, but wondered if it would be very ignorant to do so. He knocked for a third time, then waited a full minute before trying yet again. On the fourth knock the door was suddenly flung open. Davy stared. He had never seen a hairier man than the man standing before him.

"What do you want, a bloody red carpet?" snapped the man.

The movement of his beard was the only physical sign that he spoke.

Promptly the man turned on his heel and walked back into the room. Davy stood at the door for a few seconds, thought about running away, but instead decided to follow in after him. The man sat down behind his desk and with a wave of an incredibly hairy hand indicated that Davy should take the seat opposite. This seat was very low and when Davy sat down his insubstantial weight caused it to sag. He was just inches from the ground and could hardly see the Professor over the bundles and bundles of papers which covered his desk, just his great bushy head of hair and his enormous eyebrows resting along the top of his glasses. And then, even these disappeared from view as Professor Thompson hunched over to continue his writing. Davy didn't know this. Politely, he sat there, wondering what the man was doing behind the bundles, waiting for him to reappear. Five minutes passed and not a sound except grunts of concentration from the other side of the desk. Davy began to get a little twitchy, he looked around the room; from floor to ceiling every wall was crammed with shelves of books. He began to worry. Maybe he wasn't in the right place at all, maybe this was a reading-room, maybe this man wasn't Professor Thompson. Maybe Professor Thompson was waiting for him elsewhere.

"Excuse me, are you . . . "

"Shush."

"I just . . . "

"Shush."

Davy shushed and waited. He glanced at the big white-faced clock on the wall opposite and resolved to leave by quarter past three if nothing happened by that time. The minutes ticked loudly by. Three fifteen. Time to go. He got up.

"Sit down," roared Professor Thompson in a ferociously loud voice.

Startled, Davy dropped down into his seat. Professor Thompson straightened up, pushed open a gap in the bundle of papers and stared at Davy with eyes that seemed the size of raisins through his thick, thick glasses. Then he leaned forward, removed his glasses and Davy was surprised to see that his eyes were in fact the size of raisins and wondered how such heavy eyebrows could remain aloft without the aid of the frames.

"What's your name?" growled the Professor through his beard.

"Davy Long."

"So Davy Long, you want to be a librarian?"

"Yes."

"You're educated, I take it? You already have a degree?"

"Yes."

"And now you want to find gainful employment. It comes to us all. Did you bring your . . . your . . . you know your thingamajig, did you bring it with you?"

"I'm not sure."

"Christ, boy, you either did or you didn't."

"I'm not sure what you mean by my thingamajig."

"Of course you do. The piece of paper with your details. What's it called?"

"Birth-cert?" suggested Davy.

"And what would I want that for?" he

roared. "No, you know your . . . your . . . " His inability to think of the word frustrated him and he threw his eyes around the room as if he hoped to spot the word floating out there.

"CV?" asked Davy.

"Yes, that's it. Do you have your CV with you?"

"I do," said Davy and he handed his CV to the Professor. After leaving Michaela's house, he'd called back to Cathedral View on his way to the college to collect it.

Davy hated this part. In his early days of job-searching, before he'd got sense enough to leave his CV at home, he'd been through it so many times and it was always the same. He hated sitting and watching as they began to read, watching as their expression grew increasingly puzzled as they scanned down through his details until they came to the name of his referee – the Prison Governor – and then the puzzled look would be replaced by one of comprehension as things fell into place. Professor Thompson seemed to be taking an inordinate length of time to read through it; that he looked up and studied Davy every ten seconds didn't exactly speed things up. He was making Davy feel very nervous, he couldn't keep his legs still, they were hopping all over the place. Finally Professor Thompson put it down and stared at him for a whole two minutes. Eventually, he spoke.

"Well, Davy Long, I see you're not exactly a Presentation boy."

"Pardon?" asked Davy, not knowing that the Professor was referring to one of the city's private schools attended by boys from Cork's better-off families.

"Better for you. Namby-pambies the lot of them. So Davy Long, you're an ex-criminal. Very interesting. We don't see too many of them around here. Tell me, other than the desire to be gainfully employed, why does an ex-con want to become a librarian?"

"Why?"

"Yes, why?"

"Well . . . "

"Well?"

"I don't know really."

"You don't know really? Not very persuasive. Look, ex-criminals aren't exactly the sector of society we're hoping to attract onto this course, could you not try a little harder?"

"Well I think it would be a nice job and . . ."

"Working behind the men's counter in Roches Stores would be a nice job too and, judging by your clothes," said the Professor, as he looked Davy up and down, studying Colin's silk fish-motif tie and the good quality green suit, "It might suit you better." Then, spotting the line of pins along Davy's cuffs, he added. "Assuming the suit is yours and that their store detective isn't on the look-out for you."

"Thank you very much, Professor." Davy got up. "You've obviously made up your mind about me, so there's no point in wasting your time."

"Yerra sit down and don't be getting into such a huff. I'm only taking a rise out of you. I'm interested in knowing why you want to be a librarian, so why don't you tell me? And that it's a nice job isn't the answer I'm looking for. You've put down reading as one of your hobbies. Tell me, were you always a reader?"

"No, not really," said Davy still standing.

"No?"

"No, we didn't have many books at home

and I really only started reading lately in . . . well in the last few years."

"And what kind of books did you start with?"

"Anything at all. Whatever I could get my hands on. Although it's better now, I can choose what I want to read."

"And what do you choose, Davy?"

"Well, I just finished Kipling's *Plain Tales From the Hills* and now I've just started on *Of Mice and Men*."

"And which do you prefer?" asked the Professor, then added, 'Sit down, why don't you?"

Davy did, forgetting his earlier umbrage.

"Definitely *Of Mice and Men*. I like the two characters in it, they seem like real people. I can't really identify with the characters in Kipling's book." It was the first time he'd talked to anybody about reading since he'd left prison and the pleasure of doing so made him forget that he had a university professor as his audience. And he was an attentive audience too, and listened whilst Davy went on for the next five minutes retelling this Steinbeck story. As the Professor sat there in silence, Davy became increasingly animated. Finished with *Of Mice and Men*, he moved on.

"I'd read *East of Eden* before that. That was as good, but very different. You see there were far more characters and it was spread out over a longer period of time . . ." The Professor let him talk on, enjoying seeing Davy talking so excitedly. ". . . of course 'Doc' is in more books that just *Sweet Tuesday* but in that one, Mack and the boys decide he needs a girlfriend. It's a bit like *Tortilla Flat*, you know the one in which Danny inherits these old houses and him and all his friends move in and . . ."

The Professor was beginning to realise that Davy might keep talking all day, but now that he had got him to relax, he decided it was time to steer the conversation back on course.

"It's about time I reread Steinbeck," he said. "Now back to the . . ."

"Well, I can let you have *Of Mice and Men* if you like," interrupted Davy. "I can drop it over to you when I'm finished with it."

"OK, I'd appreciate that. Now, the course . . ."

"But I'd need to get it back," said Davy,

thinking of the money he'd lose out if he didn't being it back to the second-hand bookstore.

"Sure. Now Davy, back to the reason why you're here. Tell me why you want to be a librarian."

Davy was on a roll, the enthusiasm he'd expressed in talking about Steinbeck's books spilled over and he forgot the usual shyness he felt when talking about himself.

"Well, when I first went to . . . to prison it was the boredom more than anything else that got to me. I thought I'd go mental sitting around doing nothing day after day. After the first few weeks I mentioned this to my welfare officer and she suggested that I use the library. As I said, I was never much of a reader but, since there was so little to do I decided that I might as well. Anyway, the first book I took out was a Terry Prachett novel and I brought it back to the recreational room. I wasn't really used to reading and at first I was afraid I'd never get through it but, after a while I really started getting into it and when the bell rang for us to go back to our cells for the night, I could hardly believe it was that time already. Normally the nights went so slowly, but that night just flew. When I went back to my cell, I just kept reading and by the time I got to the last page, it was getting light. That morning I went back to the library as soon as I could and took out another Terry Prachett. I read all of his books and then moved on. I must have read every book in the library and they were a queer collection. Most of them had been donated by an old woman, a 'friend of the prison' though why she thought we'd appreciate Mills and Boon or Peter Pan, who knows, but it didn't matter, I read them all anyway. Later on, when the welfare officer saw how much I enjoyed reading, she suggested that I try for an 'A' level in English. So I did and when I managed to do quite well in it she helped me enrol for the open university degree course. Around the same time, the prisoner who ran the library got out so I was put in charge of it. That was the best time inside for me, I really enjoyed it in a way, you know, running the library and studying there. That set me thinking that I'd like to do something similar when I got out. I like the idea of being surrounded by books, loaning them out to people, people who can't afford to buy them. I just love the smell of books and the feel of them and the excitement I feel when I start on the first page of a new book. I love this," he ended, indicating the shelves of books all around them. Then he stopped talking, realising that he'd got a bit carried away.

The professor was staring at him

"I wonder what you were in prison for?" he asked

"Well I . . . "

"It doesn't matter. I don't really want to know." Then the professor glanced down at the CV and as if he was reading from it he began, "From failed GCSE's to a honours degree in English literature. Let me see. Father an ignorant buffoon, probably an alcoholic. Mother the same. Working-class estate on the outskirts of Belfast. Crappy school. Crappy teachers. Whole family in and out of prison like yo-yos. Definitely not a *Pres* boy."

Davy looked at him, puzzled, he'd thought things were going so well. What had he said wrong?

"So, Davy Long, how will you support yourself in the meantime?"

"What?"

"Well, the course doesn't start until next September."

"I . . . "

Professor Thompson scribbled down something on a scrap of paper and handed it to Davy.

"Here, give this number a ring. It's my brother's, he has a pub on Southern Road. You'll need a job, until the course starts. And he needs a barman, tell him I said so. We can't have you back inside for stealing food, or suits for that matter, before the course starts."

9

DAVY
AT HOME WITH BARTLEY
AND REBECCA

DAVY TRIED to walk along calmly. He tried to behave normally. Tried, but failed, for he was utterly powerless against the tremendous waves of excitement which caught him up, hurtled him along the road, catapulted him high up in the air and compelled him to punch it with his fist and shout out *"Yesssss!"* again and again. After each outburst, he tried to restrain himself; conscious of the startled looks of those around; conscious now of the two old ladies struggling along, shopping in hand, who'd stopped dead in their tracks and were staring at him as he came bounding towards them.

"Ladies," he said stopping, smiling at them – just a touch maniacally, "What will it be?" Then, with an exaggerated bow and an extravagant wave of his hand, he offered them a choice, "A Mills and Boon or a Baby Powers?" And straightening up again to his full height, he proclaimed loudly, "For I am Davy, the *librarian*! I am Davy, the *barman*!" Then, after making a low, low bow, he continued on his way leaving gaping eyes and mouths in his wake.

Another leap, another air-punch, another "*Yesssss!*"

And he continued on his merry way. On his way up to call and tell her how he got on. For isn't that what she had said to him? "Call up, I'll be dying to hear how you got on?" *She* had said to *him*. These were *her* very words to *him*. She *expected* him to call. Had *invited* him to. Why, it would be rude not to. So he was calling up to her house. Dropping in. Paying a visit. Stopping by. The way friends do.

Yessssss!

It wasn't yet four o'clock, still too early for

her to be finished work, but he knew how he'd pass the time. Southern Road, where Professor Thompson's brother had the pub wasn't far from her house, just five minutes further out of town. He'd go up there now, suss it out, see if he could spot a Professor Thompson look-a-like and talk to him about this barman's job straight away. No point in wasting time.

Over the bridge he went. Past the unusually large and extremely drunken crowd, a quick "How ya" – no stopping, none of the old fellows like Connie or Francey were around; past Michaela's yellow house – sigh and a warm happy glow; around the corner – past her husband sitting in a parked car, wearing shades, like some cop on a stake-out. What? *Past her husband sitting in a parked car, wearing shades, like some cop on a stake-out?* Davy retraced his last few steps, stopped and stared in. Colin stared out. At Davy's face first and his look of absolute hatred told Davy he'd been recognised. Then Colin's eyes travelled down, taking in his own fish-motif silk tie, his own green suit, his own brand-new £159 brown shoes and Davy saw his expression vacillate between puzzlement and anger. And Davy walked on quickly, nervously, anticipating the sound of the car door opening, anticipating quick footsteps following him, then a hand on his shoulder, a face in his face, and the words, "What the hell are you doing in my clothes?" But they didn't come. Strange, thought Davy, suspicious even. He carried on as far as the next corner, stepped into a doorway. And waited.

For what he wasn't sure. Something suspect no doubt. For some girl to arrive maybe, some girl Colin was intending to take into Michaela's bed. But why then was he sitting out on the road in his car? Maybe he was waiting for a unsuspecting stranger, some pretty girl all alone, to come along and, when she did, he'd leap from the car and force her down the road and into his house. Not such an absurd notion, thought Davy. Hadn't he seen this sexual deviant in action before?

He hadn't long to wait. Almost immediately a white van pulled up alongside Colin's car. And from the doorway Davy watched as Colin wound down his window and the passenger in the van – male, so much for Davy's theory – did likewise. Davy watched as the two men talked with "we're-engaged-in-serious-business-here" demeanours, emphasising the gravity of their conversation with their periodic curt and solemn nods. When the body of their discussion was over, Davy watched Colin hand the passenger a tiny object and as Colin turned on his ignition, Davy heard him say, "Right so, lads, I'll be off," and he drove away. Then the white van started up and went slowly down the road and around the corner. Davy hurried after it and saw it pull up outside the yellow house. The driver, a big burly fellow, along with the passenger, a little chap, got out of the van. The little chap unlocked the front door and they both went inside the house. A few minutes passed then both of them reappeared, the little one carrying a TV and the big one carrying a stereo. They loaded them into the back of their van.

"How ya," said the burly fellow on his way back into the house, noticing Davy standing there, watching them.

"Grand day," said the little chap, nodding

congenially as he followed in after his colleague.

Moments later, they both came back out, carrying boxes of CD's.

"What's going on?" Davy asked.

"Moving," said the small chap.

"I don't see a 'For Sale' sign."

"And who are you? The neighbourhood-watch?" asked the burly fellow

"No, just a . . . a friend."

"Not much of one if they didn't tell you they were going," sneered the big fellow.

"But I was in there just a few hours ago and there was no sign of them leaving. Where are they going?"

"None of your business. Now why don't you clear off and let us get on with the job. Alright!"

Ignoring him, Davy leaned into the open van and started hauling out one of the boxes of CD's. But seeing him, the burly fellow came at him as quickly as his bulk allowed, pulled the box from Davy, then pushed him to the ground.

"What the hell do you think you're playing at?" he shouted down at Davy.

The little chap came rushing in between them.

"Frank, Frank, easy Frank," he said calmly, evenly, in the kind of tone a dog-trainer might use. "We don't want any trouble, Frank. Alright?" he added warningly. Then he turned back to Davy. "Are you OK?" he asked. "Sorry about my pal here. A bit hot-headed, especially after a night on the razz. Isn't that right, Frank? A bit of a skinful last night, eh Frank?"

Frank growled in response. The little chap then turned back to Davy and helped him up.

"Look," he said. "If you're a friend, I've no problem telling you where they're going. They're off to London."

"London?"

"Yeah, Hampstead to be more precise."

"But I was here earlier and they never said a word."

"Strange. You'd have thought they would."

"London? I don't believe you."

"Yeah. Going for a year. He got some kind of promotion and his company has arranged a house swap with one of the English executives they're sending over here. We work for D-Day, the removals firm. The company your friend works for always deal with us. Our job is to go in and pack everything from start to finish. It saves them the hassle and we can do the job faster with them out of the way. *Door to Door toDay*, that's our slogan."

The man must be telling the truth, thought Davy. After all, he'd seen Colin give him what he now realised had probably been the key to the house.

"Now, are you satisfied? Will you let us get on with the job?" asked the little chap.

"Yeah," muttered Davy.

"What did you think we were doing, robbing the place?" jeered the burly fellow.

They watched him go.

"Good one, Frank. What did you think we were doing, robbing the place? Ha-ha, ha-ha."

Davy no longer had the heart to go looking for Professor Thompson's brother and instead started back for Cathedral View, thinking, as he walked quickly, how stupid he'd been to imagine that they were becoming friends when all she'd been doing was showing one of the poor unfortunates of the city a last bit of kindness before she headed off to England with her newly-promoted, high-flying executive husband. So preoccupied was he in considering just what a complete and utter thick he was that he didn't notice the pool of vomit on the bridge until he'd stepped right into it, until he felt its soft slushiness underfoot. He looked down and his initial disgust was fleetingly replaced with satisfaction when he saw the state of what were Colin's shoes after all. But then he realised that they were the only pair he now had for, no doubt, the removals men would tell him where to go if he asked them to let him back into the house to collect his clothes. He wiped his shoes on a clump of weeds and looked in disgust at the drunk lying nearby in a stupor, vomit trickling from the side of his mouth and at his friends slumped about him in various stages of drunkenness. Pathetic the lot of them, thought Davy. Miserable sad pathetic losers.

"Davy," a voice called.

Davy looked up. Sitting at the top of the flight of steps at the back of the hospital was the little girl Eva.

"Hi," he smiled up at her.

"You promised you'd play with me the next day you came," she said to him but didn't sound terribly hopeful – she'd long since learned not to expect adults to keep their promises. But it was worth a try.

"I did?"

"Yeah. You said you couldn't play the last day because you'd your own lessons to do. Remember?"

Davy looked around for Eva's father and saw him sitting on a kerb less than five metres away. His back was turned to them and he'd one arm draped around the shoulder of another drunk who was completely comatose, a fact Eva's father didn't seem to be aware of as he slurred drunken nonsense into the sleeping man's ear. Every few seconds his own head flopped as he fleetingly lost consciousness, but each time he stirred again and took up his drunken ramblings at a point he hadn't left off. Satisfied that he wouldn't notice him talking to his daughter, Davy climbed the steps and sat down beside her.

"What are you playing?" he asked.

"School, you silly," she answered,

throwing her eyes to heaven. "Don't you remember?"

"Of course," he said. Then, pointing at her collection of bottles on the far side of her, he asked. "These are your pupils, aren't they? Which one is Billy again?"

Her sitting here, playing by herself while her father spent the afternoon drinking himself into a stupor, brought back memories of his own childhood.

"I threw him away," she answered.

"You threw poor Billy away? But that wasn't very nice. I'm sure he'd like to be in school with his friends."

"But he was really, really bad."

"But if you don't let him come to school, he'll never learn to be good."

"No, he was really bad. When he got broke he hurted me. Want to see?"

"See what?"

"What he did?"

Davy nodded. She pulled down her sock and he saw the filthy rag wrapped around her calf. This she carefully unwound to reveal a long deep gash, which looked badly infected; it was red and sore-looking and seeped pus.

"Does it hurt?" he asked and she nodded. "When did it happen?"

"The day before yesterday."

"Did you go to the hospital?"

She shook her head.

"You're very brave, aren't you? Some girls would be crying non-stop if they had a cut like that. *Boo-hoo, boo-hoo, boo-hoo*, that's the way they'd be going on."

She laughed up at him.

"*Boo-hoo, boo-hoo*," he wailed.

"You're silly," she said, laughing.

The poor thing, he thought. Apart from the cut, she looked so neglected. Her clothes were sizes too small – her skirt was inches above her scratched and dirty knees. One of her elbows had come out through her cardigan. Her hair was tangled and matted and her face was filthy. And then he looked over at her father, sitting there talking drunken nonsense, just like his own father. He got to his feet, picked Eva up and carried her down the steps. He marched over to her father.

"I'm taking your daughter to the hospital. She needs to get that leg seen to."

"Leave her down and get the fuck out of here."

Davy ignored him and started to walk away with Eva still in his arms. Her father struggled to get up as quickly as his state allowed him and then he made a lunge for Davy. Grabbing him around the neck he dragged him down to the ground. Then he tried to pull his screaming daughter away but Davy held onto her tightly as he tried to get up again. The noise disturbed the other drunks, awakening even the most comatose, and, when they saw their pal Chalky trying to pull Eva away, they all clumsily got to their feet. Deciding that Chalky had caught this fellow trying to harm Eva, and fuelled by drink and outrage, they descended upon Davy. Including Chalky, there were ten of them and, once they'd got Eva out of the way, each of them pushed and shoved their way in to give Davy, lying on the ground, the kicks they felt he deserved. After suffering fifteen minutes of constant kicking, much of it aimed at his head, Davy began to lose consciousness. Two of their dogs raced excitedly around the edge of the crowd, yelping and barking, until one of them managed to get through the forest of legs. His teeth fastened around Davy's left leg. But Davy couldn't feel a thing now.

"Over the bridge," cried one of the men. But Davy didn't hear.

"Over the bridge," went the rabid chorus.

Davy didn't feel himself being hoisted up, carried along by the mob, then lobbed over the bridge. He didn't hear the cheers go up as the men watched him fall down the thirty feet and land on the burnt-out remains of the bonfire below. And he didn't feel the wooden pallette they sent crashing down on top of him.

"Word has it," said Mrs Odlum, some several hours later. "That a certain young lady, who shall remain nameless, was out partying, out painting the town red."

It was that time of a Friday night again in the Odlum house – mother and daughter time.

"What?" asked Polly crossly.

"Oh yes, there's little I don't know, Polly. My sources tell me that a certain young lady was seen out with a certain young gentleman."

"Mam, you're not Terry Keane. You don't have sources. You should give up reading the *Sunday Independent*, you really should. It gives you ideas. Anyway, what are you on about?"

"A little bird tells me that this boyfriend of yours is rather handsome."

"Boyfriend?"

"Well, that's probably an old fashioned term. Like doing a line is. It's called *jagging* now, isn't it? And people don't kiss any more, they *snog*. And they don't make love, they *have it off* with each another. Or *fuc* . . ."

"Mam!" Polly stopped her before she said it. God knows where she picked up such language, but she was forever using it, though half the time she didn't even know what she was saying. Once, Polly had heard her tell a woman in the supermarket that she thought Father Mullins was an awful langer.

"So is he?"

"Is who what?"

"No need to be so coy, Polly. If you can't talk to your mother, who can you talk to? You know I'm only interested. Anyway, a little bird tells me that he's a 'fine thing', as you young people say. And I must say he does sound rather handsome. I imagine he looks a bit like that actor, the dark-haired one, married to that one. You know, he played an Irishman in that movie, *Home and Away*. David, isn't it?"

"How do I know?" said Polly, not giving her an inch. "I don't who you're talking about. And you don't either. *Home and Away* isn't a movie, it's an Australian soap. You're all mixed up."

"No, no Polly, I'm talking about your boyfriend, David."

"Davy. And Mam, you should really keep quiet about the little birds or they'll put you away."

"Anyway, word on the street has it that this David, or Davy is very handsome indeed."

"And what else does the word on the street, or the little birdies, or your sources have to say? Or more specifically, Auntie Deirdre via Cliona?"

"Nothing much," she said.

"Well, thanks be to God for that."

"Just that's he's from the north, that he's about twenty-three and that he's doing a master's degree. He must be very clever.

Imagine Polly, you could be married to a professor!"

Polly was going to kill Cliona. God, she was such a blabbermouth.

"You should get him to give you a hand with your homework, Polly."

"Homework? Mam, I've left school. I'm in university. We don't do homework."

"Well alright, studying then. Same difference. Well, at least you've managed to meet someone nice. Not like poor Cliona."

"What?" said Polly surprised. Surely Cliona hadn't told her parents what had happened to her at the party.

"Your Auntie Deirdre met him the last time they were up in Cork. God, he sounds dreadful. Like something out of a horror movie. And really, how could anybody go out with someone named Squealer?"

"That's not his real name."

"I knew that," she lied.

"New York, you say?" said Garda Hogan, shaking his head in wonder. "Well, isn't that gas?"

"Gas," Colin agreed.

When Michaela had rung Colin on his mobile earlier in the day, he'd been in the middle of a meeting with a client in Moore's Motor Inn in Limerick. When she'd told him about the robbery he said he'd wind up the meeting and head for home as soon as he could. Since she hadn't yet rung the gardaí at that stage, he'd told her to hold off until he got there. He'd managed to make it home in little more than an hour and, within ten minutes of ringing the garda station, Garda Hogan had arrived at the house. As soon as he had taken down the details of the break-in and made a list of all that had been taken, he'd started firing questions. Question after question. Where exactly in Galway did they come from, he asked Colin and Michaela, who he'd quickly identified as fellow Galwegians. What school had they gone to? Who they were related to? What were their mothers' maiden names? Until finally, he'd unearthed someone they all knew – Colin's cousin John, who'd been in school with the young garda and who, Colin had just told him, had recently moved to New York.

"Gas," Garda Hogan now repeated, still

considering this information as he settled himself further back into the armchair, careful not to spill the full cup of tea in his hand.

On the couch opposite, Colin, sitting alongside Michaela, watched him and thought irritably that he'd be hard to shift now. He cursed Michaela for having offered him the tea.

"Didn't I meet John in the Quays there not so long ago?" the young garda continued, now that he was nice and comfy. "Well, I say not so long ago, but I suppose it must have been a couple of months back. And now that you mention it, Colin, I remember him telling me that he was going alright, but I didn't know he'd anything definite set-up."

He paused, took a sip from his tea, stretched out to take another biscuit from the plate on the coffee table, shoved it into his mouth and took another sip to get it all soft the way he liked it.

"Dmmoes hme mlimke imt thmmere?" he asked, his mouth jammed full of coconut creams.

"Pardon?" said Colin.

Garda Hogan swallowed loudly, then repeated, 'Does he like it there?"

"Yes, I believe he does," answered Colin.

"And tell me, is it Galway people he's living with?"

"Yes," Colin told him

"And would I know them?"

"Him," corrected Colin. "No, I don't think so." He was beginning to realise that the less he said, the sooner they'd be rid of him.

"Would it be Conor Twohig, they were always great friends in school?"

"No."

"Pete Flemming then?

"No."

"John Walsh?"

"No."

"Peter Maxwell?"

"No."

"Who could it be so?" He thought for a minute or two. "Was it that fellow Burke, John or James? I can't think of his first name. He used to live down the road from him."

Colin sighed, and realising that the garda wasn't going to give up, he gave in.

"Simon Field. It was Simon Field."

"Simon Field? I can't say now that I know any Simon Field."

Small mercies for that, thought Colin. But Garda Hogan persisted.

"Would he be one of the Fields that have the petrol station on the Headford Road? Or, are they Fieldings? Isn't that's terrible now, you'd think I'd remember their name. Sure I know it as well as my own. Bear with me a minute while I think."

This one would have the fool puzzling for the night, thought Colin and he yawned. He was dying to get to bed, he was shagged from all the driving and even though the garda had put his notebook away, Colin was still worried that he might revert back to the reason he was actually here – the robbery – and so, he had to sit here suffering this fool as he went on and on. And on.

"Now, that Patsy Field was a great man altogether," the garda was saying.

"Patsy Field?" asked Colin, wondering who on earth he was talking about now.

"Patsy Field – captain of the county team for five years. Or was it six? Though I don't think he's related to the Simon Field you're talking about, or to the people who own the filling station. For as far as I can remember they're not Field at all, but Fielding."

"Garda Hogan," sighed Colin, for there was a limit to how much of this kind of talk one could take, there really was, and he'd come to that limit. "We better not keep you any longer, you probably have a heap of things to be doing back at the station."

"Not at all. To be honest, we're not terribly busy at the moment. Anyway, it's great to have a chance to talk to someone from home."

Colin left out an involuntary groan, causing Michaela to look over and frown, but the visitor didn't notice.

"And do you go home often yourselves?" the fool was asking now, as if they were all emigrants in New York and not living just a couple of hours away.

"Every Christmas, God willing," muttered Colin.

"Ah, that's grand. It's good to get home, isn't it?"

"Ah, it is," said Colin. "You know, if we had a couple more of us here tonight, we could set up a little society, you know, for

Galway's diaspora. We could met once a week and tell each another news from the home county. Perhaps those of us lucky enough to receive a letter from kith or kin could read them out. What do you think, Michaela?"

Michaela looked over at him and frowned again.

"Well, I'll tell you now, you've been beaten to it," replied Garda Hogan, not catching the sarcasm. "Sure, isn't there a Galway society in Cork already, did you not know? I thought now that you'd be head and tail of it."

Colin had enough, he couldn't go on humouring this fool all night.

"I'm sorry now Garda, but . . ."

"Garda, don't mind your Garda. Call me Brian."

"Well, to be honest Brian, I think poor Michaela would like to go to bed, the excitement has her worn out. Of course, I'd love to sit here all night listening to you talking about the Fields and the Fieldings and other people neither you or I know, but maybe another night. Eh? Maybe some night down at this Galway Society."

"Ah I know, it's been a tough day for you. And here I am, gabbing away. I'll lash back the rest of my tea and be on my way."

Michaela and Colin jumped quickly to their feet, for fear he'd change his mind.

"Thanks for coming," said Colin, going out into the hall, hoping the garda will follow after him, wondering should he lay a trail of coconut creams as far as the door to entice him to leave.

"Not at all – all in the line of duty," said Garda Hogan, hurriedly collecting up his note-book and cap and popping a final coconut cream into his mouth for the road. He followed Colin out into the hall. Michaela followed after them.

"You'll let us know if you have information?" asked Colin, opening the front door.

"I will indeed. And I'll be onto you about that other matter in any case."

"What matter is that?"

"Going along to the Galway Society."

"Oh right. Of course."

Garda Hogan paused at the door as he put on his hat, surveying the street outside.

"Tell me something, Colin, have you ever

had any trouble from that lot down by the bridge?"

"No. No. They're a rough crowd though."

"They are that. They did fierce damage to one of your neighbours cars the other night – smashed in the headlights, broke off the wing mirrors and the aerial, then they did a bit of a dance up on the roof. A bad lot, no doubt about it. There mightn't be any harm in me asking them a few questions about your own misfortune."

"Oh God," said Michaela.

The two men turned to her.

"Michaela, what's wrong?" asked Colin.

Michaela's face had turned white.

"Nothing," she answered quickly. Too quickly.

"Michaela, what is it? What's the matter?" asked Colin.

"Nothing really. It's just that . . . it's just that when you mentioned the crowd on the bridge, Garda Hogan, I remembered that I'd brought one of them up to the house this lunchtime." She paused and looked over at Colin. "Now don't eat me, Colin," she said and then turned back to Garda Hogan. "He came up to borrow some of Colin's clothes. He was meant to return around five to give them back but he never showed and just for a second there I thought it might be him. But that's crazy. I know him, there's no way it is."

"You what?" exploded Colin.

"Calm down, Colin, I can explain."

"Calm down? Calm down?" shouted Colin going berserk.

"Can you describe him?" asked the garda, trying to keep the peace.

"They're no need to describe him. It wasn't him."

"Maybe not, but we'd need to question him, if only to rule him out."

"Hang on a second, Garda," interrupted Colin. "But I'd like to do a bit of questioning of my own. I'm kind of interested to know why Mother Theresa here has suddenly decided to turn our house into a welfare centre for the down and outs."

"He's not a down and out. Not really. He was going to an interview."

"Is that right? Is that what he told you?"

"If you could just describe him, please?" said the garda, trying to defuse the situation.

277

"Of course I can. But what's the point?"

"Please."

"Slight, dark, about twenty-three."

"And he was wearing?"

"What do you think he was wearing?" shouted Colin. "My bloody clothes, that's what!"

But then, remembering that he'd seen that fellow from the party earlier in the day wearing clothes that looked very like his own, he realised who Michaela was talking about.

"He just borrowed them, Colin," she was saying.

"Really?" asked Colin sceptically. Damn, damn, damn, what should he do? When Michaela had been in the kitchen making tea, Colin had made a point of telling the garda that he'd been in Limerick all day. Now, if old Sherlock Holmes here brought this fellow in for questioning, then he'd probably tell him that he'd seen Colin earlier and his lie would be found out. He might even tell him about the girl at the party.

"He is going to come back with them, Colin," said Michaela.

"Oh, he's come back already, Michaela. But not to return my clothes," said Colin, a plan beginning to hatch.

"Colin, you're jumping to conclusions."

"Hardly jumping."

The garda thought better of pursuing the matter of dress for the moment.

"And Michaela, you say he hangs around by the bridge?" he asked.

"Does he have an northern accent, Michaela?" interrupted Colin having decided that, if he implicated this character first, then the garda were less likely to believe anything he told him.

"Yes," answered Michaela.

"Remember last week, I told you that I'd stopped a fellow trying to break into one of the cars up the road, I'm sure it was the same fellow. Garda Hogan, when you asked me earlier whether we ever had any trouble, I was only thinking about ourselves. I'd forgotten that I'd seen this man tampering with the neighbour's car. Until now. I chased him away of course, gave him a few belts into the stomach as well for good measure. Now, I know we shouldn't take the law into her own hands, but I just got so mad when I saw him breaking into that car."

"Ah, I know. I shouldn't say it, but maybe if a few more people did, then we wouldn't have all the crime we have."

"Maybe not. But maybe I brought trouble on myself. He might have done this to get back at me."

"Colin, you never said anything to me about this," said Michaela looking at him puzzled.

"Sure I did, when I came in afterwards, you were in bed. Remember?"

"No."

"You must remember, I was in a right temper."

"Colin, I don't."

"Maybe you were asleep. But you did answer me."

"That tale about the interview could have been a ruse," said Garda Hogan, "To give him a chance to case the joint."

Michaela stared at him.

"Oh, for God's sake," she said disgustedly. "I think you've been watching too many

American cops movies. Anyway, it was I who invited him in."

"Still, there wouldn't be any harm in questioning him. He'll be easy to find."

Finally Garda Hogan took his leave and Michaela and Colin went to bed. After listening to Colin giving out for the best part of an hour about the loss of his set of clothes which seemed to upset him far more than the robbery itself, he finally shut up and Michaela fell asleep.

All in all, decided Colin as he drifted off to sleep, things hadn't gone too badly.

Bartley Collins wasn't one for lying-in. As soon as he awoke at five-thirty on the dot, as he invariably did, he eased himself out of bed quickly but quietly, mindful of Rebecca still sleeping. Then, not caring to turn on the light for fear of disturbing her, he dressed quickly, in the dimness feeling for his clothes on the chair where he'd laid them out the night before. He was fussy when it came to his underpants, socks and vest and changed them daily but, on working days he always put on the same pants, jumper and shirt, for there was little point in concerning himself with the state of his outer clothes, with road-sweeping being the dirty business that it is. The only real variation lay between his corporation-issue donkey-jacket and reflective jacket. The donkey-jacket it was today, he decided, though as usual he wasn't confident that he'd selected wisely.

"Rebecca," he called quietly.

"Donkey-jacket," she muttered automatically, then turned over and continued sleeping.

"Right. Donkey-jacket it is so," he said, pleased to have his choice confirmed. He put it on, then put on his heavy boots and went downstairs.

Having filled the kettle, he made his usual two rounds of sandwiches of corned beef on white bread. And, as soon as the kettle boiled, he wet a full pot of tea and, leaving it to draw, he sat at the table and ate his usual two bowls of Weetabix, doused in milk and heavily sprinkled with sugar. The Weetabix set him up for the morning. Nowadays, he rarely went back to the depot at tea-break, not since his friend Val had died. Bartley was oldest of the sweepers now, older by a few decades than most of them and he didn't really enjoy the company of the younger fellows at tea-break; he knew that he was very often the butt of their jokes, though they thought he was too thick to realise. Only one of the men, John-John, had been at the job as long, but Bartley had learnt to avoid him – the older he got, the more cantankerous he got. John-John's latest cause for constant complaint was the Corporation's decision to take on two young girls as sweepers. Bartley couldn't really see what the problem with this was, to him it made sense to take on women, they were usually better at cleaning it seemed to him. Although it wasn't a job he'd have liked to see his own daughter doing, if he had one. Or a son. But they wouldn't have worked as sweepers anyway; he used to always imagine that they'd take after Rebecca, that they'd be smart.

When the tea had drawn he added a little milk and some sugar to the pot, stirred it around, poured out a cup and brought it upstairs to Rebecca. Placing the cup on the bedside locker, he looked down at her for a few moments before softly calling her name.

"Thanks, Bartley," she muttered in response, without really waking up and he leaned over, kissed her on the forehead and went back downstairs. He poured the rest of the tea into his flask, collected up his sandwiches and left the house quietly.

Usually Bartley started work from the depot around the corner from home but John-John had been out sick all week and Bartley had been told that he'd have to fill in for him. John-John's area was on the southside and Bartley felt disgruntled now, he hated any deviation to his usual routine and the walk across town made him feel crosser still; after the revelries of Friday night, the city was filthy. It never ceased to amaze him how much dirt collected overnight; how anyone could wantonly throw chip-wrappings, or whatever, on the ground was beyond him. He was a tidy man himself. Still, he supposed, it kept him in a job. He liked cleaning his own patch on the northside – he felt responsible for it – but he had no such allegiance to the southside and he didn't get the same satisfaction at all on the increasingly regular occasions he had to fill in for John-John. Around his own area, people knew him. "Howya doing, Bartley," they'd call to him when they saw him on the street and some would stop for a chat, but on the southside he always felt like the invisible man. He felt kind of lonely over here. People passed by without even seeing him. It struck him, as it did from time to time, how in films, if the police were staking out a building, they often had one fellow working undercover as a sweeper. He could see the sense in that alright. He collected his cart, brush and shovel from the depot near the City Hall and started work.

Something else which perpetually amazed him were the things he was forever coming across lying on the ground. Now he bent down to pick up the second odd shoe he'd found in the first fifteen minutes of sweeping. As well as odd shoes he regularly came across all sorts of clothes: odd socks, hats, jumpers, even ladies' knickers. How someone didn't notice that they'd lost their shoe or, even more so, their knickers, was a puzzle to him, one that he didn't care to dwell on. On the rare occasions he did, he suspected that their loss came about in conjunction with the activities associated with the used condoms he was finding more and more of in latter years. Condoms, syringes and dog-turds were the three things he hated most. He put the shoe into the cart, shovelled up a heap of rubbish and walked on, wheeling the cart in front of him.

Passing by a derelict site he saw a notice posted on the fencing and paused to study it. He could understand the words *Cork Corporation* – after all he worked for them, it was always on his pay-cheque – but he could understand little more; he'd never been good at reading, Rebecca did all that kind of thing. He hoped it was one of those planning notices for he hated sites like this one; cleaning them was a waste of time, they were full of rubbish again in no time. Especially this one, those drunks were always throwing cans and the like down from the bridge overhead. Why people who owned sites like these just didn't build on them, Bartley would never understand. But then, they probably lived out in Douglas or Blackrock and weren't bothered by the state of their property. After all, they didn't have to live beside it. Away in at the far end of the site he noticed an old fridge lying on its side and, looking up he saw that one of the houses, some thirty feet above, was being renovated and it looked like the builders, to save themselves a trip to the dump, were flinging anything they didn't want over their yard wall and down into the derelict site. Bartley felt a rush of anger, sometimes people were worse than animals. Leaving his cart on the roadside, he climbed through the broken fencing and walked across the site, throwing a practised eye over the ground for anything worth picking up. A fellow Bartley knew ran a second-hand shop and whenever Bartley found something worth selling he brought it down to him. Only the other day the man had given him a fiver for a toaster; it had been a perfectly good one too, just jammed up with bread-crumbs. But there was nothing of interest and Bartley quickly turned around again, but as he was walking back to his cart he glanced over to the burnt-out remains of a bonfire in the centre of the site and noticed a piece of light green material sticking out from under a wooden pallet. The shop-owner wasn't keen on taking clothes from Bartley, but sometimes he did, if they were clean and in good condition. Bartley walked over. Carefully, he stepped through ashes and blackened tin-cans and over charred, half-burnt lumps of wood and the metal frame of an old car seat. Then he bent down and began to tug at what appeared to be a sleeve. But it was heavier and more solid than it should have been, and it suddenly dawned on him that there was still an arm inside it.

"Sweetest Jesus!"

He dropped the sleeve, arm and all, blessed himself, and backed back over the debris, stumbling as he went. He steadied himself, turned around and ran back to his cart. He took out his hankie, wiped the sweat from his forehead and then looked around to see if there was anyone watching. Then hurriedly, he pushed his cart along the road putting as much distance as quickly as possible between himself and the body. The last thing he wanted was be getting involved with dead people. He cursed John-John, if he wasn't for him he'd be safely over on the northside, where nothing like this ever happened to him. But then he heard Rebecca's voice in the head, "Bartley," he could hear her ask in that tone of hers, "How could you have just left him there? What if he's not dead?" "Alright, alright," muttered Bartley. He sighed and turned around his cart. Leaving it on the road he walked back over. Stopping metres from the bonfire he called out cautiously.

"Hello," he shouted, "Hello." As if he expected someone who'd been tossed upon a bonfire and was lying dead or half-dead under a heavy wooden pallette at six o'clock in the morning, was likely to suddenly sit up and answer him.

"Hello," he called again. He circled the bonfire to see if he could make out anything more without having to go nearer. He saw a leg sticking out but it provided no hint as to whether the person was living or dead. He picked up a stick and cautiously prodded the leg. It didn't stir. He prodded again and this time it moved ever so slightly. Braver now, knowing that he wasn't dealing with a corpse, he climbed onto the bonfire remains and, over the spot he thought approximated the head, he called loudly through the pallette.

"Are you alright? Hello. Are you alright?" He got no response. "This is just awful," he muttered to himself. "Awful." He caught hold of the pallette and pulled it off. Then he heaved the body onto its back. "Merciful hour," muttered Bartley recognising Davy, though he looked horrible, his face was blood-covered and badly cut and made more frightful by being blackened by the soot. "What am I going to do?" he asked aloud as if he expected poor Davy to be able to tell him. He wished Rebecca was here, she'd know what to do.

He went back onto the road, took a hold of his cart and pushed it through a hole in the fencing and wheeled it across the bumpy ground over to near where Davy lay. He tipped out its contents beside the bonfire, leaned the cart on its side and began to haul Davy into it. Once he'd got him in, he stood for a few minutes, staring at him, wondering what he should do. He thought about taking him to the hospital but he doubted his medical card would cover the expense of someone other than himself and he'd no money on him. And hospitals cost a fortune, so he'd heard. Rebecca would know what to do, he decided, and managing to right the cart again he set off home.

The doorbell woke Colin. He looked over at the clock on the locker, it wasn't yet eight. He got out of bed and, wondering who could be calling so early on a Saturday morning, he pulled on a pair of jeans, went downstairs and opened the door.

"Oh, Garda Hogan, you're back to us already?"

"Just to fill you in on what's happening," said Garda Hogan. "You don't you mind if I step in?"

And, not waiting for an answer in, he stepped in.

"Well, when I left here last night I went down to the bridge. I had a few words with some of the lads down there. They knew who I was talking about alright, although they didn't let on at first. But you'd expect that, their kind always stick together. But in the end I managed to get it out of them. They told me that our man was hanging about yesterday down by the bridge. Apparently he caused a bit of trouble – a bit of a fight, so it seems. Anyway, he lives up by the Cathedral, so they told me, so I'm going to take a walk up there now. I didn't disturb you?" He paused, then asked hopefully, "You weren't having your breakfast, were you?"

"No," answered Colin.

10

COLIN LOVES MICHAELA BUT SAMANTHA AND ANNA TOO AND NOW DENISE?

MURIEL AND Denise were always at their sourest on Monday mornings. They usually sat there, not saying a word, just sullenly banging away at their computers until they began to thaw out around coffee-break time. But this morning, when Michaela would have welcomed the silence, they were all chit-chat and it was driving her crazy. There were just so many things to worry about.

That strangers had been in her house really bothered her and, although it was illogical, since they'd already taken everything of value, she'd worried all weekend that they might come back. On Saturday evening, Colin had gone out and she'd sat there in the silence – the stereo and television God knows where. She tried to read but every little noise, real and imagined, had her on tenterhooks. The loss of the telly and the like didn't really upset her for, as Colin said, they could be replaced once the insurance came through but what did bother her was the loss of her CD collection built up so lovingly and painstakingly over the years. That she'd opened her mouth about Davy being in the house troubled her as well and despite Garda Hogan and Colin's certainty that Davy was the burglar, she wasn't convinced; someone who gave you back your purse one day didn't break into your house the next, it just didn't make sense. Garda Hogan had called again yesterday morning to let them know that he'd checked out where Davy lived and told them that he hadn't been seen around since Friday morning. The graphic description he'd given them of Davy's squalid living conditions had upset her as well. And, that she and Colin weren't talking didn't help her mood either.

He was still going on and on about her lending his clothes to Davy, claiming that if she hadn't brought that knacker – as he called him – into the house then the burglary would never have happened. On Saturday night, because she didn't want to be on her own, she'd asked Colin not to go out but he wouldn't listen, just told her that he couldn't let Ben Philips down, and anyway, he needed to get out of the house and away from her.

Now, half-heartedly, she shuffled through the basket looking for an uncomplicated letter, something with legible handwriting, to start off typing with; then she switched on her computer and resolved not to think about things.

"I'll make sure Mr O'Neill gets your message as soon as he comes in. Yes. Thank you for calling. *By-yee.*" Denise put down the receiver, switched automatically and immediately from her posh, mid-Atlantic telephone voice to her normal one and resumed her conversation. "I'm going to meet him on Saturday next. He says he . . ."

"Denise, you're skipping ahead," Muriel interrupted. "Go back to the start, tell me how you met him, I want to hear everything," she demanded.

"Well, I don't know if I can tell you . . . " Denise paused, then smiled smugly, "*everything.*"

Well, thank God for that, thought Michaela.

"OK, start by telling me how you met him then," said Muriel.

"Well, I was sitting in the lobby of Jury's waiting for Theresa, the girl I go out with on a Saturday night. We always meet there, it's really nice and they don't even expect you to buy a drink or anything. Anyway, Theresa was very late, I guessed it was because of her mother, she hasn't been very well lately, something internal, although Theresa doesn't say much about it. Anyway, just as I was beginning to wonder should I phone to see what was holding her up, this man, sitting on the couch opposite me, smiled over. Of course, I pretended not to notice but then he got up, came over and asked me would I mind if he joined me."

"Really?"

"He explained that he'd noticed I was waiting for someone and, since he was too, he suggested that the time might pass more quickly if we kept each other company."

"Hmm. He sounds a bit forward," observed Muriel, jealously.

"No, Muriel, it wasn't like that. He was just being friendly. He was the nicest fellow you could imagine. He'd a lovely manner. He was very good-looking too, had a really lovely smile."

"What does he do?"

"He's a Company Director. He owns his own soft-ware company. Employs fifty people so he does. He was staying in Jury's, you see his business takes him all over the country. Anyway, where was I?"

"He asked could he join you?"

"Oh yes. Well, before I could say yes or no, he sat down but, just after he'd introduced himself, one of the hotel staff came over and asked me was I Denise Cleary. When I said I was, she told me that there was a phone call for me at reception. It was Theresa ringing to tell me she wouldn't be able to make it on account of her mother. Of course I was very disappointed, after all my effort getting ready, not to mention the expense of the taxi into town. Anyway, I had to pass back through the lobby on my way out and I told Colin about the phone call and . . . "

"Colin? That's my husband's name," remarked Michaela.

"I didn't know *you* were listening, Michaela."

"It's not like I have much choice," muttered Michaela.

"Anyway, Muriel, I told Colin that my friend wasn't coming in and then he suggested that we might have a drink together, since it seemed like he'd been stood up as well. At first I said no, that I wasn't in the habit of going for drinks with strangers I met in hotel lobbies. Then he smiled – oh Muriel, did I mention his smile?"

"Yes, yes. Go on."

"Then he smiled and said that neither was he but, if I'd make an exception, so would he. To cut a long story short, I went with him for a few drinks in the hotel bar. Or should I say cocktails. Oh, he was such a gent, Muriel, opening the door for me, pulling out my chair, taking my coat. And he paid for everything, he wouldn't let me pay a penny all night."

"So you're meeting him again on Saturday?"

"Well, he suggested we go out for dinner. To Lovett's or Simm's Restaurant. He's going to give me a ring."

"He must be fairly well off."

"Well, he did let it slip that his company had a turnover of two and a half million pounds last year."

"How did he let it slip exactly?" asked Michaela.

"Pardon?"

"I mean did he say, 'Go on, have a cocktail, Denise. My treat, with an turnover of two and a half million pounds, I should be able to afford it.' Or what?"

"Just shut up, Michaela."

"Are you going to invite him to the Christmas party?" asked Muriel.

"I was thinking of it."

"But that's ages away, Denise," interrupted Michaela.

The two of them raised their eyes to heaven.

"Michaela, I'm talking to Muriel."

"It's alright for you, Michaela, you're

married," said Muriel. "You don't have to worry."

"I was thinking of inviting him alright," continued Denise.

"But it's only November," persisted Michaela.

Denise let out a sigh of exasperation but decided to ignore the interruption.

"Muriel, do you think I look like Elizabeth Taylor?"

"Well," said Muriel doubtfully. "Maybe. Why?"

"It's just that Colin said it was the first thing that struck him about me."

"Really?" said Muriel doubtfully.

"Did he mean the way she looks now or forty years ago?" asked Michaela.

"Michaela, I'd wish you'd stop making such snide remarks. You're just jealous."

Just then a call came through on Muriel's phone.

"Hello. Yes. Just one moment please." Muriel put her hand over the receiver and whispered. "It's for you, Denise. I think it's him."

*   *   *

"Hi, Cliona," said Polly, bumping into her cousin as she came out of her first lecture of the week. "How come you weren't on the train back up last night?"

"My nine o'clock was cancelled. I came up this morning. Do you want to go for coffee? I want to tell you something."

"What?"

"Come on and I'll tell you."

"OK, but I have something to tell you as well."

They headed to the canteen and stood in line.

"Two coffees please, Noreen," ordered Cliona, "And a Danish." Then she turned to Polly. "I'll go get a seat. Will you pay? I gave Squealer twenty pounds this morning so I'm broke until my money comes through on Wednesday."

"Ah, Cliona, you know I never have enough for the week."

"God, you are so mean, Polly!"

"I'm not. Anyway, I thought you said Squealer had got a job."

"He chucked it in, didn't suit him. It got in the way of his painting."

301

Polly paid Noreen and followed Cliona down to where she was seating.

"So," said Polly. "What have you to tell me?"

"Well, you know my friend Jacqui?"

"Which one is she? Was she one of the people I was talking to at your party?"

"No, I don't think so. But she was at it. You probably saw her. She always wears combat gear and has her eyebrow pierced."

"Cliona, that could be any of your friends."

"I see what you mean. Anyway, it doesn't matter. The important thing is that Jacqui took a heap of photographs that night and he's in one of them."

"Who? The guy who attacked you?"

"Yeah. El Creepo."

"Cliona, that's excellent. Did you bring it to the guards?"

"Well, I wasn't going to bother, what's done is done and at least Davy got there in time. But I began thinking that he might try the same thing again and, the next time, his victim mightn't be so lucky. I mean, if Davy hadn't come in when he did, there's no way I could have stopped him."

"Cliona, remember I said I thought I'd seen him before?"

"Yeah?"

"Well, I did. That's what I wanted to tell you. It was only when I was home at the weekend that I remembered where. He came into the shop with his girlfriend the other week. I'm sure it was him."

"He has a girlfriend? God, the poor thing. Can you imagine going out with someone like that." She shuddered. "Ugh. Anyway I've done all I can now. I've made a statement and at least the gardaí have his photo."

"True."

"There's nothing else I can do. Listen Polly, I'm really grateful for what Davy did, will you make sure to tell him?"

"Well . . . " Polly had to tell Cliona the truth, it was ridiculous pretending that Davy was her boyfriend, she hadn't even seen him since the night of the party.

"He's really nice, Polly."

"Cliona, you see he's not really . . . "

"Listen, why don't you two come with us out tonight? We're going to the Casket. We'll be there from about nine on."

"Well, I don't know, I . . . " Since starting college, the only other time Cliona had asked her to come out socially was on the night of her party. Her reason for doing so then, Polly suspected, was simply to make up numbers.

"Mention it to Davy anyway," Cliona continued. "If you come in, you come in. If not, then another night. Polly, I'm glad you've met Davy. He's really, really nice."

"Do you think?"

"Oh yeah. So does your mother by the way. Thinks he's very handsome."

"Don't mind her. She's never even seen him."

"She has now. I showed her his photo."

"You what?"

"There was one of you and him in the photos Jacqui took."

"And you showed it to her? When? She never told me."

"Last night. After your parents dropped you off at the station they called into mine."

"Oh good God," groaned Polly. Her mother would never shut up about him now.

"When you go home next weekend, will

you be sure to get them back from her?" asked Cliona.

"What?"

"I had two sets and she asked to borrow one."

"You let my mother take a photograph of Davy home! Cliona, how could you?"

"But Polly, what's the problem? It was a lovely one. You both look really happy in it. He's throwing back his head and laughing, as if you've just said something really funny."

"Really?" asked Polly, interested enough to forget her annoyance. For just a second. "Cliona, how could you have done this to me?"

"Polly, I don't see the problem."

"You don't see the problem? Are you stupid? You know what she's like. She's always going on about him as it is, she thinks we're practically engaged. She's probably hot-footed it into Mallow first thing this morning to get it framed and enlarged. He'll probably be staring down from the mantel-piece when I go home next weekend."

"Not if I tell her what I found out about him."

"What do you mean?"

"Oh nothing."

"You can't say something like that and then turn around and say, 'Oh nothing'. What do you mean, Cliona?"

"Well, Squealer says he's seen Davy before, up by that pedestrian bridge over by the hospital, you know, where they deal."

"And what was Squealer doing there?"

"What do you think Polly? Same as Davy probably."

"Which is?"

"Oh grow up, Polly. Buying drugs, Polly, buying drugs. You hardly thought Squealer could be that spaced out otherwise? I mean, you hardly thought he was born that way?"

"No, I suppose not. But Cliona, Davy isn't a druggie!"

"How would you know? He could be snorting cocaine right in front of you and you'd believe him if he said he was taking something for a cold. All I know is that Squealer says he's seen him by that bridge a few times."

"No, there's no way Davy takes drugs. But, telling my parents that he does might be one way of stopping them asking me to bring him down to see them all the time."

"But why don't you want to? I thought you'd be glad to show him off."

"It's a bit complicated."

"How do you mean?"

"I . . . I just don't want to yet." Somehow she didn't feel like telling Cliona the truth any more.

"What can I get you, boys?" asked the waitress smiling down at Ben Philips and Colin.

"A coffee, please," said Ben Philips.

"Same for me," said Colin.

The two of them watched the waitress as she walked away, then they turned back to one another.

"So-so," said Colin. "Seven, eight maybe."

"Nah. Too fat. Past her sell-by date," replied Ben Philips, who could well have been describing himself. "Anyway, Colin, I'm sorry about Saturday night. Your mobile was switched off and I couldn't find your home number. But there was no way I could leave Peg."

"It doesn't matter. What exactly happened to her?"

"Nothing much really. But given the state she was in when she rang from the gym I thought I'd be lucky if she was still alive when I got there."

"Was she badly hurt?"

"Not at all. She just twisted her ankle on the tread-mill. But she insisted I take her to the hospital to get it checked out and that took the whole evening. She's been in bed ever since. 'Ben, would you mind bringing me up a cup of tea.' 'Ben, it's time for my tablets.' 'Ben, my book has fallen on the floor.' It's doing my head in."

"There you are gentlemen, your coffees," said the waitress.

"Thanks," said Ben and he continued. "And I was really looking forward to Saturday night. As Phil says, you never know where, or with whom, you'd end up with on a night out with you. Did you wait long?"

"No, as it happens."

"Good, at least it wasn't a complete waste of a night."

"No, far from it."

"How do you mean?"

"There's no knowing who you'd meet in the lobby of Jury's while you're waiting."

"What?"

"Never waste an opportunity, that's my motto."

"What? Are you trying to tell me that you picked up someone while you were waiting for me?" asked Ben, looking at Colin in amazement. Colin nodded. "Man, you're unbelievable. You should run classes," Ben said admiringly. "Well, tell us, what was she like?"

"The shy, plain kind. But they're often the best bet. Very grateful. So delighted that they'll do anything to please. Yeah, we spent a very nice evening in the bar in Jury's."

"You're crazy, you know that? Did you . . . you know?"

"Not yet. She needs a bit of working on. But I gave her a call while I was waiting for you to come in."

"So you're going to meet her again?"

"Maybe yes, maybe no. I have to head to Limerick tonight. I'm going to be gone all week but I'll see when I come back. I've

309

arranged to met her at Simm's on Saturday night."

"Colin, you're mental. What are you at? How many do you have on the go?"

Colin shrugged.

"Sexy Samantha is back on the scene, isn't she?" asked Ben.

Colin nodded.

"And are you still seeing that posh one from Limerick?"

Again Colin nodded.

"And now this new one? Not to mention poor Michaela. How do you manage it, Colin? How can you even afford it? No wonder you look exhausted."

"It's not that," said Colin.

"Yeah right."

"No, we were burgled on Friday and the fool of a garda who's investigating it kept us up talking all night. Then he came around again at the crack of dawn on Saturday morning and on Sunday morning."

"And has he found the people responsible yet?"

"No, as far as I can see that's what he keeps coming around to tell me. Fierce keen, but on the dim side. It was just the one fellow as it happens. They know who he is but he's gone missing. Actually he's from your neck of the woods, a northerner."

"Yeah? What's he called?"

"Davy Long."

"Long?" Ben thought for a few seconds. "There's a notorious family in Belfast called the Longs. I wonder if he's one of them. They're unbelievable, this family. The mother is inside for drug-smuggling and I think the father is inside as well, on something drugs-related too. Whenever anything happens in Belfast the son Stephen is the first person to be brought in for questioning, although they never manage to charge him with anything. He's a real bad lot, everyone knows he runs some kind of protection racket and God knows what else besides. His wife is as bad. The Hulk, they call her. She attacked a girl with a bottle in a disco four or five months ago. It was all over the papers, the girl had to get fifty stitches, she lost her eye. What's his first name again?"

"Davy."

"Well, there is another brother, but I don't

know what he's called. He was put away years ago, when he was only fifteen or sixteen. I remember reading about him in the papers."

"Yeah?"

"Yeah, it was a horrible case. Everyone knew at the time it was Stephen Long's younger brother, even though he was never named on account of his age. He broke into this house and, while he was robbing it, the owner, an old lady, came back and he attacked her with a hammer, raped her and then tied her up. For good measure he set fire to the house. The papers were full of it for weeks. The old lady died in the fire. Do you think it could be him? Would he be out of prison already?"

"Davy love," said Rebecca. "You're awake."

Davy stared at her and then at Bartley, puzzled as to who these two old people looking down at him could be. That they did so with such obvious concern alarmed him and he looked around, anxiously, trying to figure out where he was, trying to remember what had happened and how he'd got here.

By the time Bartley had wheeled Davy across the city, brought him back to his own house and, with the help of Rebecca, undressed and cleaned him, tended to his cuts and the dog-bite on his leg, and then put him to bed, it was still early on Saturday; no later than eleven o'clock. But Davy didn't wake that day, nor the next; he just lay there unconscious, watched over anxiously by Bartley and Rebecca who took it in turns to sit by his bedside. It wasn't until now, lunchtime Monday, that he finally started to come around and, as he slowly awakened, the faces of Rebecca and Bartley anxiously peering down at him were what he saw first.

"Davy, you've had an accident. Do you remember? Do you know who I am?" asked Bartley. Davy tried to fix his eyes on him, but he couldn't keep them open. His eyelids drooped, but somewhere in his confused brain there was a flicker of recognition.

"An . . . officer . . . " began Davy.

"Davy?" asked Rebecca anxiously, fearing the worst, fearing some permanent damage from his concussion, not knowing that Davy

313

was remembering what he'd once heard Bartley call him.

"An officer and . . . " The second half of the phrase had slipped away from Davy, and his eyes closed.

"What officer, Davy?" Rebecca prompted. "Davy?" She glanced over at Bartley who was staring at Davy with concern to match her own. All that day and the two before, as they'd watched over Davy, waiting for him to come to, they'd debated whether or not they should call a doctor, but they'd held off, telling themselves that there was no need, that he was bound to wake at any moment. Anyway, they told one another, he'd hardly thank them for bringing in the authorities given the peculiar circumstances of his accident. Not to mind Davy's own odd personal circumstances, which, once Bartley had explained to Rebecca, they'd speculated over at length during their bedside vigil of the last few days. And in the end, Rebecca's faith in the curative powers of a good rest had swayed the argument and they'd held off calling in the doctor.

"Davy, I'm Bartley. Do you remember me?

I do the streets up around Cathedral View. Remember, we had a pint once in Flaherty's. Remember?"

Davy managed to open his eyes again and he looked at Bartley now. Flaherty's meant nothing to him. But he was beginning to remember Bartley. He vaguely remembered, or thought he remembered, meeting him outside his own house. He tried to think. And, though the effort tired him, it finally came to him; he remembered Bartley telling him that his colleagues in the City Hall were going to let him know when his house was due for demolition.

"City Hall," mumbled Davy.

"That's right, Davy. I work for City Hall."

"You're well in there," Davy added, now recollecting Bartley's own proud boast.

Bartley and Rebecca heaved a sigh of relief and Rebecca felt a rush of pride; such praise for her husband. And from a stranger.

"There," said Rebecca. "Do you hear that?" She looked over at Bartley fondly who looked pleased but embarrassed, neither of them thinking to wonder how Davy should be so informed on Corporation matters. "And why

315

wouldn't you be?" Rebecca added proudly. Her husband wasn't one of the brightest she knew but, in her estimation, he was one of the best and she was pleased to learn that her suspicions that he was undervalued were unfounded. She now turned back to Davy and, resting a hand on his arm, she said,

"I'm Bartley's wife, Davy – Rebecca. Tell me, love, do you remember anything about the accident?" Davy shook his head and his gaze fell down to where her hand was resting on his arm and then on, over his torso. The sudden sight of his black and blue body made him feel nauseous. As he contemplated the ugly sight of himself he was deaf to much of what Rebecca was saying.

"I've seen him bring home more birds with broken wings and lame dogs in that cart of his than I can remember. But I can tell you, Davy, when he turned up at the door and told me to take a look inside the cart, seeing you lying there gave me a bit of a turn."

"Davy, there was no other way of getting you home. The only thing I could do was wheel you across town in my cart," said Bartley, half-apologetic for the indignity of the mode of transport, but half-proud too, of his own lateral thinking. "Someone had left you there for dead. You were hidden under a wooden pallette and other bits of rubbish. It's a wonder I spotted you at all."

"I told him he was taking his responsibilities a bit too seriously; that his job of keeping the streets clean didn't extend to collecting up men he found lying about," said Rebecca, trying to hold Davy's attention. But Davy's eyes were closing again.

"Davy, Davy," called Rebecca. But he'd fallen back to sleep.

All day, as she sat in her lectures, Polly mulled over the fact that Squealer had seen Davy on the bridge, but it was quite late in the day when she finally made up her mind to go to there; if there was a chance Davy might be there, it was worth checking out. That night of the party, after Davy had hauled El Creepo down the stairs, Polly had stopped to check on Cliona and then she'd followed out after them but by that time both men had disappeared. She really wanted to see Davy again, to be sure that the creep hadn't harmed him and to thank him for what he had done for Cliona. But really, just to see him again

It was nearing five when she arrived at the bridge. It had been a dull day all day and already it was getting dark. Davy wasn't about. Nor was anyone else. Feeling disappointed and depressed she climbed the flight of steps and sat down on the top one.

Michaela's heart stopped when she saw the figure silhouetted in the dusk. For a second she thought it was Davy sitting in his regular spot but as she came closer she saw it was a girl. A young, innocent-looking girl who'd no business hanging around here on her own. Still, she decided, it was none of her concern but as she passed by the steps she glanced up at the girl and saw that she looked terribly depressed. She was staring out over the bridge, as if she were contemplating whether flinging herself off of it would be the best way to end it all.

"Are you all right?" Michaela stopped and called up. She didn't want to hear later that the girl had decided to do herself in and know that she had done nothing to stop her. She'd enough to feel guilty about as it was, what with putting the gardaí onto Davy. "You know, a lot of drunks hang about here, it's not really very safe," she warned Polly.

"You're right," sighed Polly. "I was just about to go anyway."

Polly sighed, got up and came down the steps. Michaela continued on her way and Polly began walking in the other direction

"Hey," Polly suddenly shouted.

Michaela turned and waited as the girl came towards her.

"Do you pass up this way often?" Polly asked Michaela when she reached her.

"Most days."

"They deal drugs here, don't they?"

"I don't know really. I suppose they might," replied Michaela, looking at the girl now, thinking that she looked like an unlikely drug-taker, but then you just never knew.

"You haven't seen a young guy? asked Polly. "About twenty-three or twenty-four, dark-haired, dark-skinned, good-looking and very thin. With a northern accent."

"Yes, Davy Long," said Michaela slowly. "Is that why you're here? To meet him?"

"Well, I'm looking for him."

"He sells drugs?"

"What? Oh God, he doesn't, does he?"

"No, no, I thought you said he does."

"No, I didn't. I just want to thank him. He stopped this lunatic attacking my cousin at a party and I heard that he hangs around here so I came up to see if I could find him. If he wasn't for Davy, well . . . well anyway, Davy got there in time. So you know him?"

"Sort of. But . . . "

"Can you give him a message from me if you see him again."

"Well, I don't think I will. He's disappeared."

"How do you mean?"

"The gardaí think he broke into a house, my house as it happens, last Friday and he seems to have gone missing ever since."

"Broke into your house? Davy? That's crazy. He's the kindest, gentlest person I've ever met."

"As it happens, I don't think he did either. But try telling the gardaí that."

"Do you know where he lives?"

320

"Yeah. Cathedral View over on the north-side. But there's no point in going there. The gardaí say he hasn't been there since."

Polly thought for second, then she opened her bag, searched around in it, pulled out her notebook and wrote down the phone number of the hostel.

"If they find him will you let me know? Please? Here's my phone number."

At about seven that evening, Rebecca popped her head around the door to check on Davy.

"Davy, you're awake. Are you hungry?"

He shook his head.

"I don't think so."

"You probably should eat."

She left, then came back minutes later.

"Here, see how you get on with this."

Davy pulled himself up and Rebecca handed him a cup of soup and sat down on the side of the bed.

"I'm glad things are coming back to you, Davy," said Rebecca, watching him taking sips. "But when I think of those fellows throwing you over the bridge, I get so mad. I feel like, like, going up there with a shotgun and blowing the heads off each and every one of them. I feel like . . . "

"I know," interrupted Davy, he'd heard Rebecca recount at least a dozen fitting punishments for the drunks, should she get her hands on them.

"You're looking much better," she said, calming down now. "How's the leg?"

"Not too bad. The swelling's going down."

"Bartley and I were worried about you, Davy, I can tell you. But you'll be as right as rain in another few days. Now, I know you said earlier that you want to go home, but Davy, I'd be much happier if you stayed here for a little while longer. You can't even walk yet. We want you to stay here until you're better, OK? I'd rest easier."

Rebecca left and Davy drifted in and out of sleep. In his waking moments two things became clear to him. Firstly that it was Rebecca and Bartley's bed he was sleeping in. Later, when Rebecca came back to see how he was, he'd suggested that he'd get up and let them have it back, but she wouldn't hear of it and he felt too weak to force the issue, though her evasiveness made him think they were making do with the couch. The second thing that was becoming very clear to him was that the whole episode with the removal men outside Michaela's house just didn't make any sense. The more he thought about it, the more he realised it simply didn't gel. He accepted that there was no reason for Michaela to have told him she was leaving but, equally so, he couldn't see any reason for her not to tell him. Besides, someone just about to move homes in less than a few hours' time would have been too busy to waste time getting a relative stranger kitted out for an interview. And, he figured, even if a removals firm were doing most of the work, she'd have still packed up the little items – the CD's, jewellery, ornaments – but she hadn't; her house had been in a state of everyday disarray when he'd been there. And besides, all that skulking around by Colin was a little suspicious. So, if she hadn't been moving, what had been going on? Davy wondered. And the only conclusion he could come to was that Colin had been walking out on her and taking their belongings with him.

11

MICHAELA AND POLLY
AT HOME WITH THE ODLUMS

"GOD, YOU are *so* naïve, Michaela,"
said Colin.

It was the following Saturday evening.
Colin had arrived back to Cork after spending
the week in Limerick. While he was shower-
ing, Michaela had ordered a Chinese
takeaway, enough for two, only to be told by
Colin, when the food arrived, that he'd
arranged to go out to dinner with a client.
Now, they were sitting at the table, she eating
and Colin picking from her plate.

"I am not naïve," answered Michaela
crossly. "And, there's another reason now
why I don't think he did it."

"What? Let me guess. He arrived at the door and said, 'Please, nice lady, I didn't rob your house, you've just gotta believe me.'"

"Will you shut up! For your information, I met a friend of his who was looking for him down by the bridge on Monday. When she asked me did I know him, I told her about the robbery, and, according to her, there's just no way he could have done it. She told me that . . . "

"Well, that's that then," interrupted Colin. "At last – conclusive proof of Davy Long's innocence – his friend says he didn't do it." He leant across the table and tapped Michaela on the forehead with his knuckles. "Hello, hello," he called. "Anyone at home?"

"Stop that," she snapped, pulling away.

"And you say you're not naïve? Michaela, she's his friend, she's hardly going to think he did it."

"Will you just listen to me, Colin?" said Michaela. "I wasn't finished. There's more. She told me that at a party lately, some psycho attacked her cousin and only for Davy getting there in time, God knows what would have happened. Now, I'm not saying it's proof that he didn't rob the house but, like the way he gave me back my purse, I just think it's an indication of the kind he is."

"Are you sure *he* wasn't the psycho who attacked this girl's cousin?" asked Colin.

"What do you mean?"

"You're not the only one who's been talking to people who know him. I've heard things about him too."

"Like?"

"A lot of things."

"Such as?"

"Well, for one, he comes from a notorious Belfast criminal family called the Longs. There's not a single person in Belfast who hasn't heard of them."

"So, that doesn't make him a criminal."

"No, you're right it doesn't," said Colin. He'd been looking forward to telling Michaela his news concerning Davy Long. The way she kept sticking up for him all the time really bugged him. Now with some satisfaction, he continued. "But I think you'll agree that being found guilty of burglary and arson probably does."

"What? Are you trying to tell me that Davy

was found guilty of burglary and arson?"

"Will you stop calling him Davy like he's your best friend? And yes, that is what I'm trying to tell you."

Michaela snorted in disbelief.

"And did I mention rape?" asked Colin.

"Rape? Davy?" laughed Michaela. "Oh, for crying out loud!"

"Burglary. Arson. Rape. And there was a fourth. Now what was it?" He scratched his head, pretending to think hard. "Oh yes, manslaughter, that's it. Now, I know that just because he served time for rape, manslaughter, burglary and arson, that doesn't mean he robbed our house but, I think you'll agree, Michaela, that – to use your own words – it's an indication of the kind he is."

"I don't believe you, this is ridiculous."

"Do you think so? Well, read this then and see how ridiculous you think it is. Let's see then what you think of your precious Davy."

He handed Michaela a photocopy of a newspaper article. She took it from him and began to read. All that Ben Philips had told Colin was there, with every gory detail elaborately recounted.

"This 'minor' could be anyone. There's no telling it's Davy," said Michaela looking up.

"It is."

"How do you know?"

"I mentioned the robbery to Ben Philips and, when he heard the name Long he recognised it. Ben's from Belfast. He filled me in on this Long family including your friend Davy. Apparently, even though Davy Long's name was never mentioned in the papers at the time, everybody in Belfast knew it was Stephen Long's younger brother. Stephen Long is like a Belfast version of Martin Cahill. Anyway, later on, I rang our friend Garda Hogan and passed on what Ben had told me. He checked it out with the RUC and came back to me on my mobile on Wednesday and confirmed that it was the same fellow."

"This is awful. Why didn't you tell me earlier?" Then a thought struck her. "Colin, you let me stay here on my own all week. He could have come back."

"Michaela, I only met Ben on Monday morning and then I went to Limerick. I didn't get a chance to tell you."

"No, Colin, you met Ben on Saturday,

remember? You were home all day Sunday, why didn't you tell me then?"

"No, Ben never showed up on Saturday. His wife Peg twisted her ankle and he had to take her to the hospital."

"But you didn't come home until twelve."

"Well, I met a friend – Maurice Murray," said Colin easily, without even pausing for a second, practised liar that he was. "He was staying in Jury's and I bumped into him in the lobby while I was waiting for Ben, so I went for a few drinks with him in the bar."

"Is that so?"

"Michaela, why are you looking at me so weirdly?"

"Am I?"

"Yes you are. Anyway, we were talking about this Davy Long," said Colin. "When Garda Hogan rang he told me that he'd gone back down to the bridge again, just to make sure that those drunks had told him everything they knew about Davy. As it happens, they hadn't. Garda Hogan met a fellow who told him that Davy Long tried to abduct his daughter only last week. On the same day of the robbery. It seems that while this fellow was sitting by the bridge with some of his friends, Davy Long came along and picked up his daughter who was playing on the steps when their backs were turned. Apparently he just tried to walk off with her. Thankfully they spotted him and managed to get the little girl away from him. But she was in an awful state. From what Garda Hogan says, it sounds like this fellow and his pals gave Davy Long some beating."

Soon after Colin had left to go out for dinner, Michaela went to bed, but she found it impossible to sleep. She wasn't a suspicious person but even she couldn't fail to see that the similarities between Denise and Colin's accounts of last Saturday night were weird. Denise had said she'd bumped into a man called Colin in the lobby of Jury's who told her that he'd been stood up and, together they'd gone to the bar for a drink. Colin had been in Jury's. He'd been stood up. He'd bumped into someone in the lobby He'd ended up drinking in the bar.

When Colin arrived home at eleven she was still awake. At first she pretended not to be but, as he fumbled about in the dark, cursing as he undressed, she give into the temptation to ask him a few questions.

"Hi there," she muttered.

"Hi yourself," he answered gruffly.

"Had a good night?"

"Not really."

"Where did you go?"

"Simm's."

"Nice. Who did you say you were meeting?"

"Just a client."

"Maurice Murray again?"

"No, Maurice Murray isn't a client. It was a fellow called Bernard Byrne."

"Have I met him?"

"No, at least I don't think so."

"Have I met Maurice Murray?"

"I don't know, Michaela. What's with all the questions all of a sudden?"

"Nothing, just taking an interest."

"Well, can you save your interest for the morning, I'm knackered." He climbed into bed beside her. "Go to sleep, Michaela, alright?"

As he leant over and kissed her, Michaela got a faint but very definite smell of perfume.

"What kind of aftershave does this Bernard Byrne wear then?" she asked him.

"What?"

"There's a smell of perfume from you, Colin."

"Could be," he answered. "I've always thought that old Bernard is a bit too much in touch with his feminine side. Ben Philips suspects that he wears a nice set of undies under his suit. And he's far too keen on physical contact for my liking. The minute I came into the restaurant tonight he threw his arms around me and gave me a great big bear hug. I was mortified."

Always ready with an answer, was Colin. But he had been to Simm's and Michaela was almost sure that's where Denise was meeting this new man of hers. But if she confronted him now he'd just worm his way out with lies and she wouldn't be able to prove a thing. Better to wait until Monday and talk to Denise.

Michaela didn't sleep a wink all night. As Colin slept soundly beside her, she lay awake, thinking. And, for the first time, she acknowledged to herself that their marriage was turning into a disaster and that the perfection of the first few months were well and truly over. The long hours Colin claimed he worked had nothing to do with it, there were just the excuse she'd made herself believe in. Now, he was hardly ever home and, even when he was, his mind was miles away. He hardly noticed her any more. And she realised that if, by the slimmest of chances, he wasn't seeing Denise, then there was every chance he was seeing someone else. All the classic signs were there only she'd been too stupid to see them – the nights away, the mysterious phone calls, his vagueness about his plans, that fact that he was always broke.

If she was honest with herself, she realised that she didn't even like him any more. The fact that he'd stayed away all week, not bothering to even phone to let her know that the person who'd broken into their house was a convicted rapist, was just so typical of him. What if Davy Long had come back again? If he'd turned up on the door, she'd have let him in without a second thought. She'd been so convinced by him, just like that other girl, the girl on the bridge. Suddenly Michaela remembered that she'd told the girl where Davy lived and realised that, if she was desperate enough to hang about a bridge on the off-chance he might pass by, then there was a very real possibility that she'd go up to his house looking for him. And what if she found him there? If Davy Long had tried to abduct that little girl last week, then obviously his spell in prison hadn't taught him much.

Michaela got out of bed and searched through her bag until she'd found the scrap of paper with Polly's phone number. She looked at her watch, it was only quarter to seven, she'd wait until nine o'clock before giving her a call. She looked at Colin sleeping soundly in the bed and, realising that she couldn't bear to get back in beside him, she got dressed. Quietly she left the house and went for a walk.

At nine o'clock, she made her phone call.

"Hello, College Heights Hostel," answered the young female voice.

"Hello, is that Polly Odlum?" asked Michaela.

"One second, I'll get her for you now."

Michaela heard the receiver fall to the table, heard the sounds of heels clattering along a long bare hall, and then the same voice shouting, *"Pol-ly! Pol-ly!"* Then the heels clattered back again.

"Sorry, Polly doesn't seem to be here at the moment."

"Do you know where I could find her."

"No, sorry."

"It's important."

"Well, I think she might have gone home. Her family have a shop on the far side of Mallow, on the Limerick road, I think she works there at weekends."

"Do you have a phone number for her?"

"No, I'm sorry. You could try the telephone directory."

"Thanks." Michaela put down the phone. Just as she was about to pick up the phonebook, a sleepy-looking Colin arrived into the kitchen.

"Hi," he said. "Who were you on the phone to?"

Michaela knew she couldn't bear to be around him for the day.

"Just a friend. She wants me to come down

to see her. I said I would. You don't mind?"

"No. Have you had breakfast?"

"Yeah. I've been up for hours."

She went upstairs, brushed her hair, picked up her bag and came back down.

"I'll be back about six," she told him.

"You're going now?"

"Yeah. See you."

The 11.20 a.m. train from Cork took about a half an hour and Michaela arrived into Mallow before noon. Before leaving the train station, she'd asked directions to the bus station and headed directly there, arriving just as the Limerick bus was about to leave. She hurried onto it and was glad to find that the driver knew the Odlum shop well and would drop her off right outside it. She paid her fare and sat down at the front of the bus. Immediately it took off.

"Are you a friend of young Polly's then?" asked the bus driver, looking at Michaela in his rear-view mirror as he left the town of Mallow behind and came onto the open road.

"Yes," replied Michaela. There was no point in trying to explain.

"I had Polly's grandmother, old Mrs

Odlum, on the bus during the week."

Oh great, thought Michaela, just her luck to get one of the chatty ones.

"A gas character altogether. Have you met her?" he was asking.

"No, not yet," replied Michaela.

"A character, no doubt about it. She was telling me that Polly has a boyfriend now. God, they grow up so fast. It seems like only the other day Polly started getting the bus into school. She was the smallest little thing back then, with a bagful of books nearly the size of herself. Is it from the college you know her?"

"Yes."

"She's the apple of her grandmother's eye, that's for sure. They must miss her at home, the house must be very quiet without her. But, as I said to Mrs Odlum, you have to let them spread their wings."

The bus continued on for another five miles with the driver talking non-stop. Finally he pulled up outside the shop.

"There you are now. Tell Polly I was asking for her. And the rest of the family."

"I will. Thanks. Bye now."

Michaela climbed down the steps and stood outside. Now that she was here, she felt nervous. It had seemed a good idea this morning, to come in search of Polly Odlum, for if nothing else it gave her a reason to get out of the house and away from Colin. But now she wondered had she been a little rash. A movement from inside the shop suddenly caught her attention and she realised that someone was peering out from its dark interior. What the hell, she was here now. She walked inside.

"Hi," said Polly who was sitting behind the counter. "I thought it was you when I saw you getting off the bus. You're the girl I met on the bridge, aren't you?"

"Hi, Polly."

"You remember my name?"

"You wrote it down on a piece of paper."

"Oh yes, of course I did. But this is a coincidence, seeing you again so soon."

"Not really. You told me to give you a ring if I heard anything about Davy."

"So I did," said Polly, puzzled.

"I rang the hostel this morning. The girl on the phone told me where you lived."

"Why did you want to know? I don't understand. You hardly came all the way down here to tell me something about Davy. Did you?"

"Well yes . . . you see . . . "

"Polly!" came a cry from outside.

"That's my grandmother. Please don't mention a word about Davy. Please."

"Polly, do you want to go in for your dinner?" asked Granny Odlum as she came into the shop. Then she caught sight of Michaela. "Oh, I'm sorry, I didn't know you had a customer. I didn't notice a car outside."

"Hello," said Michaela. "I'm afraid I'm not a customer. I'm a . . . a friend of Polly's. You must be Polly's grandmother."

"A friend of Polly's! Well now, I must say you're very welcome indeed. We were beginning to think Polly was ashamed of us. We're forever telling her to bring her friends from Cork down to see us, but does she take any notice, not at all. Well, I'm glad to see she has for once. Polly why didn't you tell us you had a friend coming today? So, pet, tell me, what's your name?"

"Michaela."

"Well, Michaela, go on now, into the house with Polly and have a bite to eat for yourself."

"You're very kind, but I've just dropped by for a few minutes."

"Get away out of that! I won't have it said that we left a friend of Polly's leave here with an empty stomach. Off with you!" She took Michaela by the arm and propelled her towards the door, saying as she did, "Polly, take your friend inside now."

"It must be something serious, seeing as how you've come all this way," said Polly, as they walked away from the shop.

"Is there somewhere we can talk?" asked Michaela.

Before answering, Polly glanced back and, as she expected, there was her grandmother, standing at the shop door, fondly watching Polly and her nice friend. She gave Polly a little wave.

"Do you mind if we wait until after lunch?" asked Polly, knowing that if her grandmother saw her go anywhere but directly into the house, she'd start shouting after her, demanding to know where they were off to. "We can talk in the shop after-wards," said Polly.

"Well, if that's what you want. I'll go for a walk while I'm waiting."

"Indeed you won't. Granny's right, you might as well have something to eat."

"Well this *is* a lovely surprise," said Mrs Odlum for the fourth or fifth time as she bustled about the kitchen. "It's not often we get to meet a friend of Polly's. Michaela, do you eat lamb?"

"Please, don't go to any trouble, Mrs Odlum."

"It's no trouble at all."

"Well then, lamb would be lovely." Moments later, a whopping great plate of lamb, potatoes and vegetables was put on the table in front of her. "Mrs Odlum," protested Michaela, "that's far too much. I'll never eat all that."

"Eat it up. You young ones are far too skinny."

"So, are you at college as well, Michaela?" asked Uncle Joe, sitting at the table across from her.

"No, no, I'm working actually. But I've been thinking of going."

"You should. You can't beat an education, that's what I always say," said Mr Odlum. "Isn't that right, Polly?"

"Yes, Dad, that's what you always say," answered Polly. She looked over at Michaela and raised her eyes to heaven.

"I see you, Polly," said Mr Odlum. "I see you smirking. And I hope you're not letting that Davy turn your head. Stick to your books Polly, stick to your books. Isn't that right, Michaela?"

Michaela nodded. She hadn't realised that Davy was Polly's boyfriend; she'd got the impression that she hardly knew him.

"Tell me, Michaela, have you met Davy?" asked Mrs Odlum.

"Yes, I have."

"Lovely fellow, isn't he?"

"Mam, you've never even met him."

"No, but I've seen his picture. And I found where I had left Cliona's photos. They were on the fridge all along, right under my nose. I'll go and get them now." She got up. "He's doing a Master's, Michaela," she said as she poked about on top of the fridge. "But I suppose you know that. Wants to be a lecturer. Here we are." She sat back down at the table, put on her glasses and took the photos from the wallet. She glanced at the first one – it was Cliona and a bunch of her friends smiling for the camera. "I've never seen such a load of oddballs in my life, including my own niece," she said. "She's the oddest of them all. Have you met Cliona, Michaela?"

Michaela shook her head. Mrs Odlum handed her the photograph and Michaela looked at it.

"Which one is your niece?" she asked politely.

"There, the one in the middle," said Mrs Odlum, pointing her out.

Michaela passed it on to Polly who was sitting on the other side of her, remarking as she did,

"She doesn't look a bit like you Polly."

"No, she's ruined herself, ruined herself," said Mrs Odlum. "There's the one with Polly and Davy. Don't you think they look very well suited, Michaela?"

Michaela took the photo and stared at it. At

Davy in particular. He looked lovely in it; throwing back his head laughing. It was hard to believe that he could have done such awful things.

"Of course he takes a drink," said Mrs Odlum, leaning over to point out the can in Davy's hand. "But who doesn't nowadays? There's worse he could be doing, I suppose. And that's Cliona's boyfriend," she said passing Michaela another photo. "Did you ever see such an odd-looking fish? What height did you say he was again, Polly?"

"Seven foot ten," she said, exaggerating for effect.

"Imagine. Sure Cliona's hardly five foot herself. Squealer they call him, Michaela, did you ever hear the like? Who's he now, Polly?" she asked, pointing out Colin in another photo. Colin was standing apart from a group who were posing for the camera, looking on at them with some disdain, not realising that he was included in the frame.

Polly leaned across Michaela to examine it.

"Just some creep," answered Polly. "The one I was telling you about, Michaela. Show me." Polly took the photo from her mother and stared at it.

"Why do you call him a creep, Polly? I was about to say that he was the only normal-looking man at the party," said Mrs Odlum. "Apart from Davy, of course."

"He just is."

"What do you think, Michaela?" asked Mrs Odlum, taking the photo back from Polly and passing it to Michaela. "Do you think he looks like a creep?"

Michaela stared at it.

"That's Colin, my husband."

"It can't be," said Polly. He's the one . . . " she stopped, remembering that her parents didn't know what had happened to Cliona that night. "It can't be. He came into the shop with his girlfriend the other week."

Michaela looked at the photo again.

"You're right Polly, it's not him. It was the blond hair. I just thought it was Colin for a second. I was mistaken."

"My, my, so young and married already," said Mrs Odlum. "But of course a lovely thing like you would be snapped up straightaway. I was beginning to think we'd have Polly on our hands for the rest of our days."

"Mam, I'm only eighteen. You're worrying prematurely."

"She wouldn't even go to her school Debs, Michaela. Too scared to ask anyone."

"Mam, stop it. Please."

They'd come to the end of the photographs and Mrs Odlum got up and started clearing away the table.

"Polly, why don't you show your friend around the farm," she suggested.

"Mam, Michaela isn't interested in seeing around the farm. We're a bit old for that. Besides I have to go out and let Granny off."

"Don't mind the shop, Granny and I can look after it. You'd like to see around the farm, wouldn't you Michaela?"

The girls walked down the field. For a while neither of them said a word. Eventually Polly spoke.

"That was your husband in the photograph, wasn't it?"

Michaela nodded, then, after a few moments she asked, "When I met you on the bridge, you said Davy Long stopped a man

346

from attacking your cousin – you were talking about Colin, weren't you?"

"Yes."

"What night was that?"

"Wednesday, the week before last," answered Polly.

Michaela thought for a while.

"That was the night he was supposed to be staying in Sligo, but he came home early, he was sick, with a tummy bug," she said. "Polly, when did he come into your shop?"

"About two weeks ago."

"With a girlfriend?"

"Well, that's what she seemed like at the time."

"I see," said Michaela. Then, after a minute or two, she continued. "Yesterday, I wouldn't have believed you. Now, I don't know what to think. Last night I found out that he's just started seeing one of the girls I work with and it suddenly occurred to me that he could have been seeing other women as well. He's away a lot, you see, working supposedly, but he's always very vague about where he's staying and when he's coming back."

They continued walking. Polly was at a

loss for words, she tried to think of something comforting to say, but she couldn't. She wondered how she'd feel if she found out that her husband had been fooling around. She glanced over at Michaela, she looked so sad and Polly felt like reaching out to touch her, to tell her to go ahead and cry if she felt like it. But she hardly knew her. They walked on. Polly was finding the silence awful.

"Michaela, I'm sorry," said Polly. "I just don't know what to say. Or do."

"Neither do I."

They walked on.

"I came down here to tell you about Davy," said Michaela eventually.

"It can wait."

"I didn't know he's your boyfriend."

"He's not."

"But your parents . . . ?"

"It's a long story."

"I see."

"When I started college, I thought it would be brilliant. But, I don't know, I just don't fit in. I really hate it. I don't seem to be able to make friends and I'm failing all my assessments. But there's no point in telling my parents, they're so proud of me. So I let them think I'm having a great time. And a couple of weeks ago, I happened to mention Davy, just that I liked him and for some reason my mother got the idea that he was my boyfriend. I tried explaining that he wasn't, but then I saw how happy it made her and I didn't bother any more. And, in a way, I suppose I like pretending he is."

"And you really like him?"

"Yes. I've never had a boyfriend, you know. I've never even met someone I fancied before. But Davy, well, Davy's different. He's prefect. He's so gentle. And very handsome, at least I think so. He's very funny too. And intelligent, he's doing a Master's Degree in college," she paused. "Michaela, whatever it is you have to tell me about Davy must be pretty bad, you wouldn't have come down here otherwise."

"No, I wouldn't have."

"How bad?"

"Do you really want to know?"

"Yes, I suppose I do."

Michaela stopped walking, took out the photocopy of the newspaper article from her jeans pocket and handed it to Polly. Polly took it from her and read it.

"What are you trying to tell me?" she asked. "That this 'minor' is Davy?"

"Yes."

"I don't believe you. Davy would never do these things."

"Polly, it's him alright. The gardaí have checked it out. When I remembered that I'd told you where Davy lived I was afraid you'd go there, looking for him and that he might . . . I don't know . . . that, that he might do what he did to that old lady. You see, the gardaí say he tried to abduct a little girl on the same day he robbed our house."

"I don't believe you."

"Polly, listen to me. He lives on his own in a squalid derelict house. He's just out of prison. He's robbed our house. He tried to abduct a little girl. He raped an old lady, then beat her so badly with a hammer that she would have died anyway if she hadn't died in the fire he started. And that's all we know about him, there could be a lot more. Polly, he's no good."

Michaela looked over at Polly. She was

staring straight ahead, her face expression-less.

"He even lied to you about doing a Master's," Michaela went on. "He doesn't go to college. For heaven's sake, he had me believing that he was going to be a librarian. He's probably not right in the head. I even loaned him my husband's best suit for an interview." Then Michaela shuddered. "Oh God, to think that I was alone in the house with him."

"And did he rape you?"

"No, but . . . "

"Set fire to you? Beat you with a hammer? Abduct you?"

"No, but . . . "

"Even though he had the chance? And tell me, Michaela, did you feel in the slightest bit threatened when you were alone with him?"

"No," answered Michaela. She hadn't. Not when she had been alone with him in the house. Not when she had been alone with him on the bridge. He had made her feel warm, happy. "But so what?" she asked. "I didn't know then what I know about him now."

*   *   *

Michaela's plan to get the bus back into Limerick was overturned by Mrs Odlum. She wouldn't hear of it and insisted that Michaela stay for tea. Mr Odlum, she told her, would be dropping Polly into the station later on and Michaela could travel back on the train with her.

They were finished the tea now and it was time to go.

"Thanks very much for tea, Mrs Odlum. And for lunch," said Michaela as they shook hands.

Polly was hugging her grandmother goodbye as Uncle Joe put her bags in the car boot. From the driver's seat, Mr Odlum beeped the horn impatiently.

"Come on, Polly. Hurry up," he called. "God, you'd never think she was just going for the week," he muttered.

"Well, it was lovely meeting you. I hope we'll see you again, Michaela," said Mrs Odlum.

"I hope so. Bye."

Michaela got into the backseat of the car and Polly climbed into the front beside her father. It was a silent trip back to the station. Neither Polly or Michaela felt like talking.

"The Sunday-night blues," said Mr Odlum, nodding knowingly.

They reached the station, parked the car and all three of them got out.

"Dad," pleaded Polly. "Don't try to get me a half-fare. It's embarrassing. They know what you're up to."

"But Polly, it always works," he answered, taking the bags from the boot. "Nobody would think you were in secondary school, let alone college."

They came to the counter.

"Two half-fares to Cork, please," Mr Odlum asked the man behind the glass screen.

"Has she got ID?" asked the man, looking sceptically at Michaela.

"What would she need ID for? She's only fifteen," replied Mr Odlum.

The man sighed.

"Mr Odlum," he said wearily. "She's no more fifteen than myself. Nor is your daughter. Every week, I let her off because I know you. But you're trying to make a fool out of me now, Mr Odlum. You can't expect me to go letting her friend off as well."

"Ahh, come on."

"Please Mr Odlum," said the man patiently. "I'd say something if you were short of a bob."

"Dad, just pay him the full fare," begged Polly.

Begrudgingly, Mr Odlum handed over the full amount for Michaela and half for Polly, despite Michaela's protests that she'd pay for herself, despite the man's protests that he was still being left short. But eventually, with an air of resignation, he took the money, realising that it was all he was going to get out of Mr Odlum.

"Good-bye, Mr Odlum," said Michaela as she boarded the train.

"Good-bye, Michaela," said Mr Odlum.

Michaela found a seat and watched through the window as father and daughter hugged good-bye. Then the guard walked along the platform, closing the doors of each of the carriages and Polly hurried onto the train.

"Watch this," she said, having settled herself in the seat beside Michaela. "He always stands there, long after everyone has moved away."

And he did. As the train pulled out, Michaela and Polly watched Mr Odlum waving and waving, getting smaller and smaller. The only person left on the platform.

"Didn't I tell you? Isn't he a sweetheart?" said Polly as he disappeared from view.

Neither of them said much on the train journey. A half an hour later, the train passed under the long tunnel as it came into the city, and Polly, like the other passengers, got up and collected her bags.

"I appreciate you coming down, Michaela," she said, as the they waited for the train to come to a stop. "You know, to tell me about Davy."

"But you don't believe me."

"No. But thank you anyway. What are you going to do? About your husband?"

"I don't know."

"Maybe you could stay with a friend for a while," Polly suggested, but Michaela shook her head so she asked, "Well, do you want to come back to the hostel with me?"

"No. Thanks. I'll go home. I have to face

him sometime. Although he probably won't even be there, he never is." And then she laughed sadly. "Now I know why."

"You can't go home on your own. I'll come with you."

"There's no need."

"Would it help if I did?"

"Yes, I suppose it would."

They let themselves in quietly. The first thing Michaela noticed was the note on the table. She picked it up and read it aloud. "Headed to Limerick tonight. Saves me an early start in the morning. Will be gone until Thursday. Will ring. Love Colin."

"There," said Polly. "At least that gives you some time to decide what to do. Look, why don't I run out and get a bottle of wine and a video," she suggested. Noticing Michaela slumped at the kitchen table, despondently staring into space, she felt she couldn't leave her on her own for the evening. "You can start thinking about things tomorrow," said Polly.

"The VCR's been stolen."

"Well, do you feel like going out for a drink?" suggested Polly, but Michaela shook her head. "Will I go and get some wine then?"

asked Polly. Michaela shrugged noncommittally. "OK so," decided Polly. "That's what I'll do so. I'll be back in five minutes."

"Polly, you don't need to go out," said Michaela. "There's a couple of bottles of red in the kitchen. We can have those unless you'd prefer white. "

"No, no, red's fine," said Polly relieved at not having to blow half her week's money.

Careful to steer clear of Colin and Davy, Polly had managed to fill the last two hours with words. Michaela didn't mind, Polly didn't need answers. Michaela wasn't particularly close to her brother or parents and she found Polly's numerous little anecdotes about her family amusing and, more importantly, they kept her mind off Colin, as Polly intended. But even Polly was running out of stories and she finally lapsed into silence. Michaela was lying on the couch, Polly was sitting on a cushion on the floor and now she was staring over at Michaela contemplatively.

"I don't get it," she said eventually. "You've spend the night crying away quietly and you still look lovelier than most people can ever dream of. Why isn't your face all puffy and red? And why isn't your hair all flat from lying on it?"

"I'm quite sure I look awful," said Michaela.

"No, you don't. I'd bet that you've never looked awful in your life. Colin must be mad," she said, her tongue loosened from the wine. Michaela had drunk very little and, although it seemed Polly had hardly paused for breath, she'd still managed to finish most of the first bottle and had made a good start on the second. "I mean, why would anybody with a wife as beautiful as you go on the way he does? Look at your hair, your face. You're like a model." Then she added begrudgingly "And you're nice as well. It's so unfair."

"I think you're exaggerating," said Michaela.

"No I'm not. There's no way you've ever looked in a mirror and thought, 'Oh, God I can't possibly look that bad.'"

"Yeah right! Listen to Quasimodo talking."

"I'm not quite Quasimodo. But I'm plain."

"Plain?" Michaela looked at her. "Do you really think you're plain?" Polly nodded glumly. "Oh, for heaven's sake, you're joking," said Michaela, but it was perfectly clear that Polly wasn't.

Michaela fell silent again. There was no telly to watch, no music to listen to and Polly couldn't think of anything else to say now. She tried to think of something they could both do because Michaela didn't seem to want to go to bed yet and Polly couldn't bear seeing her lying there looking so sad.

"Do you want to play cards or something?"

"Oh God no. Anyway I don't have a deck."

"Scrabble?" suggested Polly.

"No, not really, unless you want to."

"No, I don't really."

Then Polly had an idea.

"I don't know," she said now. "Even when I put on make-up I still look ridiculous. I usually go overboard like some novice drag–queen experimenting for the first time. I bet you don't, I bet you always manage to put on just the right amount. What kind of make-up do you wear, Michaela?"

"Well, I don't wear much really."

"I should have known."

Suddenly an idea, just as Polly hoped, struck Michaela.

"Why don't you let me make your face up, Polly? It'll give me something to do, I'm sick of just lying here."

"No way," said Polly.

"Please, I want to."

"Alright," said Polly showing just the right amount of reluctance. "But only if you promise I'll look like you at the end of it."

Michaela got up from the sofa, and ran upstairs. Moments later, she came back with her make-up bag.

"Now hold still," she ordered Polly, emptying the contents of the bag on the floor.

Polly held still while Michaela kneeled in front of her and went to work on her face. A few minutes passed.

"Open your eyes wide and look at the ceiling," ordered Michaela.

"What are you doing now?"

"Stop moving about."

"What's that pencil for?"

"It's to bring out the colour of your eyes. Now look up."

"The red? Michaela, you're poking it *into* my eyes."

"If you'd stop moving it would be easier."

"Show me the mirror."

"No. Not until I'm finished. Now close your eyes."

"I didn't realise you were so bossy."

Concentrating hard, Michaela worked away for a few more minutes.

"I know this part of the story," said Polly. "This is where you transform the ugly duckling into a swan and the man she loves, but doesn't love her, comes back and realises that he's been blind to her beauty all along and promptly falls in love with her and they live happy ever after."

"Try to stop talking while I'm putting on the lipstick."

"That's definitely enough," said Polly a moment later.

"One second, I'm almost finished." She put down the lipstick and started on Polly's hair.

"Stop at my hair. What's with all this fluffing up business?"

"OK, take a look," said Michaela, holding the mirror in front of Polly.

Polly stared at herself.

"Gosh! I look, well – well – I don't look like me anyway that's for sure. Mind you, I don't look much like you either." But Polly liked what she saw.

"Polly, you look lovely."

"So will my Prince come back and realise that he's been blind all along?"

"Definitely."

"And promptly fall in love with me?"

"No doubt about it."

"Imagine. And we'll live happy ever after. Do you know," said Polly thoughtfully, "I almost kissed him once?"

"Your Prince?"

"Yeah, I was sitting beside him in a lecture in college and he fell asleep on my shoulder. I spent ages looking at him, thinking about the kiss and then, when I finally leaned over, I knocked my pencil case off the counter and he woke up." Polly paused. "One day maybe," she said quietly.

They were silent for a few minutes.

"This is nice this, isn't it?" said Polly.

"What?"

"You know, doing girlie things."

"Yes, it is."

"We could be friends, couldn't we, Michaela?"

"Polly, I think we are friends."

12

MICHAELA LOVES DAVY
LOVES MICHAELA AND
DAVY LOVES POLLY

Each morning Davy told Bartley and Rebecca that he thought he was well enough to go home again but they insisted, quite rightly, that he needed more time to recuperate.

"You're welcome to stay as long as you like," Bartley had said. "Besides, Rebecca likes having you in the house, Davy."

"Now don't even think about leaving yet, Davy," Rebecca had insisted. "Anyway, Bartley likes having you around."

It was clear that both of them did like having him here. And, since he'd managed to persuade them to let him sleep on the couch, and they in their own bed, he didn't feel he was putting them out so much any more. But, it was over a week since Bartley had wheeled him back in his cart and, apart from the dog-bite, his other cuts and bruises had healed up well. He was anxious to get home. It wasn't that he didn't like staying with them. He did. That was the problem. He liked it *too* much. He was afraid he'd get *too* used to it. Yesterday, Rebecca had cooked a Sunday dinner, a proper one, better than any he ever remembered having – oxtail soup to start, then roast chicken with stuffing and gravy, roast potatoes, carrots and marrow-fat peas and, for afters, a trifle. The dinner itself had been delicious but, what he'd really enjoyed was the three of them sitting around the table together. At one point, Bartley had asked him to "Pass the gravy, son," and, even though Davy knew *"son"* was what Bartley might have called any fellow younger than himself, it still moved him and, just for a little while, he let himself imagine that they were his parents and that this was just a regular Sunday at home.

About a quarter of an hour ago, he'd heard Bartley come in from work. Now he could hear him and Rebecca talking in the kitchen and he went into them. They were sitting at the kitchen table.

"Ah Davy, it's yourself," said Bartley.

"There's tea in the pot, will you have a cup, Davy?" asked Rebecca.

"OK," he said, and he went and poured himself a cup, then sat down.

"You're looking better today, Davy," remarked Bartley.

"Much better," agreed Rebecca.

"Bartley, Rebecca," began Davy. "I know that I'm very welcome here and I really appreciate what you've done for me but, I think I should go home. I need to sort things out."

"Of course you do, Davy," agreed Rebecca. "In a few days maybe, when you're fully better. That leg of yours needs more time to mend."

"Well, I was thinking of going sooner. Today, in fact," said Davy.

"Today?" echoed Bartley. Anxiously, he glanced over at Rebecca.

"Davy, love," said Rebecca softly. "We've some bad news for you. You see, well, I'm afraid they've knocked down Cathedral View. This morning. Bartley was just down there. He says they've cleared everything away. There's nothing left."

"Nothing Davy, not even the rubble," said Bartley, shaking his head sadly.

Davy didn't say anything, he just stared at the cup of tea in his hands. All he had left in the world, he realised, were the clothes he was wearing, and they weren't even his, they belonged to Michaela's husband.

"Now Davy, you're welcome to stay as long as you like, you know that," said Rebecca.

"Thanks. You're very kind." He got up. "I think I'll go for a walk. The exercise will be good for me."

"But Davy it's nearly six o'clock. It's dark outside."

"I won't be long."

"Hold on a second and I'll get my coat and come with you," said Bartley getting up.

"No thanks. I'd prefer to be on my own. Really."

"But . . ." began Bartley.

"Bartley," interrupted Rebecca. "Davy wants to be on his own."

Bartley sat back down.

"Of course, of course," he muttered.

"You know I'm really grateful for what you've both done for me," said Davy, pausing at the door.

"Hush now, don't be embarrassing us," said Rebecca.

Davy came back over, bent down and kissed her on the cheek and then he went and put a hand on Bartley's shoulder. "Thanks," he said and he left.

"Thank you," said Bartley and his hand went up to where Davy's had been.

Rebecca went to the window and watched him walk down the path. She felt a lump rising in her throat, there was such a lonesomeness about him. Bartley came and stood beside her and put an arm around her shoulder. He guessed what she was thinking.

"Maybe he'd have been just like him," he said, he too thinking of the son they'd never had the good fortune to have.

Rebecca looked up at her husband.

"Will he be back to us, Bartley?" she asked.
"He'll be back, Rebecca."

Taking it slowly, for the weight on his leg was making it throb painfully, he began walking down into town. He passed through the centre and out the other side. At Hot and Saucy, he carried on along the main road, avoiding the short-cut over the bridge, in particular avoiding Chalky and his pals. Davy had made up his mind to go to Michaela's house. He wanted to find out what had happened to her. He wanted to know if she'd really left for England or, if Colin gone on his own, as he thought was probably the case. He turned into her road.

What Davy first noticed, when he came around the corner, was the yellow garda ribbon taped across the front of Michaela's house and the little crowd of people huddled outside it. In the dark, he didn't see the broken glass or the charred window-frames.

Colin got up from where he lay on the bed, went over to the mini-bar and took out a can of Guinness. But then, remembering that he'd already had two pints in the bar before coming up to his hotel room, he changed his mind and put the can back. He didn't want to be over the limit, he still had to drive back to Cork tonight. He looked at his watch, saw that it was nearly six o'clock and wondered what was keeping Michaela; he'd expected to hear from her ages ago. Or from Garda Hogan. Why hadn't he rung him? He picked up his mobile now from the locker, checked it, saw that it was powered up and that it wasn't showing any missed calls. Then he dialled his own home number; there was no tone. He stretched himself out on the bed and pressed the remote control to "on" but nothing happened and, realising that the TV wasn't plugged in, he cursed, then flung the remote at the wall.

Staring up at the ceiling, he lay there and wished he felt like sleeping. He wondered how long it would take for the insurance to come through. The fire was an awful risk to take but, if it got Ralph Murphy off his back, then it was worth it. Not paying him would be a bigger risk. That much had been made pretty clear to him last night when two of Ralph Murphy's *boys* had called to the house and had taken him for a drive and had explained to him what would happen if Mr Murphy didn't get his money. The house was valued at £95,000 and the outstanding mortgage was £40,000 so he stood to make around £45,000. Enough to pay Ralph Murphy the £20,000 he owed him and still have money to take out a new mortgage.

The first time Colin had heard of Ralph Murphy was when Murphy himself had contacted Colin with a view to setting up a computer system for his office. Afterwards, Colin had learnt that, although Murphy liked to present himself as a property developer, he made most of his money as a loan-shark. In the poorer parts of the city, if a mother wanted to cast a slur on another, she spread it around that the second mother's child was wearing what was commonly known as a RMS – a Ralph Murphy Special – meaning clothes bought with a loan from Ralph Murphy for the Communion or Confirmation or for the new school year. So Colin had decided to approach him for a loan, it had seemed like the answer to all his problems; it would get the bank off his back and give him a little breathing-space and nobody would be the wiser. But it was a short-lived breathing-space. He'd been depending on the commission he'd get from selling Ralph Murphy the computer system to meet the first repayment, but then Murphy changed his mind and hadn't gone through with the purchase and, to date, Colin had managed only one out of three payments. The situation he found himself in now was one he'd always associated with poor people. To think that he, a professional with an income of £40,000, was being *taken for drives* and threatened by a loan-shark's henchmen. For all his faults, his Bank Manager had never *taken him for a drive*, but then, if he hadn't refused to extend his over-draft or increase his loan, he'd never have got into this situation in the first place.

He'd never have had to do anything as drastic as set fire to the house if those other two louts hadn't disappeared off the face of the planet with all his worldly goods and, without giving him a penny of the £8,000 they'd agreed for the house contents. That £8,000, together with money he'd get from the insurance company for the robbery itself, would have been enough to clear his debts. He'd picked those two louts to rob his house because they looked like the two shadiest characters in a particularly shady bar. And how right he'd been. They'd rightly screwed him.

But then, Davy Long had came along. Like an answer to a prayer. Poor Davy Long opportunely appearing on the scene to take the blame for the robbery and to give him the idea of setting fire to the house. Who'd suspect Colin when there was a ready-made culprit waiting in the wings; someone with a record for this sort of thing already? It had been too good an opportunity to pass up, now that that those louts had disappeared along with their van full of almost everything he and Michaela owned, leaving him in a worse financial mess than ever.

As on the day of the robbery, Colin had decided to place himself in Limerick once again. He was more worried about the insurance company's investigations than those of the gardaí. He wanted them to be satisfied that he was miles away at the time of the fire. And this time he decided to go solo, he'd learnt his lesson. As soon as Murphy's henchmen had dropped him back home last night he'd headed straight to Limerick. When he arrived, he'd phoned Ben Philips' brother Gerry and asked him to come out for a few drinks. Then he'd made sure that Gerry Philips got so drunk that, for all he knew, it could have been morning by the time they'd finished drinking. After seeing Gerry Philips safety into the taxi just before one o'clock, Colin had gone back to his hotel room and had slept until six thirty. When he got up this morning, he'd slipped out the rear door of the hotel and had driven straight to Cork. Arriving there just after eight thirty, he'd parked at the entrance to the lane at the back of their terrace of houses. The lane was completely overgrown and he was confident that no one would see him slipping into the house. He'd broken the glass in the kitchen door, unlocked it from the inside and went in. He'd called out Michaela's name, but no answer and, happy that she had left for work, he'd then drenched an old pillow-case with petrol, set fire to it and slipped back out of the house again. He'd returned to his car and then raced back to Limerick. Easy peasy. A piece of cake. A little after ten, he'd turned up in the hotel restaurant, to ask the waitress if there was there any chance of a late breakfast; a heavy night, he'd said apologetically.

Now with the insurance money he'd be able to pay off Ralph Murphy. And from now on, he was turning over a new leaf. It was bye-bye to Anna, she'd clean out Donald Trump if she got the chance. The last time they'd gone out together, the dinner bill had come to £215 but which, as the waiter had snottily pointed out when Colin had questioned it, included the wine – as if Colin just hadn't enough class to see that it was quite reasonable really. And on top of that having to suffer Miss Money-bags all the way home complaining that he'd been stingy with the tip. And how she'd persuaded him to spend £3,500 on an engagement ring when he was already married still amazed him. Michaela's ring had cost him £300 and, even though he'd actually intended marrying her, he'd thought that was steep at the time. No, from now on they're be no more trips to Paris. No more weekends at the K-Club. Anna was out of his league. Anyway it was time to settle down. No more Anna, no more Samantha, no more of that bitch Denise, no more of anybody else. It wasn't worth the hassle. Maybe he had come on too strong on Saturday night, but that Denise's reaction was way out of proportion. She'd been completely hysterical.

No, it was time to pull himself together. Time to make it up to Michaela. He felt bad when he thought of how the robbery had, and how the fire would now, affect her. But he'd take out a mortgage and rebuild the house and, in the meantime, he'd make sure to find somewhere really nice to rent. Maybe out of town, somewhere by the sea, like Crosshaven from where they both could commute to work. It would be like an extended holiday for them. And as soon as the house was rebuilt, maybe they'd start a family. He liked the idea of that; him and Michaela, all settled, with a little boy and girl.

As he stared up at the gutted house, the sense of what the on-lookers were saying slowly came to Davy.

"Tragic, just tragic," said one quietly, half

to herself, half to the other bystanders.

"So young, with her whole life in front of her," said another as she wiped a tear from her eye. "Wouldn't it break your heart?"

"There wasn't a mark on her," said a neighbour. "I saw her myself this morning, before they took her away in the ambulance."

"Are you going to go along to the funeral tomorrow? I think I might, when it's someone so young, you'd like to pay your respects."

"Is the removal on tonight then?" another asked.

"Yes, at six."

Davy turned to the group.

"Where?" he demanded.

"Flynn's," one of them answered. She was about to tell him it was private, but the look on his face made her think twice. "The one on Penrose Quay."

Outside the funeral home Davy paused to catch his breath. His leg was throbbing. And for a second he wondered what was he doing here, what was the point of coming? Because he needed to see her one last time. Needed to see her lovely face – lifeless – but without a mark on it. He pushed open the door and came into a room, heavy with grief, full of little groups of people whispering sorrowfully, crying softy, in the face of such tragedy. He looked around and at the back of the room he saw the open coffin. He began to push his way through the people.

He didn't see the old lady emerge from one of these huddles and walk over to him slowly. Not until she spoke his name.

"Davy," cried Granny Odlum softly. She came right up to him and put her arms around his waist, and laying her head against his chest, she began to sob quietly. "Davy, love, we didn't know where to find you. Our poor baby. Davy, how will we ever stick it?"

Confused, Davy gazed down at her white head but, reacting to her grief, he put his arms around her.

"You were all she talked about, Davy," said Granny Odlum weeping. "Oh God, your poor heart must be breaking."

Then Mrs Odlum walked over. She put an arm around Granny and the other around Davy. She brought both of them in close to her.

"Davy, Davy, Davy," she moaned. "She's gone from us."

Bewildered, Davy stood there as the women cried. Who were they? How did they know him? Then across the room he saw a head of curly auburn hair. Michaela's sister? Just at that second, perhaps feeling the intensity of his stare, Michaela turned around and a look of shock crossed her face when she saw him staring over. He watched as she came towards him and wondered if he'd sustained more damage than he'd thought from that fall. What was going on?

"Granny Odlum, Mrs Odlum," said Michaela gently to the two women. "I'll take Davy outside. Explain to him what happened."

A knock came on the door. About time, thought Colin, he'd called for room service ages ago. He got up, bounded over to the door and opened it. In the doorway stood three gardaí, two he didn't know and Garda Hogan lurking in the background.

"Mr Colin O'Neill?" asked one of the unknown ones.

"Yes?"

"I'm Superintendent Thompson. From O'Connell Street Garda Station, here in Limerick. This is Sergeant Evans and you know Garda Hogan, they're both from the Anglesea Street Station in Cork. I wonder sir, if you'd mind accompanying us to the station."

"What?"

"We'd like to question you in regard to two alleged assaults on young women in Cork City. One at a party, at Washington St on the night of November the second, the other on Saturday night last outside Simm's Restaurant. Sir, formal complaints have been lodged against you in connection with both incidents."

"What?"

"And there's a second matter as well, sir. Even more serious, I'm afraid. We'd also like to ask you a few questions about a fire. A young woman by the name of Polly Odlum died in a house fire in Cork earlier today. We've reason to believe that you might be able to help us with our enquiries. Would you come with us, please?"

* * *

Davy followed Michaela outside and into the pub next door. They sat down at a corner table, facing one another. Davy couldn't stop staring at her. He reached his hand out to her face.

"Don't touch me," she said sharply and slapped it away.

"Sorry," he said. "It's just . . . it's just that I . . . I thought you were dead."

"I wish I was," she said grimly, her eyes filling up with tears.

"Michaela, I don't understand," he said. "Who are those two old women? How do they know me? Why are you crying, Michaela?"

She didn't answer.

"Michaela, please will you tell me what's going on?"

"Their daughter is dead. They think you're her boyfriend. You'll have to go along with it. It's the only thing to do."

"What?"

"At least until the funeral tomorrow."

"Michaela . . . "

"Just shut up!" She paused and looked at him scornfully now.

"Michaela, look I . . . "

"If you don't pretend for their sakes, I'll tell everyone in this pub what you did in Belfast. Let's see how far you get then. God, just looking at you makes me sick. You're just scum. Do you think you were a hard man then, Davy Long, when you were hammering that old woman to death?"

"Michaela . . . "

"Shut up. All I want is an answer from you, will you pretend?"

"I don't understand."

She ignored him.

"Even when I showed her the newspaper article," she said, puzzled now, thinking of Polly. "Even when I told her what you tried to do to that little girl on the bridge, she wouldn't listen to me."

"Who wouldn't listen to you? And what little girl? What are you talking about?"

"Don't be so pathetic. As if you don't know. The little girl you tried to kidnap on the bridge."

Davy looked at her even more bewildered.

"Eva?" he said, comprehension beginning to dawn. "I was taking her to the hospital, she'd hurt her leg."

"Really?" said Michaela clearly not believing him. "Whatever. I didn't come here to listen to your excuses. I don't want to hear anything you have to say. All I'm interested in is letting Polly Odlum's parents go on thinking that you were her boyfriend."

"Polly Odlum?"

"Yes, Polly Odlum."

"Polly Odlum?"

"God, I haven't the time for this. Yes, yes, yes, Polly Odlum. Oh please," said Michaela looking at him. "Come on, don't sit there looking like your best friend died. You hardly knew her."

"Polly is dead?"

"Come on, I don't have time for this . . . this show of concern."

"How did it happen?"

"As if you care."

Davy reached over and caught hold of Michaela's hand.

"How did it happen?" he demanded so loudly that the other people in the pub, bar a single deaf man, turned to stare at them.

"Let go of me."

"How did it happen?"

"Let go."

"How did it happen?" His face was so close to hers that she could feel the words on her face as he spat them out.

"Let go," she demanded. "And I'll tell you." And when he'd let go, she went on. "Last night Polly stayed in my house. I left her sleeping this morning and went to work. But on the way I remembered I'd left my cheque book behind and that I needed it, so I turned around. As I came over the bridge, I saw the flames. I managed to get into the house and drag her out. She was alive when they took her to the hospital. But she died this afternoon. Of smoke inhalation."

Michaela stopped talking, she couldn't go on. Davy reached out to her hand on the table, to comfort her, but she pulled away.

"Don't touch me," she said through gritted teeth. Then, though she was barely able to keep talking, through her tears, she said quietly. "Polly is dead because I asked her to stay the night. The gardaí say it was arson and the only reason I know you didn't do it, and you can be sure you were the first person I suspected, was because one of my neighbours made a positive identification. The gardaí know who did it."

"Who?"

"They wouldn't tell me. They said they had to question him first."

"I can't believe it." He paused, then sadly, thoughtfully, he went on, "Do you know that Polly was the first person I've met in Cork who I could imagine being friends with."

"Please, just shut up."

"I remember thinking that when I went to a party with her." He fell silent as he remembered her. Then he looked over at Michaela. "But I don't understand, why do you want me to pretend to be her boyfriend?

"Polly loved you . . . "

"What?" interrupted Davy.

"Yes, Polly loved you. She was mad about you. Don't ask me why, but she was. She talked about you all the time to her family. They know everything about you. Or all that you chose to tell Polly about yourself. And now for their sakes I want you to tell them how happy Polly was these last few weeks with you."

"Lie to them?"

"Yes, they need happy memories. And for once in your life you can do something decent. You can start by telling them that you met at a lecture, that you fell asleep on her shoulder. It's only partly a lie. You did once fall asleep on her shoulder. She told me last night. She said that she'd spent ages looking down at you sleeping, wondering if she dared to kiss you."

"I don't believe it!"

"So will you do it?"

"Polly loved me?"

"Oh please, pass me the box of hankies. Polly didn't even know you."

Suddenly it was Davy's turn to get angry. Polly was dead and all Michaela could do was heap accusation after accusation upon him

"And neither do you! Listen to me, I didn't kill that old woman, my brother Stephen did, but the RUC couldn't nail him so they were happy enough to get me for it instead. Alright?"

He paused, and suddenly aware of the pin-dropping silence, he looked around. Everyone in the pub was still staring at them; it was better than any TV drama: mistaken identities, kidnapping, murder. Even the deaf man, though he wasn't catching much of what they were saying, was staring now. Davy got up and shouted.

"Get back to your pints! This is a private conversation!"

They averted their eyes for a second and Davy sat back down again. The wife of the deaf man turned to him and fiddled with his hearing aid, turning it up.

"Michaela, the only reason you have to hate me is because I had a fight with your husband, not because he robbed your house, which he did but . . . "

"Oh, come on."

"I saw him, Michaela, I thought he was leaving you, that's why I was coming back today, to see if he had. I couldn't come any sooner, I wasn't able to walk. Look."

He put his leg up on the table and pulled

down his sock to show her the dog-bite. She looked away, disgusted. Davy looked around the pub again.

"Why don't you all come over and have a better look!" he shouted at the gaping faces.

The deaf old man, taking him at his word, began to get up quickly.

"Sit down!" roared Davy. He turned back to Michaela and said quietly. "As strange as it might seem to me that Polly loved me, maybe I know a little of what she was feeling. I have loved you, Michaela, since the day I saw you coming towards me on the street, with the sunlight playing on your beautiful, beautiful hair. All those days I spent sitting on the bridge waiting for you to pass by. And that night of the bonfire, that was the happiest night of my entire life. But you didn't know I loved you, might never have. Just as I didn't know loved Polly me and might never have, except, except . . ."

He didn't finish his sentence. Instead, he got up.

"You're wrong about me Michaela, I didn't touch or harm that old lady. Or Eva. But that's not important right now. As you say, there's something I need to do."

He left the pub.

Michaela sat there for a few moments, then she looked up.

"The show is over! Why don't you turn on the telly or something?" she shouted at the barman.

Then she got up and followed after him.

From the door of the funeral home she watched. She watched him go directly to Granny Odlum, watched him take her tiny hands in his, then stoop to kiss her tenderly on the top of her neat white head of hair. She watched him as he let go of her hands, watched him enfold her in his arms, watched Granny Odlum bury her head in his chest as he whispered words of comfort. And Michaela tried to imagine him raise a hammer to another frail old lady. She couldn't.

Then she watched Mrs Odlum bring her husband over to him. Watched Mr Odlum awkwardly shake hands with Davy, and then watched Davy, Polly's Davy, put his arms around the old man. And she watched Davy hug him tightly as the tears ran freely down both their faces. He was the kindest, gentlest person, she'd ever met, Polly had said. And Michaela knew that Polly had been right.

A garda approached her.

"Michaela O'Neill," he said, his face solemn with the news he was about to impart.

"You've some news about the fire?"

"Yes. And I'm afraid it isn't good news. The undertaker tells me that we can use his office."

Sitting in the office listening to the gardaí, Michaela didn't see Davy walk to the coffin.

She didn't see Davy gaze down at Polly, lying there, completely and utterly still, her warm breath stilled for ever more; gazing down at her and remembering her on that night of the party; her eyes popping out of her head as he'd enlightened her on the ways of the body-piercing fraternity; the way she'd gone on and on, asking question after question about his "thesis", not satisfied with his evasive answers. These past few month, he'd thought that it didn't matter to anyone whether he lived or died, thought that

nobody cared. And now, when it was too
he'd learned that Polly had. Polly had care

Slowly, Davy brought his hand down to
her hair and he gently curled a strand around
his finger. He paused. She didn't wake and he
brushed away a tear from where it fell to just
below her left eye. Delicately he stroked her
rosy cheek. Then little by little, he turned
her head towards him, and then he paused to
study her lips before kissing them. And he
bent forward.

Until his lips touched hers.

The End